ENDEAVOR

Book Two in the Legends of Ralladin
Gunner Long

Dedicated to Christian martyrs, who boldly lived their faith until their last breath. It will be an honor to meet you in heaven.

PREAMBLE

IT IS YEAR 320. Five years have passed since the insurrection at Loronis, and in that time, much has taken place.

Jayfor has become king of Faldon, and Trenson aids his rule as his right-hand man. After months of toil, the confusion and division caused by Jayfor's brother, Xavson, has been resolved, and all vestiges of Xavson's insurrection have disappeared. Jayfor and Trenson continue the fight against Elara and Kallary, but despite their strategic maneuvers and gambits, Faldon is losing the war, so much that the victors of this long conflict may be in sight.

Elara continues to grow and expand its reach. The dominion of the Shadow Empire only grows. Its armies have taken almost every region below Faldon's capital, leaving no survivors as they ravage cities and take territory. Faldon's army is reduced to almost nothing, a handful of men against the thousands of Elara, and the threat of total annihilation looms.

Compared to the other two kingdoms, Kallary has made little progress in the last five years, still consumed by infighting and turmoil. However, they have managed to conquer some land in Faldon's territory directly below the Endless Mountains. The days of the city-states may be over, though, as powerful rulers start to rise and gain control over larger parts of Kallary's land.

The years of war will soon be over. Elara has almost eradicated Faldon's presence completely from the world, and unless the last kingdom of the United Empire of Ralladin is victorious in their last stand, the years of darkness will prevail.

PROLOGUE

T HRALL SWUNG HIS DARK sword around in a sweeping arc. The blow was brutal and would have been unstoppable for any mortal to deflect, but his opponent met the blow easily with his own sword. The two blades, one black, the other white, clashed with an explosion of light and sparks. Thrall's sword was parried to the side, and his enemy now had the advantage. Thrall cursed under his breath.

In the brief moment before they reengaged, Thrall looked at the battle swarming around him. The scene was plains, green plains, that stretched as far as the eye could see. Unlike his home in Elara, the sky was clear, and the cheerful blue sky and yellow sun shone down on the vicious battle ensuing below.

The two sides of the battle couldn't have been more different. On one side, in black armor and bearing shadow-clad weapons, were the Knights of the Dark Order, or Krenors. On the other, in shining armor and bearing radiant swords, were the Senver, the Knights of Va'ar. The two sides were locked in a fierce clash, with the tide of battle changing uncertainly back and forth.

However, much to Thrall's satisfaction, it seemed like the battle was finally coming to a conclusion. Although their own losses were heavy, it was nothing compared to the Senver's casualties.

He witnessed Senver falling to the ground dead, then radiating blinding light before they abruptly disappeared. The Krenors were winning.

Thrall turned his attention once more to his opponent. The Senver showed no fear as his comrades fell to the ground. He rushed at Thrall with his sword in both hands, poised to strike.

It was what Thrall was waiting for. As soon as his opponent got close, Thrall pushed the Senver's blade aside with his hand and, with blinding speed, thrust his dark blade into the shining armor of the Senver, the blade going deep into his midsection and exiting out of the back.

The Senver gasped with pain. Thrall extracted his sword from his foe and stood back, staring at the Senver through the empty eye slits in his helmet. The Senver dropped his sword to the ground as he stumbled back and clutched his midsection. There was no blood; instead, a dark ring and black wisps appeared where Thrall had pierced his armor, contrasting the white armor.

"Did you really think that anyone who challenges me will live?" Thrall said in a cold voice.

The Senver looked around and watched as his last comrade fell to the ground. Then he turned his fearless eyes on the dark commander. "I would be more concerned... with the One that you have challenged."

"Ha!" Thrall snorted. "My lord is more powerful than the One you serve. I have slaughtered hundreds that stood for Va'ar, and did their faith in Him do them any good?"

The Senver sank to his knees and looked one last time at Thrall. "Va'ar can use anyone to accomplish His will... Even you."

The thought of being used by Va'ar to achieve His purpose was revolting, more than he could bear. Thrall cried out in fury and brandished his sword, preparing to end the life of this defiant Senver quicker, but the Senver fell to the ground, glowed brilliantly, then vanished before he could reach him.

Thrall stopped, looking at the empty ground where his enemy once lay. Then he huffed and sheathed his sword, the blade making a familiar clang as it fit into place. "Fool," he muttered.

The remaining Krenors approached Thrall. Although some of the Krenors were defeated, the Senver had suffered fatally, with not one Senver left on the field. The Krenors, finished with their work, now regrouped around their commander. One of them, Thrall's second in command, came before him and bowed. "General Thrall," he said, "The Senver line protecting Faldon has been destroyed."

Thrall nodded. "Very good. Lord Tar-Raw will be pleased to hear of my success."

The second-in-command stiffened at Thrall saying *my* success, and not *our* success, but knew better than to mention it.

Thrall continued. "At last, we have broken the Senver line guarding Loronis. For too long, have we had the means to obliterate those filthy rats in the capital, but those accursed warriors of Va'ar stood in our way." He looked around at the Krenors surrounding him, each one in identical black armor. "But now that path is clear. There is nothing stopping us from achieving victory."

He looked directly at his subordinate. The captain couldn't help but feel the involuntary fear that came when Thrall stared at him. "It is almost time. The master feels it. The rule of Faldon will end, and we, my brothers, we will stand victorious, with our foot on our enemies' necks!"

A guttural chorus of agreement rose from the warriors.

"We march for Loronis immediately. This time we will not be stopped! No one shall be spared! The kingdom of Faldon shall burn, burn into ashes, and we will rise over the embers and rebuild the world!"

Every warrior of the Dark Order showed their enthusiasm by raising their weapons high and cheering, Thrall's words giving them new power and morale, the thought of Faldon's destruction rejuvenating them.

Thrall raised his voice to a shout. "We will not be denied! Va'ar and his filth will at last be cleaned from the world, and the Hope will never succeed! We march for Loronis, and when we arrive, the ground of Faldon will be watered by the blood of our enemies!"

And the Krenors cheered louder than ever.

I

R ANDOLPH LOOKED OVER HIS shoulder at the healer. "How is he doing?"

The healer placed his hand on Jayfor's forehead, then shook his head. "The fever is getting worse. He needs elixirs and herbs that I don't have, and soon."

Randolph frowned. "We should arrive in Loronis in a few hours. Do whatever you can until then."

The healer nodded, but the look on his face told of his anxiety. "I will."

Randolph sighed. He was exhausted, not just physically, but mentally as well, the last few weeks of chaos draining him. He couldn't wait to get back to the capital and to finally be at ease. Then he realized there would be no rest even when they did reach the capital; there was always more to do. This only made him feel more tired.

It didn't help that the sky was a bleak gray and there was not a trace of wind in the air. The army was returning home to Loronis after a bitter defeat, their spirits downcast. A few weeks ago, they set out on this expedition with stout hearts and an eagerness for battle. Now they felt neither.

Norman rode beside Randolph. Both barons were on horseback. Norman looked at the figure of the young king behind them, lying supine on a cot being carried by four knights, one on each corner, with the healer standing beside the cot, mixing herbs and doing everything possible to improve the king's condition. "He shouldn't have come," Norman said absently, looking forward. "We almost lost him. We might lose him anyway; most men have died from what he suffered."

Randolph knew he was talking about Jayfor. "Thinking about him dying won't help at all," he replied, trying not to let his dreariness show through his voice. He couldn't tell if he was doing a good job or not. "Once we're back at Loronis, they will be able to do more to help him. He will make it, you'll see."

Norman nodded but didn't turn his head. Randolph recognized the look in Norman's eyes. After large battles, with carnage and death on either side, it took time for those involved to move on and accept what had happened. The more battles a warrior had been in, the easier it was to get past the feeling. Norman, compared to Randolph and the other knights, had been in relatively few battles. And after a massive fight like they had been in, with countless dead and utter defeat, even the bravest warrior was shaken at how much they lost.

Randolph knew that talking helped men to put memories like that aside, so he continued. "Jayfor led us bravely, though. I've never seen anyone so young show such skill and courage."

Norman looked at Randolph with blank eyes. "He did," he replied.

Randolph knew that he should say something else, but he didn't know what. After thinking hard on this, he shrugged and decided to give up. Norman would get over it, eventually. He saw Norman reach into this saddlebag and pull out a familiar box, pry open the lid, and start eating the pink candies inside slowly, one by one, chewing thoughtfully.

Randolph turned his eyes to the road ahead. He had some thinking to do as well. The left and right motion of his horse lulled him into a reflective state as he remembered how it had happened.

It was two weeks ago that they first set out. Elara was taking over more and more of Faldon's territory. For most people, Elara seemed like a distant evil, and understandably so. The Shadow Empire was so far away, and the battles took place so far from the capital that, for most people, Elara was like a distant threat. Not anymore. Their armies were approaching the Donlar river, the closest major river to the capital. The threat of annexation loomed, and so, at the advice of his most trusted war counselors, Jayfor decided to attempt a counter-offensive attack. The idea was that if they could not hold out on the defense, maybe an offensive attack would change the momentum of the war.

They amassed the troops and set out. But Jayfor did something that his advisors did not agree with: he decided to lead the attack personally. No one thought this was a good idea. The capital was already chaotic with its own affairs, and the kingdom needed a leader in times like these. To lose Jayfor, the last of the king's line, would seal Faldon's destruction.

But even with the advice of his advisors, Jayfor left Trenson to steward in his place while he rode out to battle with the rest of the men.

Now, looking at Jayfor's pale face, listening to him moan and breathe in gasps while unconscious and stretched out on a makeshift cot, Randolph wished more than ever that Jayfor hadn't come.

The battle took place across the bridge on the Donlar river. After a week of traveling, they reached the bridge and prepared for the arrival of the Elarian army. Jayfor set up the battle lines, with the calvary in front, spearmen next, normal militia after that, and archers in the back. Norman and Randolph were to lead the frontal charge beside Jayfor, and they would engage the enemy in a calvary charge and general fighting.

Randolph stopped his train of thought. He didn't like thinking about what had happened next, even though he had replayed it in his mind countless times. But he couldn't stop himself from remembering that battle, no matter how many times he tried to ignore it.

The Elarian army came like a dark cloud, moving steadily over the ground. Randolph had heard the stories. They were slaves. The Darkness crushed their free will, and they would do whatever their lord told them to do. They had no emotion. They killed, then moved on, without any pleasure or remorse. But what seemed to be the most disturbing were their eyes. It was said that there was something different about them, something... unnatural.

Randolph was sure that these were just myths. He was a seasoned general, and his experience had been that people tended to dramatize things. This was even more likely with the unstoppable force that Elara seemed to be, so Randolph wasn't expecting what the stories said. Until the army approached them.

They wore no armor. Randolph was stunned. They wore dreary common clothes, ripped and torn, the type a peasant would wear, hardly something a knight would enter battle with. Yet they didn't look like knights at all. They were just common people. Common people with axes and cudgels and swords and spears.

The myths were true. Their monotonous marching and cernuous posture made it clear that they had no free will. Their blank faces held no emotion. But none of these things unnerved Randolph as much as the cold stare of their eyes. It was said that eyes are the gateway to the soul. If that were true, then these people had the darkest and most twisted soul — if they even had a soul — that Randolph had ever seen.

Randolph involuntarily shuddered at the thought. His horse sensed his apprehension and whinnied softly. Randolph patted the animal's neck, more to soothe himself than the animal.

Once the army was within a hundred yards, the king didn't wait to sound the bugle of battle. Jayfor charged forward, spear raised high in the air and with a war cry, and the rest of the army followed close behind, chorusing their own battles cries. The sound of the calvary's hoofbeats shook the ground, but it did nothing to faze Elara's army. The dark force simply stopped and held their weapons ready, staring down Faldon's army with empty eyes.

Faldon's army crashed into Elara's with the sound of clanging armor and screaming horses. The Elarians tried to resist the onslaught, but it was no use. Since they wore no armor, it was easy to smash through the lines and allow the horses to plow through the enemy. Jayfor led the army in the front as they completely destroyed the front lines of the enemy.

At that point, Randolph's hopes were high. Calvary charges rarely worked this well; most of the time they were resisted or stopped by the time they broke through the first line of soldiers. But they pushed on and on, destroying the second line, the third line, the fourth line, all the way through to the eighth line of soldiers before their charge was stopped and they disbanded into individual fighting. Randolph was extremely optimistic and thought to himself, *this battle has already been won.*

The rest of the battle was a blur. Randolph remembered stabbing and striking down opponents left and right. The enemy was slow, slow enough that Randolph was able to cut down his foes before their weapons were raised. Even now, as he remembered the battle, he felt a wave of guilt crash when he grasped that he was killing regular people, people who didn't want to fight or kill him. But they had no choice. The Darkness had crushed their freedom, and now they were puppets, doing whatever the Darkness told them to do. And the Darkness had told them to kill everyone who stood in their way.

It was chilling how they fought and died. When struck down, the Elarians didn't cry out in pain or even change their expressionless faces. They just fell to the ground, like a puppet whose strings were cut off. Likewise, when they killed someone in the Faldon army, they didn't show any sign of victory. They just moved on to the next one, and the next one.

The valiant charge that had destroyed the first major lines of the enemy had then halted as each man fought for himself. Randolph saw Jayfor fighting courageously, spear whipping around and killing multiple enemies with a single swing. Norman used his horse as a lethal weapon itself, kicking and crushing all who came close. They had the upper hand. All they needed to do was keep fighting and victory was theirs.

But then *they* entered the battlefield.

Randolph didn't know what to make of them. They were dressed in full black armor, with barbute helmets and spiked armor, with a strange symbol on the breastplate that Randolph had never seen before — a mountain inside of a twisted square, a symbol in red paint. They stood at least eight feet tall. They had axes and war hammers, and flails — a weapon consisting of a spiked ball at the end of a chain attached to a rod. When these figures first emerged from the enemy lines, the fighting almost completely ceased. Something about them was unnerving, and it wasn't their height or black armor or foreboding weapons. Their presence made you feel raw fear. It shattered your resolve; it made your heartbeat become loud and ring in your ears. It told you that you simply could not survive against these monsters of shadows. Even Jayfor stopped and stared at the new arrivals, and Randolph could tell that the king felt the same fear that he did.

Then the black knights started to attack. There was only about one of these warriors for every fifty normal soldiers, but that didn't make any difference. You couldn't kill them. They strode forward and swung their weapons, and no one could resist the urge to run. The axes could cut five men in half with a single swing. The hammers would send half a dozen men flying high into the air. And the flails could clear a circle in a ten-yard radius, making it impossible to get close to them without getting killed.

In only a few minutes, Faldon's army had suffered more than double the casualties they had suffered before the dark figures appeared. And soon, that number would grow until there was no one left to add to that number.

Everyone kept their distance from the dark warriors, but it was no use. They came for you. If they wanted you dead, then you were as good as dead. Some knights were actually able to get close to them and land blows, but to no avail. Any weapons bounced off the armor as if it were solid stone, and even the gaps in between the plate armor were impenetrable.

The Faldon army was being destroyed. Jayfor called out to rally the troops, but no one would dare stand against these silent beings of shadow, and some began to turn and flee. These were followed by more and more.

Randolph remembered as one of these giant knights walked towards Jayfor, swinging a flail around his head in anticipation, the spike ball making a particular *whomp-whomp-whomp* sound as it spun in the air.

Jayfor stood stalwart against the massive knight, keeping a steady hand on the reins as his horse whinnied and shook its head in fear. The warrior swung the spiked ball around in a sideways arc straight towards Jayfor. There was no time to react. Randolph screamed, "Jayfor!"

Jayfor tried to back his horse away from the approaching weapon, but it was coming too fast. With a sickening crash, the spiked ball collided with Jayfor's side and sent the king flying from his horse, and he hit the ground hard and rolled before coming to a stop, his spear clattering to the ground only to lie as still as Jayfor beside him.

"No!" Randolph cried. The army saw that their king was down, and that was all it took. Every Faldon soldier fled towards the bridge, away from the enemy, away from the dark warriors. Randolph charged his horse towards the fallen king, but Norman got there first. The baron of Ronar fief jumped down from his horse and picked up the limp form of Jayfor. The king's eyes were open and incoherent. Randolph stopped his horse in front of Norman. "Hand him to me!" he said.

Norman heaved the king into Randolph's arms. Randolph held Jayfor carefully across one shoulder and looked back. The towering knight with the flail was coming towards them, still swinging his flail around in anticipation as he took one step after another towards them.

Randolph didn't wait for him to come. Along with Norman, he spurred his horse towards the bridge behind them and galloped to catch up with the rest of the fleeing army. The banners they had once carried so proudly now lay on the ground and were trampled by the feet of the knights fleeing. The dark warriors and the rest of the Elarian army didn't pursue them; they stood and watched as their enemy fell over each other trying to get away.

Randolph's heart felt like a heavy stone in his chest as he urged his weary horse forward. They lost.

Now, more than a week later, Randolph's heart was still heavy. He looked again at the king. The left side of Jayfor's armor, where the chained ball hit him, was battered and crumpled. There were puncture holes through the plate armor where the spikes on the ball had pierced through. Jayfor's left arm lay awkwardly by his side. At that moment, Jayfor groaned in his sleep, shifted his weight on the cot, and then groaned again at the pain it caused. The healer took a cloth and soaked it in some water before placing it on his forehead. The king was in dire condition. They needed to reach the capital soon.

Thankfully, Loronis was in sight, at long last. There was a general murmur of gladness from the knights when they caught sight of their capital. Even Norman stopped eating candy and remarked in a brighter tone, "There it is. We're finally back."

Randolph smiled, staring at the inviting, secure walls of the capital in the distance. "Yes, my friend. We are finally home."

II

"**S**IR..." THE SECRETARY URGED Trenson, not for the first time that day.

Trenson groaned and picked his head up off the table. He looked at the secretary with pleading eyes. "Does all of this really need to be read and signed *today*? Can't some of it wait until tomorrow?" He tried to assume his most innocent face, hoping that the secretary would relent.

The secretary, however, was vicious. "I'm afraid not, sir. You said the same thing yesterday and the day before that. Now you've reached the end of the deadline, and all these things *must* be signed and addressed *today*." Even though he was vastly inferior to Trenson, who had been named steward while Jayfor was off at war, it was his job to make sure that everything that required the king's attention received it.

At the moment, however, Trenson was being rather uncooperative, which made his job all the more challenging.

Trenson continued to weasel out of it. "My hand is killing me from all this signing," he complained.

The secretary nodded. "I can understand that, sir. But if you had split this work up into several days, rather than doing it all at once at the last possible moment, your hand would be fine."

Trenson shot a baleful look at the secretary. "Always an optimist."

"I prefer to see things as they are, sir," the secretary replied evenly. "And what I see right now is a pile of paperwork that needs your attention."

Trenson sighed. There was no way he was getting out of it this time. With great reluctance, he picked up the next parchment and briefly scanned it, reading only enough of it that he got the general idea. It was a new law, requiring all apprentices in apothecaries to have at least five years of apprenticeship before being qualified as a master and run their own business. It seemed reasonable. After all, when your life was on the line, who would want a green healer who barely knew what he was doing to care for you? He picked up the quill and dipped it in the inkwell beside his desk, then signed his name: *Trenson, steward under king Jayfor, on the fifteenth day of the third moon in year three-hundred twenty-five.*

Trenson blew on the writing to make it dry faster. After he was certain that the ink was dry, he rolled up the parchment and set it to the side of the desk. He breathed a sigh of relief. Then he looked at the massive stack of rolled-up parchments on the other side of the desk, balancing haphazardly on top of each other, and the sigh turned into one of weariness.

Trenson stretched his arms over his head. "I'm pretty hungry," he said. "I think I'll grab something to eat from the pantry."

The secretary was on his last straw. "My lord—"

Just then, the door burst open, and a guard stood holding the door. "My lord!" he said urgently. "The army has returned!"

"At last!" Trenson said, glad for the excuse not to do more paperwork, but even more glad to see Jayfor and the two barons. He had figured out that being a king was more work than he had anticipated and was eager to return the role to Jayfor. He rose from the table.

"There's more, my lord," the guard said. He looked uneasy, not exactly sure how to break the news to Trenson. Trenson looked patiently at the guard, waiting for whatever it was he had to say next.

The guard finally found words. "The king... Jayfor has been severely wounded. We're not sure if he will live."

Trenson's light heart instantly disappeared.

***

After the drawbridge was lowered, Randolph and Norman solemnly led the remains of the army across the wooden bridge, under the stone archway, and into the streets of the capital. The usual business of the city was immediately silenced as all heads turned to the procession filing into the capital. The people filtered to either side of the street and watched as the knights passed them. The onlookers knew by the empty faces of the soldiers that they had lost the battle, and at great cost.

There was not a single light heart as the knights silently passed the human corridors on either side. For those that still believed in Va'ar and fighting against the darkness, this battle was considered the last stand. Of course, many more battles would be fought regardless of whether it was won or not, but the bridge at Donlar river was the last barrier between them and Elara. This was their chance to push the enemy back. It hadn't worked.

But more people than not didn't feel any sorrow about Jayfor's condition. They considered the entire fight with Elara a lost cause, and didn't believe in Va'ar. Randolph could pick their faces from the crowd, with their smug looks and expressions saying *I told you so!* Randolph currently wanted to throttle them, but restrained himself.

It seemed like forever before they reached the steel gates before the palace. There was no need to request permission to enter: the enormous gates were already opened, and an entourage of soldiers were standing before it. Word traveled fast. Randolph was glad, for the sooner they got Jayfor under more beneficial care, the better.

Without a sound, they rode amid the throng of guards, nodding at familiar faces as they went through. The soldiers acknowledged Randolph and Norman with a slight tilt of the head, which the barons returned. The immaculate structure and vibrance of the palace seemed dull, dull like the dreary gray sky above, dull like the hard cobblestone which the hoofs of their horses clopped across.

About halfway between the steel gates and the doors of the palace, the doors opened, and Trenson stepped through, wearing not only his steward garbs with the star of Faldon on the right shoulder, but an expression of worry on his face. He ran forward towards the group. Randolph and Norman stopped, and in turn, all the knights behind them stopped.

"It's good to see you back again," Trenson said when he stopped close to the group. "I was worried that you may never come back.

You all still seem to be in one piece, though." He tried to lighten the mood with the last line, but it fell flat. No one stirred.

Trenson cleared his throat. "Where's Jayfor?" He already guessed that the king was being carried or unconscious, but he asked anyway, just to make sure.

So he was not surprised when four knights emerged from the group, each one carrying a corner of an improvised cot. They walked forward, but they didn't need to go far, because Trenson ran forward and met them halfway. He saw the stricken face of the king, red with fever, and the smashed armor that he wore, as well as his left arm, which lay at an awkward angle. Trenson couldn't help but gasp. He never expected it to be this bad.

The healer, who Trenson was unaware had walked beside the cot and was looking down on the king beside him, broke the silence. "He's in a dire condition. We really must get him moved to the infirmary right now."

Trenson snapped out of his trance. "I — of course. Get him moved immediately!" he said urgently. The soldiers holding the cot began walking — far too slowly. "Faster! He's at death's door!" he yelled. Although he didn't know if this last part was true, it had its intended effect: The soldiers immediately picked up the pace to a jog, and ran through the doors of the palace, leaving the healer, who wasn't used to running, calling out, "Slow down!" as he panted after them. The soldiers didn't slow down.

Trenson turned to Norman and Randolph. "Head to the barracks and dismiss your soldiers there. After you're ready, meet me in the chamber." He ended his order abruptly. Before the barons could respond, Trenson turned and broke into a dash, running back inside the palace and after the knights and healer carrying Jayfor to the infirmary. He didn't look back.

Randolph waited a few seconds, watching the doors of the palace close slowly. The doors came closed with a thud, and the guards returned to their positions by the door.

Then Randolph looked over his shoulder at his company. "We make for the barracks! The faster we get there, the faster we can rest, so I suggest you make all haste, because I'm not waiting for you!"

***

The royal parlor, better known as simply "the chamber," was a spacious and well-furnished room. It was originally used to entertain important guests who were visiting the capital. However, the definition of "important guest" changed, until it was basically used for small meeting or planning, because it was a more comfortable place to sit and discuss plans than the long-tabled meeting hall. Large windows gave natural light to the room, while several cushioned chairs formed a half-circle in the center. A map of Faldon was attached to one of the walls, being so big that it almost took up the entire wall.

Trenson was sitting in one of the chairs now, rubbing his hands together. He was waiting for Randolph and Norman to come in so that they could discuss what was to be done next. There was a lot that needed to be addressed, especially with Jayfor in the condition that he was in. Trenson was unsure of exactly what they would do now. He didn't know this as a fact, but he was almost positive that the battle Jayfor had fought had been lost. The faces of the knights looked anything but happy, which gave Trenson all the evidence he needed.

Trenson found his mind drifting into the past. It had been... He counted the years... Five years since they had retaken Loronis from Xavson. Five years. It seemed like only yesterday they were fleeing from the chaotic city, recruiting help from the barons, rescuing Jayfor from the bandits, sneaking under the city through the secret passage, fighting Xavson in the throne room, and Agrond revealing himself as a Senver and saving his life.

He marveled at how much had happened since then. It took months to restore order and remove the last of Xavson's influence from the kingdom, dismissing the remaining mercenaries and sending word to all the generals and soldiers who left that they may return, banning all the laws that Xavson had created, releasing all those who had been put in prison for resisting him — the work felt like it would never end.

But even after they finished erasing all the results of Xavson's insurrection, their work had only begun. Elara was attacking more frequently and vehemently than ever. The war had only gotten worse in the last five years. Rarely did they hear news of a battle won or victory achieved; it was defeat, almost every time. Kallary had also taken over a fair amount of ground, especially since the kingdom was starting to settle its internal wars and dominate rulers emerged, but it was nothing compared to the progress of the shadow empire.

The doors of the chamber suddenly opened, breaking Trenson from his thoughtful trance. He looked up to see Norman and Randolph enter the room. He met eyes with the men and nodded towards the chairs. The two barons took their seats directly across from Trenson.

Norman was the first to speak. "How is Jayfor?"

"We're still not sure," Trenson replied, his voice heavy. "They gave him a tea made of bynal herbs, which is supposedly the most healing herb in Ralladin, but they don't know for sure. They're confident that he'll survive, but they're still not sure exactly how serious his injuries are." He sighed. "You know healers. They take forever to get anything done. I told them to inform us when he wakes up." Trenson almost added *if he wakes up,* but checked himself.

Norman nodded. "I'm glad they think he will live. Hopefully, they're right; I don't know what I would do if the king died."

"If that were to happen," Randolph commented, "Then Trenson would most likely take his place as king."

Trenson shook his head violently. "Being a steward for two weeks was hard enough. Let's hope it doesn't come to that, for Jayfor's sake, and mine."

Randolph huffed and leaned back in the chair, crossing his arms. He didn't voice it, but he agreed with Trenson: he would probably make a terrible king. Not saying anything against him, but ruling a kingdom took a certain skill, a certain deftness in politics and the ability to spin many plates. Trenson, although a great right-hand man, didn't hold many of those skills. A period of silence followed.

Then Trenson asked, with caution, "What happened in the battle?"

Randolph looked at Norman, who returned the look. Then they both began explaining how the battle went, along with breaking through the enemies' front lines easily, how the dark warriors had arrived at the battle and started demolishing their forces, how Jayfor had been struck down by one of these warriors, and their retreat and flight back to the capital. Trenson listened to it all with a face of stone and nodded silently throughout the story.

When they finished, Trenson was silent for a time. He didn't know exactly how to respond. He didn't want to state the obvious, *that was a crushing defeat,* but he had no idea what else he should say. He finally decided. "We're going to need to make a new plan if we are to survive this war. Elara is gaining ground faster than we can manage."

Randolph nodded. "That was my thinking. We can't keep sending troops into the field, only to return in defeat with their numbers cut in half, like we have been doing." He scratched his chin, thinking.

"What other way is there to fight?" Norman said. "We have used every tactic and gambit we could think of. If we can't beat them then, what else can we do?" His nervousness showed through his voice.

Trenson understood Norman's fear. "I don't know. Maybe Jayfor will have better ideas about what to do. I've already sent out more forces, including some of our last reserves, into the field, which should hold them back for now. But I'm afraid that there is a potentially greater problem at hand."

Norman and Randolph immediately looked at Trenson, a questioning look in their eyes. Their expression sent a clear message: How can anything be worse than Elara at our doorstep? Patiently, they waited for an explanation.

Trenson soon provided one. "The people have a different attitude towards us than they did five years ago. The admiration and honor they once felt towards us has disappeared, and they are drifting into a new state of mind: they are starting to lose faith in Va'ar."

The two barons glanced at each other. "But hasn't it always been that way?" Norman asked in his usual timid voice. "I mean, there have always been many people in Faldon who don't believe in Va'ar. Why is it worse now?"

"Because that number is growing significantly. Now only a handful of people still believe. And this isn't one of those usual swings, where the people will believe, then don't, then will, and so on. The trust we once had in Va'ar has been deteriorating for too long, and now the people have almost completely turned their backs on their protector."

Trenson sighed and ran his hand through his hair. He considered it a miracle it hadn't turned gray by now, with all the stress and anxiety he had been put through.

"How do you know this?" Randolph asked.

"I sometimes go through the city in disguise, so I can get an idea of what the people like and don't like. It—"

"Wait one second," Randolph interjected. "Did you just say that you sneak through the city in disguise?"

Trenson shot a dubious look at Randolph. "I don't 'sneak,'" he retorted. "I merely walk through the city and listen to what is being said."

"In disguise?" Norman asked, starting to pick up on the conversation.

Trenson shot Norman an equally dubious look. "I wear a cloak with a hood! If I paraded through the city without one, then everyone would know who I am and be on guard and not talk as much, which would make it even harder."

"I don't know," Randolph mused out loud. "If a suspicious hooded man was stalking around while I was talking, I don't think I would feel any more open."

Trenson stared hard at Randolph. "I know what I'm doing," he said in a cold tone.

Randolph held up his hands innocently. "If you say so."

Trenson waited a few seconds to see if Randolph or Norman felt like commenting any more, but, to his delight, they were silent. "Anyway," he started again, annoyance evident in his voice, "I've found that there's a man by the name of Kylor who is becoming extremely popular in the city lately, and he has amassed a ridiculous amount of 'followers' who believe anything that comes out of his mouth."

"Kylor?" Norman said, "I think I have heard of him."

"Me too," Randolph added, "and it's always been in glowing terms."

"Trust me," Trenson said, "he's anything but glowing. He may have the charisma and rhetoric that wins people over, but there's an underlying message in his words."

"I heard he was a great orator," Norman said, "but that's all I know."

"He is," Trenson replied. "It's no wonder the people idolize him. He has wit and words, and would be a great herald, if he wasn't so bent on leading Faldon to its destruction."

Randolph frowned. "What do you mean?"

Trenson took a deep breath. "Kylor believes that reason and intellect are the true rulers of the world, and that Va'ar is not needed. He also thinks morals are demeaning, claiming that right and wrong are different for every person, and we are to choose what we think is right or wrong."

"Ridiculous!" Randolph exclaimed. "Right and wrong are fundamental truths, not labels to excuse behavior!"

Trenson nodded. "I know. And yet, as senseless as his words are, the people can't get enough of him. Obviously, when right and wrong are opinions, you are free to do anything you want, which is very appealing to most. Like I said, he has a posse that shadows him and does whatever he pleases."

Randolph sighed. "Great, more problems. It's enough to worry about Elara closing in, but now the people are turning away from Va'ar, who is the only reason we win battles in the first place!"

"We can't deal with both at the same time!" Norman said. He looked at Trenson. "What are we going to do?"

Trenson shrugged. He knew that shrugging was not very leader-like, considering that the weight of the kingdom and the fate of those who still believed in Va'ar were resting on his shoulders, but he honestly didn't know. "Jayfor will probably have more ideas," he replied. *Or at least I hope so.* "But until then, I say we just see how it plays out. Elara is on the move, and I'll deploy what little troops we have to fight back. Kylor isn't as imminent a threat as Elara, at least not now. You two can return to your fiefs, and I'll inform you if anything happens."

Norman quickly got up from his chair. "At last!" he said. He had been waiting eagerly for the conversation to end. "All this dreadful talk of battles and whatnot. I cannot wait to return to my fief and have some peace for a change."

Randolph chuckled and rose from his seat as well. "I was thinking the same thing."

The barons both began to walk towards the doors leading out of the chamber. Trenson stood and began walking toward the doors as well.

Before they opened the doors and parted ways, Randolph commented, with a rare smile, "Have fun stalking the streets in our absence."

Trenson merely grunted a reply.

III

JAYFOR THRASHED HIS ARMS violently to keep his head above the surface of the water. He couldn't swim. He struggled for air. The water seemed to wrap itself around him and pull him down with an unescapable grip. Jayfor flailed his arms and kicked his legs, trying to churn the water to keep himself up, gasping for air, but he was growing tired, his body weary and spirit almost broken.

He gasped again for air, but he sunk a little too low in the water, and instead breathed in a mouthful of water. He choked and sputtered. He felt cold. It was almost over. In one last effort, he reached his arms up into the air, trying to reach for something, anything, to escape, but his hands gripped only air. Slowly, he sank down, water enveloping him, filling his nose as he held his breath, as he tried to stay alive just a little longer. His lungs were the only thing not cold — they felt on fire and about to explode. The water was cold and grew colder as he sunk deeper and deeper.

Then, when Jayfor felt he could last no longer, he felt a hand encircle his wrist. Hope sparked in him. The hand gripped him tightly, and, with surprising strength, began to pull him up. He felt himself rush upwards; the hand pulling him up higher and higher with increasing speed, until he broke through the surface of the water, fresh air filling his lungs and—

Jayfor awoke from the dream with a start, the faces of three healers all looking down on him.

"He's awake!" One of them exclaimed.

Jayfor, still panting from his dream, looked around. He was in the infirmary, laying on one of the cots there. Why was he here? He tried to sit up, then yelped as a wall of pain hit him hard. He slumped back into the bed, wincing. "What happened?" he asked. His mouth and throat were both dry.

"Just hang on, my king. We'll have you back on your feet in no time," one of the healers said, not answering his question. "Get him some water," he ordered another healer.

A cup of water was soon brought, and the healer put it to Jayfor's lips and tilted it up. Jayfor relished the cool water as it traveled down his throat. After he had swallowed the last of the water, he asked again, "What happened?"

The healer frowned. "You were almost killed in battle," he said. "You took a flail to the left side of your body, and it knocked you unconscious. Don't worry," he quickly added, "we are almost certain that you'll survive."

Jayfor nodded and picked his head up to look at himself, then gritted his teeth in pain and decided it wasn't worth the effort, and rested his head back on the pillow, looking up at the wooden rafters of the roof.

"Don't worry, my king," he heard one of the healers say for the third time in the few moments he had been awake. "We will do everything in our power to make sure you survive." Then he heard another healer whisper, not realizing Jayfor could hear, "I hope it's enough." Jayfor didn't hear much more, as a wave of exhaustion swept over him. Too tired to resist, he let himself fall back into a blissful sleep.

***

Or rather, blissful for a few minutes. He woke up a few minutes later to the sound of a voice. "You said he was awake!"

Then another voice said, "I didn't say that! He said that."

"Well, *he* came into the chamber saying that he had woken up. He doesn't look very awake to me!" Jayfor recognized the voice: Trenson. Although ecstatic to see his friend, Jayfor kept his eyes closed. He wanted them to think he was sleeping, just to see if he could catch any interesting conversation.

"I merely told him to inform you that Jayfor was indeed alive," the voice was the chief healer. Jayfor could imagine him staring dubiously at the servant who had delivered the message.

"Wasn't he alive when you brought him here?" Trenson.

"Yes, he was," Healer, "but he was hanging on to life by a thread. His heartbeat was so quiet and his breathing shallow that I was honestly expecting him to get worse. But just recently, his breath and heart rate have returned to almost normal."

"So he's improved?" Trenson asked.

"In short, yes," the healer replied.

"Well, why didn't you just say that? You ran into my office dancing a jig, singing, 'He's alive!'"

This time, another voice responded. "Well, technically, what I said was true!"

"In any case," the healer's voice reigned in the conversation, "he's improving."

"That's it?"

A pause. "Yes, that's it. Were you expecting any different?"

"No, but I mean, well... how soon until he will be able to do things?"

"Like what things?"

"Like... paperwork, for example."

Jayfor couldn't hold it in any longer. His eyes flicked open, and with a large grin, he said, "Never."

The healer jumped like someone had poured cold water down his back. Trenson's reaction wasn't much better. Both men stared at Jayfor. Jayfor, meanwhile, was grinning uncontrollably, looking down at the two men standing at the end of his bed. The rest of the healers in the room all turned to look at Jayfor, most of them surprised.

Jayfor tried to laugh, but it came out more like a wheeze, and he winced while smiling through the pain. "Got you," he said.

The expressions from the healer and Trenson couldn't have been more different. One was elated, and came to Jayfor's bedside and started bombarding him with questions about how he was feeling. The other stood rooted in place, and shrugged sheepishly at Jayfor, but was inwardly thinking, *the healer never did give me an answer.*

***

Over the course of the next few days, Jayfor remained in the infirmary, barely able to move or do anything without help. The healers had a better idea of what Jayfor's condition was now. A few of the king's ribs had been broken, but they would mend in a few weeks, with the help of some herbs.

It was Jayfor's left arm that concerned them. It took a serious blow from the flail, and for days Jayfor couldn't move it. When he tried, it caused him so much pain that they told him to stop. They were certain it was wounded, but to what extent, they were still unsure.

So until further notice, Jayfor was stuck in bed, his every need pampered by the healers or servants. It drove him crazy. He wanted so badly to walk around or go outside or do *something*. But every time he tried, he would be met by an avalanche of pain and the scolding of the healers and would be forced back into the bed by both.

What kind of king was he? How could he be expected to rule the kingdom if he couldn't even get out of bed?

His only condolence was Trenson, who was doing as much as possible to bear the burden of being king. Jayfor knew more than anyone that being the ruler was an extremely tough and exhausting job, but Trenson handled the role with skill and tenacity, although Trenson did complain about the paperwork and huge demand of his attention, but Jayfor couldn't blame him for that.

"When do you think you'll be better?" Trenson asked Jayfor one day. "As in, better enough to take back your role as king."

"If it was up to me," Jayfor replied sourly, "I would be out of here and riding back into battle with the rest of my men. But my overseers won't let me." Overseer was the term Jayfor used for the healers that kept him in bed and watched his every move.

"I'm sure you'll get better before long." Trenson said.

Jayfor smirked. "Of course you do. The only reason you want me better is so you can pile all the responsibility back on me."

"No, that's not the only reason. Just one of them."

Jayfor chuckled, but the chuckle became a wheeze of pain, and Trenson's smile became a frown.

Jayfor swallowed hard a few times to ease the coughing. "What do you plan to do now?"

"I've been thinking about that. At your command, I sent our reserves of soldiers to the battle lines, but it will take some time to hear the status of Elara's army. Until then, I have another threat I need to deal with."

Jayfor's eyes lit up. "Kylor."

"Exactly. He has a new philosophy that has taken Loronis by storm. Now he's saying that Elara may not be the bad guys. Since right and wrong are completely up to you, Elara can be the good guys or bad guys, and Faldon is the same. Ridiculous."

Jayfor shook his head. "It's only gotten worse in the past weeks. To think that five years ago, when Xavson took over Faldon and announced to join Elara and Faldon, the people rioted and died fighting against it. Now they want to have the same ideals as Elara, and see us as enemies in their way!"

"I know," Trenson replied. "That's why I have a plan." He let the sentence hang in the air for a few seconds, trying to build suspense and see if Jayfor would prompt him to continue.

And prompt he did. "Well?"

"Well, I plan to head into town and see if I can't find this Kylor. I've never actually seen him, only heard the rumors. Maybe I could have a few words with him."

Jayfor raised one eyebrow. "Don't you think that your presence in town will draw a crowd?"

"I'll be in disguise, of course," Trenson replied.

Jayfor's other eyebrow rose to the same level as the first one. "Disguise?"

Trenson looked skeptically at Jayfor. "I go through town in disguise all the time."

"All the time?" Jayfor exclaimed. He had heard nothing about this, and was starting to wonder if Trenson was keeping anything else from him.

"Well, not all the time... Anyway, I'm going to see him for myself. I shouldn't be gone long."

With that, Trenson turned and started walking towards the doors out of the infirmary.

"Be careful!" Jayfor called after him.

Trenson looked over his shoulder. "Since when have I not been?"

Jayfor rolled his eyes. "Too late."

IV

From his vantage point in the back corner of the room, Trenson had a clear view of the entire inn. He let the hood of his long, dark cloak drape over his face, but not so much that he couldn't see. He held a pipe in one hand, hovering the mouthpiece close to his mouth, but didn't smoke it, as it wasn't lit or even had any tobacco in it. It merely served to add to his persona. He reclined nonchalantly against the wall and kept his arms crossed, scanning the room.

As far as size was concerned, the tavern was exceptionally large. It was about twice the size of most inns. Like most taverns, there was a counter with an innkeeper behind it, refilling tankards; there were serving girls running back and forth with plates and an assortment of food; there were large windows that let light stream into the room.

But in the center of the tavern is where the action was. A large group of people formed a tight circle around a table, a table that a man was standing on, a handsome man with a clean-shaved face and a voice that reached everyone and that seemed to talk to each one individually, and made everyone immediately believe that no matter what this man said, it must be true.

"Does anyone here believe that they are wrong about something?" Kylor said, glancing around the room as if waiting for someone to reply. "Anyone? Is there not one person who knows that they believe something that is wrong?" He had a strong voice and an honest expression. This clearly wasn't his first speech.

Heads turned in the crowd as everyone looked around to see if anyone would say something. But no one did. Kylor let the silence drag for a few more moments, knowing exactly how long to let it hang to make it most effective, then spoke again.

"I thought not. But see, that is the point. If we knew something was false, then we wouldn't believe it. It's very simple. How could you believe something that was false? You can't, because if it was false, you wouldn't believe it. Truth and opinion are one and the same."

A murmur of revelation flowed throughout the crowd. Trenson couldn't help but huff. People were wrong all the time. Old ideas and inventions that were once thought to be the truth were constantly being replaced with better ones. It was obvious that people could be wrong — or obvious to Trenson, anyway. Yet the people were hypnotized by Kylor's honeyed words and believed it.

Trenson thought about speaking up and asking Kylor why it was that people were wrong all the time, but he held his tongue. His goal was to assess Kylor for himself and determine how much of a threat he was. Revealing his identity would compromise his mission. So he kept silent.

"This discovery is not the end, though. Far from it. This discovery is the key to open more doors and truths. The revelation that everything is opinion allows us to shake off the bonds that those in power put on us. We are indoctrinated to think a certain way, to act a certain way, to do this and not do that. But who are they to tell us what to do? Are we merely animals to be hounded by those who consider themselves high and mighty?"

Kylor's voice rose with fervency. "Far from it! We are people, people with free will and the ability to decide for ourselves what right and wrong is! No authority or king can tell us what is right and what is wrong, for they are merely his opinion. Take no man's words to be true until you have found them to be for you. Everything, I say, is simply opinion!"

Oh really? Trenson sarcastically thought to himself. *Nothing is true? Does that include everything you just said? And you just told us what to do.* The self-contradicting nature of Kylor's arguments would have made Trenson chuckle, if the rest of the people also saw just how absurd Kylor's words really were. But they didn't. They mindlessly believed his words and stood huddled around the table, silent, listening for more, like dogs waiting to be handed food. Trenson eyed the figure of Kylor from under the hood of his cloak, waiting for more.

"This discovery on truth means that we no longer have to argue in circles about what should be done about the kingdom. Take the threat of Elara as an example. There are some who believe that Elara is evil, and that we must do everything to stop them. Others think they are not quite as bad as they seem. And still others view Elara, not as an enemy, but as a possible ally. But why must we bicker about which is right? The zealots who believe everything associated with Elara is evil have no right to tell you what you should believe."

Another chorus of agreement rose among the crowd. Kylor paused, and Trenson saw an almost unperceivable hint of pride in the orator's features. But he masked it skillfully. Kylor cleared his throat, and the whole room instantly fell silent once again.

"This rule applies not just to us, my friends, no! The king and those in power are no exception! Let us use Jayfor as our example."

Trenson immediately tensed at hearing the name. His guard was raised, and he listened more intently. Other people also perked up. Kylor had sidestepped making any claim against the king in the past, to avoid the inevitable retribution that would follow. But it seemed that he wasn't using an indirect approach anymore.

"Our king, I am afraid to say, does not know this truth. He does not believe that we have the right to think and do whatever we wish, and so he chooses to spend his time forcing his agenda and ideals on us. He tells us he does this by 'Va'ar's' command and admonishes that we are abandoning Va'ar and should turn back to Him. But I say that they are both wrong! Jayfor can't tell us what is right and wrong, and neither can Va'ar!"

The crowd roared in approval, raising their fists high in the air. Kylor was so absorbed in his speech that he looked like he had gone mad, his eyes wide and spit building on the edges of his mouth. The easygoing expression he had when he began the speech was gone.

Trenson felt his blood start to boil at the remarks about Jayfor and Va'ar. If only he knew, he thought, if only he knew what Jayfor had gone through to save their necks from Elara. He clutched his fists and had to bite hard on his tongue to prevent himself from bursting out and tackling Kylor where he stood.

"It pains me to use such strong words, but there is no excuse to how those zealots of Va'ar treat us. The way they talk down on us is more than an insult. It is inhuman! We will not be treated this way for standing up, and will never relent our pursuit of freedom! We will not submit to Va'ar's bigoted philosophy that everything is his to decide. We are the people! Va'ar has no authority over us!"

It was too much for Trenson. He hardly heard the roar of approval from the crowd. He was so mad. All pretense of this being a covert mission was out the window. He stood straight and tall, the hood of his cloak falling back and dropping his pipe to the ground in the process, and yelled above the crowd, "Kylor! When's the last time you did a reality check?"

Instantaneously, it was silent. The sound of Kylor and the people ceased completely. Every face of the crowd turned toward this man who once was sitting peacefully in the corner, but now spoke with a sort of frenzy in his eyes. There was a suspenseful silence. Who would dare speak against such a man as Kylor?

Kylor quickly turned and scanned the room, looking for the source of the voice, and quickly found it to be a man in a long cloak, with a sword at his hip and a defiant look in his eyes. Kylor's eyebrows knitted together. He wasn't expecting resistance. He was hoping for an easy speech and a few more supporters. He never anticipated anyone speaking back.

Although... Kylor looked closer. He had a feeling that he had seen this man somewhere before. Someone in the crowd spoke up, "It's Trenson!" Then recognition hit Kylor. So *that's* who he is. The lapdog of Jayfor himself is here! The right side of Kylor's lip turned upward in a half smile. This might provide a valuable opportunity.

Trenson knew there was no turning back now. His cover was blown, and he had everyone's attention, so he might as well speak his mind. "You speak of freedom and of Jayfor condemning others, but you are condemning others yourself by saying that! You speak of right and wrong being mere opinions, but why is it good for you to judge what Jayfor and Va'ar do if they are opinions? And all you people don't see this? Have you all lost your mind?!"

Trenson's zeal got the better of him. He usually wasn't a very loud or talkative person, but the sheer absurdity of Kylor sparked the fire inside him. The words just seemed to pour out of him. His ears started ringing from the volume of his own voice.

Kylor's even-tempered expression was replaced with a frown. An audible gasp emitted from the crowd. Trenson simply stared at Kylor, waiting — daring — him to reply.

He never did, though. A few men emerged from the crowd and started stalking toward Trenson. "You keep that smart-aleck mouth of yours shut!" Trenson instinctively backed away and reached for the sword at his hip, then realized that he couldn't kill anyone justifiably. He decided he would have to run for it — all too late. Before he could escape, two large and husky men had grabbed him by each arm. "You're just a pawn to that stuck-up king!" Trenson struggled to free himself, but both men had a steel grip. "At least Kylor has a mind of his own, and isn't forced to do someone else's bidding!"

The crowd started to jeer and mock Trenson, calling him names and telling him to mind his own business. Trenson felt the two men start pulling him towards the door. Trenson let his feet drag and desperately tried to move his arms, but that only made it hurt worse and did nothing. Kylor stood tall, watching the scene from the tabletop with a stoic look, but there was a trace of a smirk on his features. He kept silent. The people were doing all the work for him. This was exactly what he had hoped for.

Trenson's arms tingled from the circulation being cut off from the grip of these men. The crowd parted, allowing Trenson to be drug through it and towards the door. The mass of people taunted Trenson relentlessly on either side as he struggled to get free. "Kylor!" Trenson screamed over the crowd, "this isn't over!"

The jeering of the crowd increased. The door of the inn loomed before Trenson. Behind him, he heard the voice of Kylor, almost unperceivable above the noise of the people. "So you see now just how the fanatics of Va'ar wish to destroy our rights to think differently—"

Trenson heard no more, for he was dragged before the door of the tavern, the door was kicked open, and the two men threw Trenson out of the open doorway. Trenson flew forward and landed hard on his chest on the rough ground of the city. He simultaneously felt relief in his arms from being freed from the men's grip, and pain from his rough landing.

He heard laughing behind him. He rolled onto his back and saw the two men laughing for a brief second before the door closed. The noises of the inn were now a faint hum from outside.

Trenson slowly rose from the ground and got to his feet. He shook his arms in an effort to make the tingling stop, then brushed the dirt off him. He looked up at the tavern one last time before pulling the cloak's hood once more over his face and walking in the direction of the palace.

Well, that went well.

V

"And then," Trenson said passionately, motioning with his arms to add to the drama. "And then, the two men threw me out of the inn and into the street, laughing their heads off the whole time!"

Jayfor nodded patiently, pursing his lips. "Yes, I know," he said simply.

The king's lack of concern startled Trenson, and he cast a sideways look at Jayfor. "What do you mean, 'I know?' This is bad!"

Jayfor nodded, with no change of expression. "I know this is bad. But the story was a little more exciting the first time you told it to me. After the second or third or fourth time, it gets old."

Trenson opened his mouth to respond, then realized Jayfor was right, and closed it in defeat.

Trenson was back in the palace and explaining the tavern scene to Jayfor — not for the first time. Jayfor was still in the infirmary, but his condition was improving rapidly. He was in good shape and young, and with the help of a few herbs prescribed by the healers, he was improving daily. His ribs still caused him pain when he ate or bent in any direction, but the healers said that would go away.

At this point, the only reason Jayfor was still confined to the infirmary was because of his arm. The bone wasn't broken, the healers finally figured out, but merely fractured. This was great news, because it meant that Jayfor's arm wouldn't be crooked when it healed. There wasn't much the healers could do about a broken arm, other than hope it wouldn't mend the wrong way. A fracture was much better. It would practically heal itself.

Since Jayfor was much better than that, he was able to return to his duties as king, something that Trenson was exceedingly grateful for. And since Jayfor was right-handed, he could sign all the documents that needed to be signed, too. Trenson's mind still ached from all the things he had to multitask and think about, not to mention the cramp in his hand from signing scrolls. He handed the position back to Jayfor readily and returned to being his right-hand man. Jayfor offered to let Trenson continue doing the paperwork, seeing how much he enjoyed it, but Trenson responded with enough threats that Jayfor took back the offer.

The healer was mashing up some herbs in a bowl and sprinkling them into a cup of steaming tea. Satisfied, he walked to Jayfor and gingerly handed him the cup.

"There you are, my king. It's hot, so be careful."

Jayfor took the cup and offered a half smile to the healer, which failed miserably. Trenson grinned. Jayfor frequently complained that he was made to drink this disgusting tea for 'healing purposes.' Trenson had asked earlier if he always drank the tea. Jayfor had avoided the question and changed the subject.

"Thank you," Jayfor replied, rather bluntly. The healer bowed, then returned to the table to make more herb powder, presumably for more tea.

Trenson eyed the tea, which was a pale brown color, then Jayfor, and a wry look danced in his eyes, even though he didn't crack a smile. "Well? Drink up!"

Jayfor frowned at Trenson. He knew exactly what Trenson was doing. "It's hot," he said simply. To add to the effect, he stuck his finger in the cup. Surprisingly, it wasn't as hot as he had expected, and was probably cool enough to drink easily. But Trenson didn't need to know that. Jayfor pulled his finger out of the cup and shook his finger like it was burned. "Very hot," he added.

Trenson wasn't buying it. "What? It can't be that hot! I don't even see any steam! Let me see." Then, to Jayfor's horror, Trenson reached forward over the bed, reached out his hand, and stuck his own finger in the tea. Jayfor almost dropped the cup in surprise. Jayfor quickly moved the cup out from Trenson's finger and held it on the opposite side of the bed. "Trenson!"

But it was too late. "See?! That tea isn't that hot! It's the perfect temperature!" Trenson put on an accusing face, but inside he was brimming with pride. Most of the time it was Jayfor pulling his leg and forcing him into these situations. Now the tables had turned, and he knew that Jayfor knew it.

Jayfor feigned anger. "I can't believe you just did that. You stuck your finger in my drink. That's disgusting!"

Trenson wiped his hand on his garb and kept his mouth in a straight line, not letting a trace of a smile escape. "I was just checking to see if it was hot!"

"I told you it was!"

"But it wasn't!"

Jayfor sighed. How did he get here in the first place? Now he was starting to wish more than ever that he hadn't gone out in battle in the first place, only to end up in this situation.

Trenson continued. "In any case, it's not hot. So you best drink it all before it gets cold."

With a cold stare, Jayfor returned Trenson's seemingly innocent face. Trenson thought he won. But Jayfor wasn't done yet. "I can't drink it now! Who knows what your hands have been on today? What if you touched something that will give me a terrible illness? I can't risk it."

"What?" For once, Trenson's brows knitted together as he realized Jayfor had the upper hand. "I mean — I haven't had my hands on anything not clean, I promise. I—"

"No, no, I don't think it would be a good idea. I think I will just have to skip this one." Jayfor set the cup on a table beside the bed.

Trenson was showing signs of distress, and was about to say something when the healer who had given Jayfor his tea came over. "Is something wrong?" he asked, a questioning look on his face. Trenson and Jayfor had no idea that their bickering was loud enough to attract the attention of pretty much everyone in the room — from the servants to the healers.

Trenson turned to the healer. "Yes, in fact, there is. It seems Jayfor won't—"

"No, there isn't," Jayfor interrupted, smiling at the healer. "I simply burned my tongue on that tea. You were right, it was hot!"

"Oh!" The healer smiled, totally ignorant of what actually happened. "My apologies. I thought something must be wrong."

Jayfor shook his head. "No, we're fine. I appreciate your concern, though."

The healer bowed. "It's my duty, your majesty." Then he walked off, heading back to his concoction-making.

Jayfor waited until the healer was out of earshot. Then he looked at Trenson, a giant grin on his face. Trenson had his arms crossed and was staring at the floor. After a few more seconds, he met Jayfor's eyes and said steadily, without humor, "Sometimes I wish I could fire you." He didn't try to hide the defeat in his eyes.

Jayfor clicked his tongue. "You gave up your role of king too early, it seems."

***

Kylor stood in the woods outside of town, waiting patiently. He leaned against the smooth bark of an oak tree and enjoyed the shade, along with the cool breeze that wafted through the tree limbs. He scanned the surrounding area, waiting for someone.

This job was almost too easy. It sometimes puzzled him why he was hired to do what he did. There was nothing special about him, and yet his contractor had specifically chosen him to do this. He didn't know to what end his contractor was using him for, but whatever it was, he didn't care, so long as he got paid.

It sure beat his life at the academy. Kylor remembered his earlier years, when he was enrolled in a university in Loronis. His father was a wealthy merchant and well versed in politics, deciding that he wanted his only son to be educated in the most advanced school in Faldon.

Kylor applied himself to his studies diligently, and soon rivaled his teachers in knowledge, though not very much in wisdom. He was sometimes labeled a troublemaker, and Kylor took this name to be a badge of honor. He wasn't ashamed of breaking rules; in fact, he rather enjoyed it. His father didn't care about his behavior as long as he passed the exams, so his conduct was never checked. His teachers, most of whom weren't the most moral either, did nothing to change his ways, and some of them even encouraged him in his activities.

If there was one thing that Kylor could do better than anyone else, it was speak. Even he didn't know exactly how he did it, but when he wanted to, he could lull a crowd to sleep or pull them into a frenzy. It was a natural talent, but he never cared much for it, only using it when it allowed him to achieve his goals.

After many years of study, he graduated. He was offered a teaching position at the academy, but declined, as now he had the freedom to do whatever he wished. At first, his newfound freedom was something to celebrate. He could do whatever, whenever, with whoever. But his money didn't last forever, and in a blink of an eye he was broke and in need of food. He tried to look for another way to earn money and continue his lifestyle, but found none. He was so desperate that he started considering taking a real job to make ends meet.

Thankfully, before he was forced to do that, he was offered a different sort of job. Unlike a monotonous all-day occupation, he was offered so many coins that it made his head spin thinking about it. He could live for years on it and have as much fun as he wanted. And there was only one requirement: Whenever the contractor told him to, he would go to taverns and speak about whatever it was the contractor wanted him to. That was it. In return for his service, he would be paid handsomely.

Kylor chuckled to himself. What a boring life the rest of the world lived. He was happy and rich, and could do whatever he pleased. If only those people who called him a troublemaker could see him now.

Finally, after waiting for some time, he saw who he was looking for: a large warrior in black armor, emerging through the underbrush in the distance. Kylor smiled. It was time to be rewarded for his work. He started walking towards the towering knight. The soldier walked through bushes and hedgerows as if they weren't even there, plowing through them with ease.

When they were within a few yards of each other, they both stopped. Kylor spoke first. "I expect you brought my payment?"

The warrior merely grunted and produced a large bag from behind his back. He tossed it to Kylor with ease, who caught it and almost dropped it from its weight. He heard the jingle of coins inside and felt a ping of satisfaction. He looked up at the warrior, who stared back at him through empty eye holes. Then Kylor undid the bag's string and looked inside. His eyes reflected the hundreds of gold coins glimmering in the bag.

Kylor looked at the warrior, a disappointed look on his face. "This isn't the amount that we agreed on. Not even close."

The warrior crossed his arms. "Do you really think that we would pay you for your work before it was finished? How else would we know that you will carry out our commands?"

Kylor shook his head. "The whole reason we're meeting now is for you to pay me for my services. In fact, I thought after this, I would be done."

"No. Not yet." The warrior turned and started pacing from left to right, not looking at Kylor. Kylor watched him skeptically. "Plans change. We require your services a little longer to ensure our success. Consider this a down payment. There is much more to come — if you indeed continue to do as we say."

Kylor straightened at the prospect of more money. "I'm listening."

"You have already made exceptional progress in swaying the people. Continue to do what you are doing. Give speeches and rally the people, and create as much an uproar as possible. This time, however, direct your attacks on Va'ar as much as possible. For example, call Him a tyrant and talk about how those who serve Him look down at the rest of the world. Anything antagonistic about Va'ar or the king will do." The warrior continued pacing and talking, not looking at Kylor as he did, as if he were talking to himself. "This will be the final stage of our plan. After this, we will no longer need you."

Kylor nodded, still gripping the sack of money. "So do what I'm doing, just more against Va'ar, until you give the word?"

The warrior abruptly stopped and turned his helmeted head towards Kylor. Not for the first time, Kylor felt chills as the black mountain of a warrior stared at him, but he shook off the feeling. "Yes."

"Then I will be paid in full?"

"Then you will be paid in full."

Kylor nodded again. He liked the sound of that. "Consider it done." He furrowed his eyebrows. "You better keep your side of the bargain and provide me with payment."

The warrior stared down at Kylor. "We always keep our word."

Kylor wasn't completely sure; nothing about this knight said "honest." But it was so much money promised in the end that it would be impossible to refuse. He shrugged inwardly and opened the bag again, his eyes lighting up again at the sight of the coins. He stuck one hand into the bag and ran his fingers through it, feeling thrills as his hands passed through the gold and the shine reflected onto his face.

"This is almost too easy," he said offhandedly, still looking at the coins in the bag. "I don't even believe everything I'm telling them. Yet they believe what I say, and I'm being paid to say it!"

He heard the warrior's voice. "What you believe or think you believe is none of our concern. We only need your charisma to make the people have faith in what we want, and so long as your thoughts do not interfere, you may do whatever you please."

Kylor wasn't really paying attention to the warrior's words. He was too busy fingering his new gold. Then a thought suddenly occurred to him, and he stopped. "Why are you making me do this, telling the people what to believe? What is it you gain from it?"

There was silence. Kylor looked up from the bag, expecting to see the dark knight, but instead he saw only grass and underbrush where he was once standing. The warrior was gone.

VI

THE INFLUENCE OF KYLOR only grew. Every day, reports about another speech given, another dozen people added to Kylor's posse, another group of people gathering and protesting that Jayfor's rule was unfair and that they deserved justice. Hardly was there any good news worth telling of.

"Five years ago, I risked my life to save these people from Xavson's tyrannical rule," Jayfor commented one day to Trenson. "They praised us as their savior. Now they act like I'm worse than he was."

Trenson shook his head, exasperated. "I know," was all he said. He couldn't believe it either. He had a hard time processing it, the fact that it only took one man with a way with words to change the views of all Loronis. Faldon prided itself by allowing the freedom of speech, no matter how radical or controversial the speech was, but that also meant that Kylor could say whatever he wanted and not be arrested for it, so long as his speech didn't incite riots or cause fights. Kylor was getting very close to crossing that line, however; taverns were buzzing with people talking over Kylor's latest speech.

Jayfor looked Trenson in the eye, not even trying to hide the inner turmoil he felt. "Be honest, Trenson, am I really a worse king than Xavson?"

"What?!" Trenson was shocked that Jayfor would even consider the possibility. "No! Of course not! Faldon has never been better. You have lowered the tax rate while simultaneously increasing trade and improving the economy. New inventions and great victories have been achieved under your rule. You even invented a mill powered by water current which has revolutionized the process of milling. Xavson did none of these things."

Jayfor offered a weak smile. "Thank you." His smile disappeared. "But the people don't think so. And it is by the people that a king must rule. If I were to eliminate all of Elara single-handedly, and the people didn't like it, then I would have failed as a king."

"But you would have succeeded as a person," Trenson said. "And your duties as a follower of Va'ar come before those of a king."

Despite the situation they were in, Jayfor couldn't help but grin. "Since when did you become so wise?"

Trenson shrugged. "I surprise even myself sometimes."

Jayfor laughed. "Well, I'm glad that you're here to make me feel better about myself."

Trenson shrugged again, then changed the subject. "So, what is it you plan to do now?"

Jayfor's good humor dissipated into a serious countenance. He had thought about this for some time. "I've been thinking about that. Everyone wants me to give an answer to Kylor's accusations, so I'll give them one. I've already planned to give a speech to the people in another week, and will announce I will do so today. No doubt Kylor and his lackies will show up, and I'll show them just how absurd he really is."

"That ought to do it," Trenson agreed. "I like the sound of that. Do you really think Kylor will give up?"

"No, of course not. But my goal isn't to change Kylor's views; it's to show everyone that Kylor really isn't as smart as they take him to be. If I can explain to them how the notion that there is no right and wrong is self-refuting and convince them to turn back to Va'ar, then I will consider it a success."

Trenson nodded. "Sounds like a plan."

"It's the only thing I can think of doing. The people have completely turned from Va'ar and abandoned the very foundation for all reason. As a result, they believe whatever some man with sly words says." Jayfor ran his hand through his sand-colored hair. "This might be the last chance for the people to see how wrong they are." He met eyes with Trenson. "I have a feeling that something big is about to happen — something that can never be undone. I don't know," he raised his hands in a helpless gesture, "maybe all this work is getting to me."

Trenson frowned. "I think you're right. Not about the work getting to you, but about something big coming. It's almost like there's a storm cloud over us, and at any moment, the bottom will fall out."

***

Later that day, along the long gray walls of the city, all was quiet. That was usual. On most days, there was nothing worth telling of, and the sentries would spend the day walking left and right, left and right, switch positions with their comrades for a different side of the city, eat a mediocre lunch, then walk back and forth for another six or seven hours before they were relieved by the night guards. It was boring, they all admitted, but it paid well, and had a certain prestige to it, so it was better than nothing.

One of these guards was particularly bored. He had recently changed shifts with another guard for a different part of the wall, and now was counting the seconds until he could leave and catch up on some much-wanted sleep. He leaned nonchalantly against the opposite side of the wall and stared out at the open plain before him.

He didn't find this section of land to be any more interesting than the previous one, other than this one had more trees than the last one. It was unfortunate that he didn't find trees very in-teresting. He was guarding the front gate of the capital, which, considering there were still a few solid hours until nightfall, was unnaturally quiet. There were still people strolling into or out of the capital, mostly merchants or couriers. He could tell the difference because the merchants usually wore bright colors and had carts pulled by horses or donkeys, while couriers wore darker outfits and rode on horses.

It was odd, the guard mused, for there to be this little activity outside the walls. He was slightly disappointed. Watching people go in and out of the city was one of the few activities that he could do on guard, but there was almost no one out. He sighed. This was looking like a more boring day than ever.

Actually... He glimpsed something in the distance, riding towards the capital. It was close enough for him to tell that this was no courier or merchant, but it was still too far away to tell what exactly it was. He could tell that this wasn't one of the small, quick messenger horses that couriers rode. The horse was bigger and bulkier, and ran with a somewhat slower gait, more like a battle horse. He could also make out a figure riding on the animal's back.

Now intrigued, the guard squinted and leaned forward over the crenelations on the wall. There was also something unusual about the person riding it. As the horse came closer, he could tell that the rider was slouched forward strangely in the saddle, like he was sleeping while riding,

The horse came to the drawbridge and began to trot across it, its hooves clopping hollowly against the wood, and that's when the guard saw that the rider really *was* sleeping in the saddle. But what puzzled him the most was the fact that the person in the saddle was wearing full armor, and he looked more like he was dead than sleeping.

The horse passed through the gate and into the city, and the guard quickly changed to the opposite side of the wall to watch him. The horse and its unconscious rider sauntered through the streets of the city. People stopped and stared.

The horse made it about a hundred yards through the city. Then the rider slid sideways out of the saddle and tumbled to the ground and lay still on the road. The horse kept trotting a few paces, then sensed its rider was gone and stopped, and stood still in the middle of the road, a few yards from its fallen rider. The knight didn't move and lay in a heap of armor on the ground.

Well, the guard thought, *my day just got a lot more interesting.*

***

News spread fast. The unconscious knight was brought to the palace by some compassionate passersby, and he was taken into the infirmary. But it was useless. It didn't take but a few minutes for the healers to know that he was dead, and had been for some time. The servants called for Jayfor and Trenson, who came as soon as they could.

When they went into the infirmary and saw the knight, they couldn't help but gasp. It was Sir Turner, a respected general that was sent a few weeks ago to the front lines against Elara. After Agrond left five years ago, he had taken over his role and had been instrumental in several key victories against Kallary and Elara. He was a lighthearted man who cared deeply about those under his command, and always used his authority to help others, rather than bring them down. He wasn't just obeyed by his men, but respected, and was seen as a father figure to most of his men. But now he lay still, his heartbeat quiet, his breathing stopped, his eyes open like he was still watching everything that happened around him. He was dead.

But that wasn't why Jayfor and Trenson gasped. On Turner's forehead, branded in black letters the color of coal, was a message: *I come for you.*

VII

"THERE'S ONLY ONE THING left to do!" Randolph exclaimed, slamming his fist down into the table of the council room to emphasize his point. "We need to summon every fighter and every man bearing a weapon to the front lines in a final stand against Elara. It's gone on for too long! Pull out all the stops and give them everything!"

Trenson, Jayfor, Norman and Randolph, along with many other generals and commanders in Faldon's army, were seated along the edge of the long table of the council room. They were gathered here today to discuss what should be done next against Elara, and exactly how they should go about doing it. The fact that they were on the brink of defeat was obvious. But what they did next would determine if the kingdom survived or died, and the weight of that decision made the atmosphere in the room heavy.

Sir Turner's death and the ominous message branded on his forehead only served to dampen everyone's spirits further. The death of the major general was a heavy blow to the army's morale, for everyone looked up to him and trusted his leadership even when the odds were against them. His arrival yesterday, already dead and bearing a cruel message, showed just how ruthless their foes really were. They reverently buried the honored captain that night in the graveyard, along with so many other captains and leaders who had given their lives for the kingdom.

Trenson broke the silence after Randolph's statement. "I'm not sure an all-out frontal assault is such a good idea."

Randolph shot him a withering look. "It's the only thing left to do! After suffering a dishonor such as this, we need to retaliate swiftly and teach them a lesson!" Randolph was fuming that Elara would dare treat their general like this, and looked like he was about to charge and face all of Elara by himself if no one agreed with him.

Trenson tried to calm Randolph down. "Be realistic, Randolph. If we blindly sent every man in Faldon against Elara, do you really think we have a chance of winning? Do you think that would 'teach them a lesson'?"

To the contrary, Trenson's rebuttal only served to fuel Randolph's fire. "Well, it would be better than sitting here, twiddling our thumbs and feeling sorry for ourselves! I'd rather die with honor!"

Despite how reckless Randolph's call to action was, a few commanders around the table nodded their agreement. They shared the baron's view of valiant and romantic battles, no matter the odds, and in their opinion, so long as they died in battle, they didn't really care if they won or lost. They were ready to head out and fight anytime.

Jayfor spoke. "We're all upset about what happened to Turner." He took a deep breath. "Believe me, I would like nothing more than to charge into Elara and avenge Turner's death. But while emotions are great advisors, they are terrible rulers. We must step back and look at the big picture before deciding on what should be done."

"I have!" Randolph rebutted, "and I've made my decision!"

Norman spoke up, his small voice barely reaching all sides of the table. "But we can't just abandon the kingdom! It would be too risky, and if we lost, then there would be no hope of saving the kingdom!"

"Norman is right," Jayfor said, before Randolph could reply. "While I do believe a counterattack of some sort needs to happen, we can't afford another frontal assault. Last time we did that, I almost died, and you two," he looked at Norman and Randolph, "had to carry me back. Another one is nothing but asking for more casualties."

"I agree," another captain at the table said, "We need something strategic, something that will stop Elara's momentum."

Randolph looked at the other commanders in anger and was about to say something, but then realized they were right. He was smarter than this; the last thing they needed was another disastrous frontal assault. He grunted and sat back in his chair, crossing his arms. "As long as I get to fight them," he mumbled, "I don't care what plan we use."

Jayfor breathed an inward sigh of relief at having quelled Randolph's ranting. Although he didn't agree with Randolph, he could relate to what the baron was feeling. After their general was treated so wrongly, he felt a desire to storm out without a plan and attack Elara single-handedly as well. But unlike Randolph, he didn't let his emotions interfere with his reason.

Trenson pointed to the large map spread across the table, with corresponding blue and black tokens on it to denote their forces and those of Elara. "Elara has gained so much of our territory, and is so close to our capital, that we need nothing short of a miracle to push them back."

"How many soldiers are in their main army?" One of the generals piped in.

Jayfor replied, "We don't exactly know. We rarely get feedback from our spies on their forces since they always find and kill them. But it is clear from the few reports that we do receive that it almost beyond count. Some say one, two, or even five hundred thousand troops are in their army."

The captains' eyes all grew wide as they looked at each other and murmured in disbelief. Five hundred thousand! That was over a hundred times more than the troops they had left. Nothing they could do would leave a dent in an army so massive.

One of the captains at the table stood up from his chair, anguish in his features. "What is there to do?" he said desperately. "No matter what we do, Faldon will surely face extinction against a force so large! There is no way we can win!"

Some commanders raised their fists in approval and shouted their agreement. The others did the same, but in opposition. Another commander stood up, pointing a finger at the first captain. "You have completely lost faith in our cause!" he shouted. "You are no better than a traitor for your lack of belief in our cause! I would rather die than live with dishonor!"

The other captain's face turned red with anger and he slammed a fist into the table, making it shudder. "Then die you will, along with all your comrades who march blindly into battle! At least I have enough common sense to not rush into every battle that is within reach, or to fight for causes which have no hope!"

An uproar immediately ensued, and the tranquility of the room shattered into chaos. Every commander was split in one of two factions, one side vehemently supporting the need to continue the fighting, even if that meant certain death; the other side saw continuing the war as hopeless and advocated that they needed to settle this with a peace treaty, surrender, or even abandoning the capital and moving to re-establish Faldon. Randolph, the loudest in the room and on the side of fighting to the death, was in another general's face and shouting with a crazed look in his eye. Norman sat in the corner, eating candies from a side pocket in his outfit and watching the action, not taking part of it in any way.

Jayfor buried his head into his hands. He felt like giving up. Not only did the people hate him, but he also couldn't even keep his own generals unified. He gripped his hair hard in frustration. Kylor was right: he couldn't do this. He couldn't –

"Silence!"

An extremely loud voice pierced through the noise. All the turmoil immediately ceased, along with all the noise. The fighting stopped dead in its tracks. Every head turned to hear the voice's source. Jayfor lifted his head and looked beside him to see Trenson standing tall, looking over the group with a strange look in his eyes. His countenance commanded respect.

"Listen to yourselves, squabbling over our next plan of action. Don't you see that if we can't even stand together as one, that we have no hope of winning, whether you wish to flee or fight? If we bicker among ourselves and fight against our friends, then who really is our enemy? We will all be killed without drawing a sword if we choose to fight our allies rather than face the enemy, who is approaching towards our capital, intent on letting not a single soul escape."

There was a spark in Trenson's eyes and a determination that almost left Jayfor in awe, for never before had he seen his friend like this before. The commanders were equally shocked, and just as equally ashamed of their infighting as Trenson's words reached their hearts. Everyone was silent as they absorbed Trenson's words, while Trenson continued.

"And if we choose to flee rather than fight, we have already subjected ourselves to the same death as we would have in fighting. Elara wants every Faldian dead, and after they take the capital, they will not be satisfied until they have rooted out and destroyed every remnant of our kingdom. By running away, we are merely sealing our doom for another time."

Some of the commanders who had sided on fleeing saw the sense in Trenson's words and nodded in understanding. Still, others huffed and shook their heads. But even if they didn't agree with Trenson, they couldn't help but have a feeling of admiration towards him as his words reached their hearts.

"But let us not, my friends, think we achieve either victory or defeat by our own actions. Nothing could be farther from the truth! No, we need to return to the reason this war began, and why we are still fighting it. We need to return to the fact that we fight for Va'ar, not just to save our own necks! Va'ar determines if a battle is won or lost, if a soldier lives or falls, if a kingdom prospers or is brought to ruin. If we abandon Him, then it is impossible for us to win this war. If we turn our backs on the author of victories, is it not certain that he will not grant us the victories we desire?"

All the generals looked down, as if there was suddenly something interesting about their shoes. Trenson's words cut into them like a knife as they were forced to grapple with their own convictions. He was right: they *had* abandoned Va'ar; that was why they were losing. Maybe not openly or all at once. If you asked them, they would answer that they served Va'ar. But saying those words was the only time they served Him. Their life was no different from an unbeliever. Many in the room felt repentance. But some still didn't see the reason they had lost so many battles, and blamed it on Va'ar rather than themselves, and they felt anger towards Trenson for calling them out.

And they were even angrier that Trenson wasn't finished. "If we should all stand together in unity, and fight not only under Va'ar's banner but under His command, then we have already won the battle. If we are to conquer, and drive Elara back, and reclaim our territory, then thanks be to Va'ar! But if we should all die by Elara's sword and our kingdom fall to ashes, then we have still won, for we died serving Va'ar, and there is no truer commitment than one who is willing to die for his king."

Trenson paused for a moment, looking around at the faces staring at him, some in anger, some in shame, some in committed resolve, but all in awe of Trenson's words. Trenson, the spark leaving his eyes and his voice returning to normal, spoke one last time, his voice soft. "Will you fight beside us?"

Silence. Jayfor continuing staring at Trenson. He tried to take in what Trenson just said, or rather, what he just did. Trenson couldn't write a speech to save his life. Jayfor had tried to help, because for someone of Trenson's rank, it was important to be able to present yourself in front of lots of people. But Trenson never could manage it without summarizing, repeating the same thing over and over, or adding lots of "uhhh's" and "ummm's." But he had just delivered the most compelling call to action that Jayfor had ever heard.

Jayfor looked around the table quietly, looking for someone to stand up and give their support. Each captain sat in suspense. For some, they knew they would fight for Jayfor and Va'ar to the death. For others, they could not decide what to do, and were wrestling with their convictions. A few scowled bitterly at Jayfor, actively showing that they considered fighting worthless and they would not side with Va'ar.

Then Randolph stepped forward from the crowd, his face firm, and drew his sword with a *shing*. The blade was large and reflected the light. He held it before him for a second, then gently placed it on the table, on top of the map. Still holding the blade's handle, he looked at Jayfor with a look that testified to his commitment and respect. "I am with you, my king."

The sound of other swords being drawn rang out, and one by one, other generals came forward to place their swords on top of Randolph's, the swords forming a circle of steel around the middle of the table, a pact of their oath to continue fighting for Va'ar, no matter what it may cost them, for it was worth it to serve their lord.

Trenson drew his sword as well and placed it on the table, giving Jayfor an encouraging nod while doing so.

Norman, lost in his own world with his candies, suddenly realized that everyone was putting their swords on the table. He wasn't really listening to Trenson's speech, as he drowned it out along with the generals fighting before that. But now everyone was putting their sword on the table. Maybe he should, too. Hastily, he shoved the box back into his pocket, drew his sword and placed it on the table with the others, but he fumbled with the blade as he set it in the pile, and so the weapon stuck out much farther than the others. Norman hoped nobody noticed. Unfortunately, they all did.

A group of four generals stood separate from those gathered around the table. They scowled at their companions' decision to fight, and when the last general supporting the king placed his sword on the pile, everyone turned towards them to see what they would do.

The look of anger on their faces only intensified. "Don't think that because of his speech, we'll change our mind!" one of them responded indignantly. They started walking towards the doors of the chamber, each one of them sneering back at the captains around the table, notably Jayfor and Trenson, who watched them leave with great sadness and regret on their faces. The room was silent save for the quick footsteps of the generals' leaving.

When they reached the doors and pushed them open, they stopped and turned to look at the faces staring back at them. "Kylor was right," one of them threw defiantly. "You have all completely lost your minds!"

And with that, they departed the room and let the doors slam hard behind them.

The room was silent for a period. A gloomy atmosphere pervaded the room, the departure of the generals only adding to the feeling of hopelessness that they could ever win against Elara. But nobody mulled over the generals' leaving for very long, because every eye soon turned to Jayfor, waiting anxiously to see what the king would do now.

Jayfor looked back at every face staring at him, not showing any fear or sadness or worry. There was only resolve, a firm resolve that said that no matter what came, no matter the consequences, no matter what it might cost him, even if he lost his life, he would stand.

Slowly, Jayfor drew his brilliant sword from its scabbard, the hiss of steel echoing in the room. Trenson watched the light of the room flicker off the silver edge of the blade and reflect off the gem in the hilt guard's center, sending light flashing across the room. Jayfor held the sword up for a few seconds, his eyes taking in the majestic craft of the weapon, then firmly placed the sword on top of the others on the table. The king's sword easily outdid every blade under it.

"Even if this kingdom shall fall and we all perish, I shall die fighting for the only cause worth dying for." Jayfor's words were simple, yet the weight of his words were heavy.

"As will I," every general replied in unison. There was no hesitation.

Jayfor nodded once. "Thank you." He then retracted his sword from the pile and slid the blade easily back into his sheath, ending the pact that had just taken place. Trenson, Randolph, Norman, and the other commanders took their swords back as well and placed them back in their scabbards, until the table was empty, and, besides the fact that four generals had left the room, there was no sign that anything had taken place. But the atmosphere in the room had changed. Instead of being gloomy and hopeless, now there was newfound courage.

Jayfor returned to business and pointed at the map. "The next battle we fight will very likely be the last hope. Elara is probably less than two weeks away from here. By the time we can gather the soldiers and meet them on the field, they will almost certainly be between the Ashdin woods and the Idonia mountains." He pointed at the plains between the two locations. "That is where we will meet them in battle."

"But how?" A general spoke up. "They have over one hundred times our numbers. Meeting them in a frontal assault would be suicide." The rest all mumbled their agreement.

"I have a plan," Jayfor said with a cunning smile. He waited a few seconds to make sure everyone was listening. By the way they stared at him, it was clear they were, so he continued.

"I have seen this myself: Elara has no archers, calvary, or any unit whatsoever beside infantry. We can use this to our advantage." He met each general in the eye. "Since this battle is the tipping point, I will send every one of you into the field. Each of your leadership will provide a moral boost to the troops and will help ensure our success."

"You're not going with us?" Norman asked in disbelief.

Jayfor shook his head. "I would like to, but… I have matters to attend to here, and with the people begging me to give a speech, I can't afford to leave." Desperately, Jayfor wanted to join them. His heart longed to go with them and fight in this decisive battle, but he couldn't. The memory of an earlier conversation with Trenson flashed into his mind.

"Jayfor, you can't go. I won't let you."

"Why not? I am the king of the last region fighting against Elara, and we are on the verge of defeat. It's my duty to go with them for this battle."

"It's too risky. You know as well as I that we won't win."

"I believe we have a fair chance."

"Don't dismiss the obvious. There is an extremely small chance that we will win that battle. As much as you wish to avoid it, you must see that if we were to lose you, it would seal the destruction of Faldon without a doubt. That's why you can't leave."

"Trenson, I will not abandon them! I will *lead them into battle, whether you like it or not. You will stay here and act as king in my stead. If I don't return—"*

"That's what I'm trying to tell you! Even you know that if you head into battle, it is very unlikely you will ever return."

"And what if I don't return? At least I will have fought for my kingdom, instead of prattling in my palace while my kinfolk are being slain! And I have ridden out to battle before; this is no different."

"I know more than anyone that the last thing you want is to abandon your army in such a pivotal battle. But let's say we did end up winning the fight, and completely vanquished Elara's army. If we lost not a single troop or general, but you were to fall, then nothing

we could do would ever be able to rebuild Faldon. Without you, the kingdom would crumble by itself, even if we won every other battle against the Dark Order. Those battles were different - the situation wasn't so dire."

"That's not true. You could rule just as well as me."

"You know that's not true. After just two weeks, I was about ready to call it quits on being a steward. The kingdom only got worse while I was in charge, and I doubt things would get any better with you gone permanently."

In the end, Trenson made Jayfor promise not to ride out to battle. Jayfor felt a stab of shame pierce him now, standing before the generals, feeling guilty that he was sending them to what very well may be their doom. However, unknown to him, each of them understood why he couldn't come, and agreed inwardly with the king staying behind, not because they didn't want him to lead them, but that it would be another risk to take.

Jayfor continued. "Anyway, we will divide the army into layers. To ensure that we will not be surrounded, the front lines will be stretched farther than normal. Onagers and trebuchets will be stationed at the rear, while infantry will make up the center and spearmen and archers will take the front lines. We will still use what little calvary we have, but they won't come in until the first part of my plan has taken place.

"Once the lines have been drawn out and the enemy is in sight, the archers in front and siege weapons in the rear will launch a fusillade, which should clear off a few hundred Elarians at the minimum. The siege weapons will continue to launch missiles throughout the battle, but once the enemy is within a hundred yards, the archers will return to the rear flank and launch arrows from behind.

"Then, once the melee has initiated combat, the battle will proceed normally, except under one circumstance. Elara likes to swarm their enemy with sheer numbers. If their army starts to form a half circle around our army to close in, the calvary will charge out on each flank and repel them from both sides. Once you have cleared them from both flanks, you will return to the middle until they try to surround again. The process will repeat until we have won."

Every face in the room slowly lit up as they realized the brilliance of Jayfor's plan. Besides the dark warriors, sheer numbers are the only advantage Elara had. And Elara was known for surrounding their enemy with those numbers. The calvary charge on each flank would keep them from swarming them, and effectively neutralize their only advantage.

"I like it," Randolph announced, breaking the silence. He didn't say anything else, but he was smiling, which was a rare enough sight to make it clear he thought this was a good plan.

A chorus of agreements filtered throughout the generals. With a plan like this, maybe victory wasn't so far away after all. Even Trenson, who was the master of seeing holes and flaws in plans, was impressed. *This might work,* he thought.

One of the generals spoke up. "With a gambit like this, we may turn the tides yet!"

"Aye!" another said. "Those Elarians won't know what hit 'em!"

Excitement built in the room. The gloomy atmosphere was replaced with enthusiasm and eagerness.

Then Norman stopped eating his candy and spoke up. "What about the dark warriors, Krenors? What are we going to do about them?"

Like a curtain, the buzz in the room dropped. No one had thought about that. The Krenors were the other big reason they lost almost every battle; nobody could harm them. They all turned to Jayfor, seeing how the king would solve the problem.

Jayfor sighed. "Nothing we have ever done has stopped or even remotely slowed them down. I honestly don't think that anything we can do will stop them. A calvary charge might slow them down, or even possibly bring some of them down, but besides an onager landing a boulder on one of them, I don't think there's anything we can do. Let's focus on the normal forces. Then the Krenors will turn back if they're the only ones left."

It wasn't a favorable response, but it was the only option. There was nothing they could do against such powers of darkness, so everyone just had to accept that fact.

A general spoke up. "Maybe Va'ar will send a Senver to help us fight the Dark Order, like He did with Agrond."

Jayfor offered a half-smile. "Maybe," was all he said.

"When would we set out?" A general asked.

"As soon as you're ready," Jayfor replied. "Most of the levies have been called upon anyway, so besides packing the rations, which will take a few days at most, everything is in place. And thank goodness it is, because Elara is almost knocking at our door."

Silence encompassed the room. Trenson ran through the battle plan in his head, committing it to memory, even though he wasn't going off to fight. There was nothing else to be said. Jayfor looked up.

"Well, I think that's it. This meeting has officially ended."

VIII

After some closing comments and discussing minor details about how they would organize when they set out, the council was over. The generals said they would start the preparations at once. The two barons, Randolph and Norman, had to return to their respective fiefs to assign stewards and settle things, but they would soon return to the capital with their share of soldiers once again.

Trenson noticed that Jayfor didn't get up from his seat when the council ended. This was a little strange, as Jayfor was usually the first one to rise when meetings were over. But this time he didn't, not even when the generals started to leave the room. Trenson gave the king a questioning look, and Jayfor replied with an expression that said, *there's something I want to discuss with you, privately.* Trenson understood and waited in his seat until the last general left the room.

When they were the only ones left in the room, Jayfor turned to Trenson. "What in the world was that?" he asked.

The question was so blunt that Trenson was puzzled. "What was what?"

"That speech! I spent years teaching you the basics, trying to help you become a better speaker. And then, as soon as I don't think there's any hope, you come out with a brilliant call to action, with no practice, no rehearsing, nothing!" Jayfor was teetering between pride and frustration. Pride, that Trenson stepped up and delivered the speech that he did, and at the just the right time. Frustration, that Trenson was never paying attention when Jayfor tried to help him in speech, and in order to talk like that, Jayfor would probably have to practice many times.

"Oh... that. I don't really know." Trenson was very casual about it. "It just came to me at the moment. They started arguing and fighting, and things were about to get out of control. Suddenly I felt like I should say something. So, I did."

Jayfor shook his head, the frustration side showing more of itself. "You just all of a sudden felt the need to start talking?"

"Basically."

To be honest, Trenson was a little surprised at himself too. Everyone, including himself, knew that he wasn't one to talk. He preferred to keep quiet and leave that to others. But he had just felt a strange urge to start talking, and when he did the words just poured out. He didn't even think about what he was saying. It felt like someone else was talking for him.

"Well, seeing as you can just 'basically' throw out speeches like that, maybe you can deliver addresses to the people after all." Jayfor smiled cunningly.

Trenson scowled and shook his head quickly. "That was a one-time thing. I'll leave that to professionals like you."

Jayfor huffed. Trenson wasn't going to agree no matter what, so he let it drop.

There was a brief period of silence before Trenson broke it. "So this is our final plan? Possibly our last battle against Elara?"

Jayfor nodded, returning to a solemn mood. "It depends. But you're right, this is the last chance to push them back and turn the tides. Even if we lose this battle, I guess there could be more skirmishes, but they would be a lost cause. Elara is so close now, and our army so small, that this will be the tipping point."

Trenson understood. "And you think it will tip in our favor?"

"I don't know. Of course, I desperately hope that it will, and I know if it is Va'ar's will, then we have nothing to fear. But I can't deny that the odds are stacked against us."

Trenson thought about Jayfor's words. He felt the same way, wondering if they could turn this war around this close to the end. His mind lingered when Jayfor said *Va'ar's will,* and a thought suddenly came to him. "What if it's not Va'ar's will that Faldon will survive?"

Jayfor raised an eyebrow, confused. "What do you mean?"

Trenson was trying to figure out the best way to say this. "What if Faldon is going to be destroyed anyway? What if that is His plan?"

"I... I guess that's an alternative. But what makes you think that?"

"It's something I just thought of. Don't get me wrong, I'm sure that it's Va'ar's design for us to win this battle, but if we didn't, I feel sure that it wouldn't be the end; that there would be some other way."

Jayfor thought about it for a few seconds. "Maybe," he said. "But let's hope it's His plan that we win. I don't want the last of our generals and men to go into the field for nothing. And mentally, I don't know if I can take another loss."

***

The generals who had openly opposed Jayfor's decision to fight left Loronis a few days later. They were given no order to leave by Trenson or Jayfor or anyone; they simply packed their things and left without giving a word. Nobody was very sad to see them go.

"Really?" Trenson asked Jayfor after their departure. "They just left?"

"Just like that. Didn't say a word to me or anyone. We didn't find out until today, when we tried to find them and their rooms were empty."

"Traitors," Trenson said with disgust. "I can't believe they would call us a 'lost cause,' after fighting with us for so long! We trusted them, and they fought and won our battles! How could they forget that?"

All Jayfor could answer with was a shrug. "People change."

The only downside to them leaving, however, was the fact that it reduced the number of generals for Faldon from ten to six, including Randolph and Norman, who had both taken roles as commanders and left stewards to rule their fiefs in the meantime. In order to efficiently command a force of a few thousand, every general would be sent out to fight, leaving them none if they lost the battle. This is why it was considered the last hope, for there was no way they could rebuild after another loss.

The next few days were spent in preparation. There was a lot to do: supply wagons had to be filled with food and extra equipment, weapons needed to be sharpened, and soldiers needed to be gathered and prepared for war. Jayfor did most of the work coordinating, but Trenson, Randolph and Norman did whatever they could to help as well, which Jayfor was grateful for. Randolph and Norman had individual preparations as well. They were the primary leaders of the battle, so their armor and weapons were in top shape.

Finally, a week after the defense council took place, the army marched from Loronis and towards the Ashdin woods, on the other side of which the enemy was.

Jayfor and Trenson met the two barons in the barracks a few hours before they were to depart. The scene was a busy one: knights ran back and forth, preparing weapons and armor, loading up the supplies, double-checking everything to ensure there wouldn't be any delays. Everyone was anxious, not just about getting everything ready, but about the battle ahead of them. This was a critical battle, one that would determine the fate of the kingdom. But Jayfor couldn't think of two better people to lead it than those standing in front of him.

"Is everything ready?" Jayfor asked. He already knew the answer. He knew every detail about the army down to the smallest detail. But it was a good way to start the conversation and break the ice.

Randolph chuckled. "You wouldn't think it by looking at the way these soldiers scramble like ants, but yes, almost." Randolph himself had finished arranging everything at his fief to be in order.

The last thing he wanted was to come home to find his castle in chaos. But his steward was an old friend, and he trusted him.

Just as a precaution, he gave instructions to the steward on what to do in case he didn't return home. This was unusual for him. He knew it was always a chance he took, going out to battle, but he never gave detailed instructions to the one he left in charge. He felt the need to this time, though. He knew how deadly this battle would be, and how slim his chance was at returning home. And he had a bad feeling about this battle, anyway. Better safe than sorry. He didn't know it, but Norman also made sure his castle was in order, in case he didn't return.

Jayfor nodded. "Very good."

It was an awkward silence. Jayfor wasn't exactly sure what to say next. For all he knew, this might be his last time talking to the barons. He felt like he should make it count. Of course, the one time he felt like he should say something, he was tongue-tied.

Out of all people, it was Norman who said something first. "What will happen if we win?" It was a thought that lingered in his mind. He always liked to know what could happen in the future.

"I'm not exactly sure," Jayfor replied. "It depends to what extent we defeat Elara. If we can defeat at least half of the army, then Elara will probably retreat. And if they retreat, then we can regroup, and after that it's a matter of what Elara does."

"So what we do afterwards is dependent on Elara," Randolph summed.

Jayfor nodded. "Exactly."

"And what if we lose?" Norman asked.

Jayfor smiled. "We're not going to, remember?"

Norman returned the smile nervously. "Right, right…" He didn't try to hide the fact that he wasn't confident at all in this battle.

But Norman wanted to fight. Just to make sure, after the war council, Jayfor told Norman that if he didn't want to fight, he didn't have to. Jayfor would find someone else to take his place. Jayfor wanted his generals to go willingly into the field; he wasn't forcing any of them to do it; he was asking. Norman shocked Jayfor by telling him that he wanted to fight and lead the men. Jayfor had already mentally lined up men to take his spot. But the baron wanted to fight. Jayfor didn't ask any questions or press the matter; he was so thankful that Norman had agreed to go that he didn't want to say anything that might change his mind.

Trenson said, "We can't wallow in what we are afraid will happen. We just have to go into battle, give it our all, and leave the rest to Va'ar."

"Exactly," Jayfor agreed. "It's like the wise person said: you can't steer a ship while watching the waves around you."

Trenson raised an eyebrow. "What wise person?"

"Me," Jayfor replied. "I can be very wise at times."

Trenson grunted a reply. Again, everyone was quiet for a time.

Then Randolph said, in a somber voice, "I think we should get to the men. We're going to be departing soon, anyway." Although he was enthusiastic about most battles, and he was certainly ready to fight this one, the danger and importance of this battle dampened his excitement. For all he knew, this could be his last time talking to his friends.

He looked first at Jayfor then at Trenson. "If we don't return, know that it was an honor serving by your side all these years. We achieved so much in the past five years." Trenson thought he saw the baron's eyes get moist, which he was not expecting. "It's only now that I realize how much I've lost, and gained, and taken for granted. Hopefully, I will look back on this battle in the future with pride, but in case I can't look back at it, know that you gave this baron a life to be proud of."

Jayfor opened his mouth to say something, but no words came out. Now he felt his own eyes getting moist. He swallowed hard, then found his voice. "I didn't give it to you, you chose it. I'm glad you have fought with us all these years. I became a better king and better leader with you at my side." Then Jayfor smiled at Norman. "And you too, Norman."

Norman sighed in exasperation. "How am I going to beat what Randolph just said? Everyone is being so inspirational, and I'm here thinking the same thing everyone is saying, but I can't think of how to say it originally!"

Jayfor chuckled. "That's alright, it's the thought that counts."

"Thank goodness for that." Norman said. He fiddled with the collar of his chain mail. He didn't have his candies – they were in his saddlebag, which was on his horse — and so he was having to resort to other stress-relieving habits.

Randolph took a deep breath and clapped his hands together. "Well, we're off. Va'ar willing, we'll see you in in a few weeks."

Trenson was the first to reply. "Good luck. Knock out some Elarians for me." But inwardly, he was thinking, *Va'ar willing, it won't be in paradise.*

***

About an hour later, Jayfor watched thoughtfully from the walls of Loronis as the large army marched away, the sound of thousands of feet hitting the ground simultaneously slowly fading away. It was a large gray mass in the distance, slowly moving away from the capital — towards the enemy. "Do you think we will ever see them again?"

Trenson, who was standing beside him, shrugged. "Maybe. Maybe not."

Jayfor grinned, despite the seriousness of the topic. "You've never been one to be optimistic, have you?"

Trenson only shrugged again.

***

Jayfor and Trenson had little time to mull over the army's departure, for they now had something else to prepare for: Jayfor's address to the people, concerning Kylor and the war with Elara. The people had grown extremely hostile to Jayfor and virtually anyone connected with the crown lately, thanks to Kylor's influence in the city. Whenever Trenson or anyone associated with the king went into the city, there was always a crowd that followed them, hurling insults or even rocks to show their opposition. It was getting out of hand.

They almost had enough evidence to arrest Kylor. Through his words and prompting, he had almost incited a rebellion in the city against the monarchy, but it still wasn't enough to arrest him. No one had ever been injured or hurt in any way, although there had been some close calls. In order to arrest Kylor as a dissenter, he or one of his supporters would have to attack, or at least try to attack, one of Jayfor's men.

But until that happened, Kylor was protected by Faldon's law of free speech. He had the right to say and do whatever he wanted, until someone influenced by him started a fight. Trenson waited every day for a report to come that it had happened, that someone had gotten hurt while protesting, but it never came.

"Kylor is sly," Trenson commented disdainfully to Jayfor one day. "He knows he can get away with anything, so long as no one gets hurt."

Jayfor shrugged. "Kylor technically hasn't done anything unlawful. There's no legal reason for us to arrest him, anyway."

Trenson stared at Jayfor, shocked. "How could you say that? After everything he's done, turning the people against us and causing uproars, even leading them away from Va'ar, you seriously don't think he should be punished?"

Trenson was bewildered that Jayfor could hold any sympathy for Kylor. In Trenson's mind, Kylor should be locked in the deepest prison, with the key thrown away. It infuriated Trenson to hear Kylor speak so boldly against Jayfor and Va'ar and their kingdom, like he knew exactly what he was talking about. Kylor was clueless as to how much Jayfor had gone through and sacrificed to protect them.

Jayfor kept a cool countenance. "He will face punishment for his deeds eventually, just like all of us. Va'ar is a just ruler and will judge us according to our acts, whether good or bad, and you can rest assured that Va'ar will not let Kylor get away with this."

Jayfor's calm words did nothing to calm Trenson down. "I know, I know. But as rulers of the people, we have a duty to judge too, right? Va'ar doesn't want us to overlook crimes, and so we can deal with him, right?"

"Yes," Jayfor said patiently, "we can, if they don't obey our laws. Kylor has broken a countless amount of Va'ar's laws, to be sure, but think about it: can you name one law that Kylor has broken in Faldon's laws?"

At this, Trenson stopped. He thought about a reply for a few moments and soon came up with one. "Lying."

Jayfor sighed. "Trenson, that's no law against that."

"Well, there should be! Why not call the council, and we can get some new laws put in place?"

Jayfor stared at Trenson with a withering gaze. Trenson shrugged and ignored looking the king in the eye, then said, "I don't see why lying shouldn't be banned. It would make life a whole lot easier."

"Trenson, we would have to build a cage around the entire kingdom to keep in all the prisoners. Name one person in the world who hasn't lied."

"Well, how am I supposed to know everyone's—"

Jayfor interrupted. "Don't act like I was born yesterday. You know as well as me that no one in the world is perfect. Faldon's laws are *civil*, not *moral*."

"I don't see anything wrong with putting some moral laws in place," Trenson rebutted. "By the sun, the people need to start treating each other better. Faldon could use some morality."

Jayfor sighed again and ran both hands through his hair. He couldn't believe he was having to explain this. "Va'ar gives everyone free will. If people want to blasphemy and lie, then they have the choice to do it. It doesn't mean it's right, it just means they can do it if they want to. We can't take away their free will."

"I don't want to take away their free will," Trenson replied. "I just don't want them to do... Well, what they're doing right now! Rising against us and causing total pandemonium."

"And they can do that if they want to." Jayfor concluded.

Trenson eyed Jayfor in exasperation. "I'm starting to realize there is no way I am going to win this argument."

Jayfor couldn't help but grin. "Arguing with kings is usually a hopeless endeavor."

IX

JAYFOR NEVER UNDERSTOOD THE expression "butterflies in the stomach." He personally had never felt anything like it. He had been nervous before, of course, and being a king didn't help. But he never quite felt anything like it. He had wondered what it was like.

Now, standing upon a high podium, facing dozens, hundreds, thousands of people, all staring back at him, none of them looking in a good mood, the entire multitude of Loronis waiting to hear from their king, his words having the power to bring back the kingdom from the brink of destruction, Jayfor could confidently say that he had butterflies in his stomach.

He swallowed hard, trying to force the lump that was in his throat to go away. He had recited what he was going to say countless times, and a few hours before, he had been in a good mood, completely confident about his speech and ready. The few hours flew by, and with it Jayfor's nerve.

The rollicking crowd of people buzzed with anticipation, but once everyone had caught sight of the king standing on the stage, the noises dropped, and an impatient silence prevailed.

He took a deep breath. He was ready. This was it.

"Citizens of Faldon, men, women, and children alike. I thank you for gathering here today." He swept his gaze across the crowd, assessing his audience. All sour faces and bitter scowls.

He continued. "I will skip the formalities and get to the point. The issue that I'm addressing today is of great importance to our kingdom, a turning point in our history. Future generations will either honor or regret this point in history. Our decisions will have a ripple effect that will shape the future. And this is why we need to carefully consider our next action."

By their steely gaze, it seemed like the crowd had already decided their next action: to get rid of Jayfor. It reminded Jayfor of a predator, patiently watching its prey, being able to strike and kill at any moment, but waiting for the most convenient time to do so. Their faces of stone remained fixed on Jayfor, and the thousands of cold glares being focused on him did little to soothe the butterflies in his stomach.

"No doubt you know exactly what I'm talking about. The issues are twofold: the threat of an invasion from Elara, and the influence of Kylor over the city. These two issues are connected, and I will start with the matter of Kylor."

Jayfor paused. He would have to choose his words carefully. If he worded something the wrong way, or used derogative terms to describe Kylor and the ideas he was promoting, then any hope of uniting the people and leading them back to the true path would vanish in an instant. Keeping this in mind, he raised his voice once again.

"Faldon has always prided itself on our right of free speech. In neither Kallary nor Elara does anyone get to openly speak their mind without punishment. It is a law I am proud of, and would never seek to revoke. I am trying to clear any confusion that I am some tyrant trying to keep people who speak against me under my boot. If anyone one of you think that I deserve nothing better than to be dethroned and exiled, then please, tell everyone! I will never keep you from sharing your mind."

Jayfor waited for the people to denounce him angrily, or to murmur optimistically among themselves, or at least do *something*. But doing something was the one thing they didn't do. Besides a baby crying in the distance, there was no sound except Jayfor's ringing voice, and no expression other than the passion in Jayfor's eyes when he spoke.

"I am bound to this right as much as you are. I may speak my mind freely, without threat of punishment. I can share my opinion just as much as anyone. I should not — will not — be hounded by what the majority thinks. I can use my free will just as well as the next man."

Jayfor's voice rose in volume the longer his speech went on. "And I will use my free will now to ask you something that has been on my mind for a long time: why you have abandoned Va'ar? Naught five years ago, you abhorred Xavson for dishonoring Va'ar, for treating you like you were dirt and taking away your freedoms. And now I hear rumors that you would gladly take him over me!"

The carefulness Jayfor had when he started this topic flew out the window. His zeal for Va'ar and his anger towards the people had boiled inside him for months. Now he could not stop himself from letting it out. And let it out he did.

Now the people were reacting. Unfortunately, it wasn't the way Jayfor hoped. The thousands of people in the crowd began to churn, like a storm brewing. A few angry shouts rose, then more, until most of the crowd was shouting and raising their fists towards Jayfor. Jayfor looked the mob boldly in the eye and continued, the throng growing silent to hear the king's words.

"Listen to me! Kylor has poisoned you with his smooth words and robbed you of your reason. His words are absurd! To say there is no such thing as truth — truth would have to exist in the first place for those words to be true! Five years ago, this never would have been tolerated, but now, now you flock to him as your commander and teacher!"

An outburst of opposition exploded from the throng. Jayfor cut them off. "Don't you see? This is why we're losing this war! We have abandoned the whole reason why we're fighting in the first place! Va'ar is the one who determines all victories and defeats, and if those who once served Him dishonor Him like this, is it not natural that He will not grant us victory? Elara is winning this war because we have already surrendered! We have deserted our Supreme General, and with it, all of our reason!"

Suddenly, another voice sounded above Jayfor's. "Who are you to tell us how evil we are?"

Instantly, the clamor of the throng hushed. Jayfor stopped short and gazed through the crowd, trying to find the speaker. He didn't have to look for long. The crowd close to the podium shuffled backwards and formed a half circle around the man who had raised his voice: Kylor.

The great orator shook his fist at Jayfor. "You abuse your authority as king of Faldon! To think that the one made to protect and encourage the people is now slandering and shaming them publicly! The king has the right — no, the *command* — to support the people, to assist them in their endeavors, to promote what they are striving to achieve. Instead, you throw our ideals, our virtues, our goals to the dirt and spit on them!"

The people aroused into a storm at Kylor's words, hurling their most vile insults and throwing their fists towards Jayfor, who stood resolute, looking the crowd boldly in the eye.

The voices that spoke were numerous now. "Down with the monarchy!" "You had your chance to rebuild our kingdom, and you have failed us!" "Let Kylor be our king! He will lead us to a new future!" "You oppress our freedoms!" "We deserve more!" "Tyrant! Down with the tyrant!" "Down with the tyrant!"

Jayfor looked down at Kylor, who stood staring back at him. Despite his noble appearance, Jayfor caught the subtle hints of a smirk in Kylor's face. It was a look that said, *I have won. You have lost for the last time.*

Jayfor opened his mouth to respond, when a rock struck him hard on the right side of the face. He stumbled backwards, dazed, throbbing pain radiating from his right cheekbone. He heard the solid thud of another fist-sized rock hitting the podium and bouncing a few yards from his feet. Followed by another. And another.

A larger rock slammed into Jayfor's stomach, the force pushing him back and almost knocking the breath from him. The crowd cheered on sight of the king being injured, and sought to couple it with more as many more rocks came flying towards the stage.

"King Jayfor!" One of the royal guards standing on the side of the stage ran up the steps and held his arm up to deflect the oncoming missiles. "We must get you out of here and to the palace!"

A sharp rock smashed into Jayfor's shin, causing Jayfor to take in a breath sharply. He nodded in agreement and, holding his arms up to ward rocks from his head, he walked quickly towards the stairs on the side of the podium, the guard accompanying him. The crowd let out another cheer seeing their king retreating, but didn't let their barrage of rocks slow.

Before he descended the stairs, Jayfor glanced under his arms at Kylor, who was standing still as a statue, watching him. The orator made no attempt to hide his smirk now, and his eagle eyes followed Jayfor until he vanished from sight behind the stage.

Once behind the stage, Jayfor reached his other guards, twenty in all, who formed a circle around him, waiting for his orders. Trenson stood in this circle, his teeth and fists clenched, his face red with fury. "That's it!" He exploded as soon as Jayfor reached them, briskly leaving the group and heading to the side of the podium, the side on which the surging throng was. "I'm settling this once and for all!" He drew his sword and held it ready in his hand.

Jayfor knew exactly what Trenson was going to do. "Trenson, stop! You can't kill him!" Seeing the Trenson had no intention of stopping, he turned to two guards standing close. "Restrain him and bring him back!"

The warriors nodded and ran after Trenson, reaching him just before he could turn the corner. Trenson had no idea what was happening until the iron grip of the guards grabbed each arm and pulled him, his feet dragging on the ground, back to Jayfor. Trenson cried in protest and waved his sword in the air in front of him, as if hoping Kylor would appear in front of him so he could chop him down.

Once the knights returned with Trenson, still waving his sword in the air, the captain of the guard spoke. "We must make for the palace, and quickly, before things get ugly."

Jayfor nodded. "Agreed." He looked around at the stern faces of his entourage. "Form up! Make for the palace with all speed."

They needed no prompting, and soon formed a circle around the king, spears ready. Jayfor looked at the two guards holding the still-struggling-and-protesting Trenson. "Can you hold him the rest of the way back?"

"Of course, my lord. He is not very heavy."

"Good." Jayfor fixed his eyes on the distant but still looming figure of the palace. "Then let's go."

X

"I don't think I've ever been more embarrassed in my life."

Back at the palace, a few minutes after the large doors closed behind them and they were safely inside, Trenson broke the silence and threw off the arms of the guards, standing up straight and sliding his sword indignantly back into its sheath. He looked like a bird who had its feathers ruffled, disheveled and out of temper.

Jayfor cast a glance at Trenson. "If you wouldn't have been difficult, then you wouldn't be so embarrassed."

Trenson held his hands up in a helpless gesture. "It was the best idea I could think of! Actually, it still is!" He pointed a finger at Jayfor. "You of all people should agree with me! The entire city is trying to kill you! Don't you think we should eliminate this uprising at its source? Kylor is the whole reason we're in this mess. Getting rid of him would solve everything!"

"On the contrary, that would only make everything worse!" Jayfor rebutted. "Killing Kylor would only serve to fuel the people's rage and give us more problems, something we don't need!"

He was about to continue, then saw the guards standing around him, waiting to be ordered. "Dismissed," he said with the wave of his hand. The knights all saluted, then walked quickly down the hallway towards the direction of the barracks.

Trenson wasn't finished. "You say that all the time! Do you expect that if we let him live, things will get any better? They clearly haven't so far! It's time we stopped waiting for a miracle to happen and the people to return to reason. We need to arrest him!"

"Trenson, calm down!" Jayfor almost shouted in reply. "We will arrest him! Kylor has breached our laws now, and I will send a detachment out to detain him at once. Are you happy?"

Trenson relaxed a little. "You mean we can lock him up now? And throw away the key?"

"Well, besides the key part, yes. By his influence, he caused a public assault on the monarchy, meaning that he's responsible for the chaos that ensued. He's also the reason for an assault on an innocent bystander — me — so we have ample evidence to punish him."

Trenson was elated. "Finally! That liar will get what he deserves."

Jayfor eyed him mirthlessly, but held his tongue. To be honest, feeling the throbbing pain of the bruises from flying rocks, he was thinking the same thing.

***

Of course, the next day, when Jayfor sent an assembly of knights to capture Kylor, the orator was nowhere to be found. He was not at his usual tavern making his speeches, nor was he at any other establishment in town. The people were tight-lipped, and usually responded with rebuke, but a few people, after they finished with their verbal abuse, claimed they had no idea where he was.

Jayfor was baffled. Why would Kylor, at the height of his power over the people, suddenly disappear without a trace? Maybe it was because he knew that now he was eligible for arrest and was hiding in fear. But Kylor wasn't one to shy away from being in public, and, Jayfor knew, arresting Kylor would only incite the people more, so being arrested actually turned in his favor. But whether he realized this or not, there was not the slightest trace of Kylor anywhere in the city.

A reward was promptly offered for the capture of Kylor or any information on where he was. Heralds shouted the reward to the people on street corners. The people responded by assaulting the heralds who proclaimed this news, which resulted in many heralds quitting their jobs. Jayfor and Trenson were both confident that at one point or another, the pot-stirrer would show himself. And, they both agreed, if Kylor decided not to return, that would be just fine with them as well.

***

And it started to seem like that would be the case, as the days went on. Almost ten days had passed and still no sign of Kylor. Jayfor and Trenson were in the sanctum, discussing the topic.

"Of course, the instant we can deal with Kylor, he disappears," Trenson said crossly.

"You should be glad he's gone," Jayfor said, somewhat surprised. He had expected that Trenson would be jubilant about Kylor's disappearance. Oddly, it was the opposite.

"Well, who knows what Kylor's doing now! At least we used to know exactly what he was doing and could watch his movements. Now he's running wild without our surveillance! Probably concocting more evil schemes and plotting to overthrow the kingdom."

Jayfor sighed. Trenson's hostility towards Kylor was unmatched. "Let's just be glad that he's gone," he concluded, trying to drop the subject.

Trenson, however, wasn't playing along. "Don't get me wrong, I'm as glad as anybody that he's gone — gladder than most. I just have a feeling that we haven't seen the last of him. He'll probably return just when things are settling down and whip the capital back into an uproar."

Inwardly sighing, outwardly nodding, Jayfor said passively, "Maybe." *Since when did Trenson become so chatty?* he wondered.

Trenson looked like he was going to say more, but it seemed he picked up on the evidence that Jayfor wasn't interested, and instead, he mumbled something inaudible to himself. Jayfor was relieved.

"How's your arm?" Trenson asked, changing the subject.

Jayfor shrugged. "It's fine. It doesn't hurt anymore, which is a relief, and besides this..." he rubbed his hand over a spot near his shoulder on his right arm. There was a slight lump, where one of the spikes from the flail pierced his armor. "I can hardly tell I was hit in the first place."

"That's a relief," Trenson agreed. "When you were brought back from the battle, the healers told me they were skeptical that they wouldn't have to amputate your arm."

Jayfor drew in a sharp breath. "I would have kicked them all out of the palace if they did that."

Trenson let out a single laugh. "By the way you complained about how overbearing they were, I'm surprised you didn't do that anyway."

Jayfor grunted a reply. A short period of silence followed.

Then Jayfor moved on to another topic. "We should receive word about the battle before long."

Trenson, who was still mulling over Kylor to himself, looked up at Jayfor. "The battle? Oh right, the battle."

"Yes, 'the battle,' the one on which rests the fate of the entire realm of Faldon. Not very important or memorable, really."

"Sorry! My mind's been focused on other things lately."

"That makes sense. After all, mulling over how much you disdain Kylor and how to deal with him probably takes lots of attention."

Trenson furrowed his brow. "Since when did you become sarcastic?"

Jayfor chuckled. "I'm learning."

From who? Trenson wondered. He didn't ask, however, as he thought it might be better if he didn't know. "Anyway, now that you bring it up, I do wonder how they're doing."

Jayfor nodded. "If my estimates are right, then they should have met Elara's army around five days after leaving from here, so…" Jayfor mentally counted the days. "It's been two weeks since our army departed, so five days to get there, one day of battle, five days of return... They should have been here three days ago."

Trenson replied, "Well, in a perfect world, that's how it would go, but of course they likely got delayed, or maybe their travel speed wasn't as fast as you thought. Armies travel at the pace of the slowest soldier. Maybe one soldier was exceptionally slow."

Jayfor huffed. "True. Too bad this isn't a perfect world, else we wouldn't be dealing with... any of this."

Before Trenson could respond, the sound of the doors of the sanctum opening caught both of their attention. They turned and saw a servant poking his head through the crack made between the two doors. "My lord, there's..." he fumbled for the right words. "There's a soldier who needs to talk to you."

Jayfor raised an eyebrow. "A soldier?" Most people that requested an audience with the king were couriers or merchants or politicians. Soldiers and other army men went to their commanders when they needed something. For a soldier to request to see the king himself told Jayfor this was no ordinary circumstance. "Of course. Admit him at once."

The servant nodded once, then closed the door.

"What does a soldier, of all people, want to talk to you about?" Trenson asked quizzically.

"If I knew," Jayfor responded without missing a beat, "then he wouldn't have to talk to me in the first place."

Trenson nodded and crossed his arms. "Good point."

After another few seconds, the doors opened again, and this time two people entered: the servant, and... the most bedraggled, tattered, broken-spirited soldier Jayfor and Trenson had ever laid eyes on.

<u>XI</u>

Involuntarily, Jayfor and Trenson both gasped. The soldier was still in his armor, but the chain link was broken in several places, the loose ends hanging towards the ground. He was dirty, his face and torso smeared with dried blood and dirt and grime. He didn't stand or walk upright, but hunched over, like there was an iron weight around his neck pulling him down.

When the soldier stood still before Trenson and Jayfor, and barely looked up enough to see both of them through his long hair, stuck together in clusters with sweat and grease, Trenson saw the soldier had a look of both terror and sadness. It seemed like at any moment, the soldier could break down and cry. It was moving.

Jayfor felt it too. "What happened?" he asked anxiously, directing the question at the soldier. "Who did this?"

The soldier remained inactive for a few more seconds. Then, still barely looking up enough to see the room, the soldier looked slowly to his left, as if looking for someone, then slowly to his right. He was shaking slightly, Trenson noticed. Then he looked back at Jayfor.

"We were outnumbered," the soldier said, brokenly and unevenly, emotion thick in his voice. He paused for a few seconds and took a few ragged breaths, the memory of what he was recounting being almost as painful as the event itself.

Jayfor shot a look at the servant, searching to see if he had any hints of what he was talking about, but the servant's face remained blank and awaiting orders. Then it hit him, with sickening realization. "Are you..." he breathed, not wanting to hear the answer he knew was true, "You're not a soldier from Randolph and Norman's army... are you?"

The soldier looked back down at the ground, quivering more now, and emitted a single sob. He nodded his head quickly, almost in unison with his shaking.

"No," Trenson said breathlessly.

"We were outnumbered," the soldier repeated, in the same shattered voice as the first time. "They came, many of them, so many, so many... We were outnumbered. H-he — Randolph, Norman, the captains, they led us. We — we fought." The soldier paused to emit another sob and to gather himself to continue. Trenson's heart broke to see a man reduced to such a state.

"We fought — and — and — they killed us. They surrounded us. We couldn't hold them — hold them back. We fell, so many, so many of us died." The soldier swallowed. "Then — th-th-they came."

The knight shook violently. "They wore black. Black armor, helmets, weapons. Swords, axes, f-flails... W-we couldn't stop them. They killed — they — they killed everyone." Another few sobs escaped him.

Jayfor's eyes widened. "Everyone?" he asked. His mind teetered on the edge of hope and hopelessness, desperately gripping onto the little hope that remained, trying not to fall into the chasm of despair that opened at his feet. The soldier didn't respond immediately, so he asked, "Norman?" No response. "Randolph?"

The knight looked up at Jayfor, and the king saw a single tear appear on the bottom of his eye and roll down his face. "I-I saw it... Randolph fell from his horse, and — the black knight — took — a sword, and..." He looked back down at the ground, closing his eyes tight, as if trying not to see the image the memory brought up.

In an instant, the hope Jayfor was gripping disappeared, and he fell headlong into the chasm of despair. "No!" he gasped. Anguish swept over him like a wave, drowning him, making it hard to breathe.

More tears escaping the knight's face, he nodded. "M-many times, it pierced him, even — even after he was dead. Our forces faltered, but we still — we still fought... and then Norman — he was struck from his horse, and — they — they..." It was too much. Falling to his knees, the knight burst into sobs, weeping uncontrollably, putting his hands over his face, shaking intensely.

Trenson wasn't one to show emotion, but he felt a phantom punch in the gut as much as Jayfor. He had to swallow hard to prevent tears from running down his face. Jayfor wasn't as successful, and his eyes began to brim with water, threatening to overflow.

With every heart now as broken as the soldier's, a gloomy silence pervaded the room, broken only by the moans of the knight on the floor. Randolph and Norman were more than just allies or generals. They were friends. They had both helped to retake Loronis from Xavson when no one else would. Over time, the bond between them only strengthened. Now the chain was severed, and everyone felt the emptiness in the loss.

The knight looked up through a tear-streaked face, mustering the will to speak. "I — I was — I was knocked out in the fight. When I woke up, I was surrounded by — my brothers, comrades, they were all — all dead. I was the only one left. But then..." The knight shut his eyes tight, grimacing at the painful memory. "A black knight — he found me, and grabbed me, and — and he — he said t-to, to tell you," A few gasps escaped the knight. "He said, 'I-I am coming to break you. I will conquer, and your — your kingdom is mine."

Another passion of weeping overcame the knight. Trenson looked at Jayfor with wide eyes, and saw the king was no less disturbed by this ominous message than he was.

Another period of silence followed. No one knew exactly what to say next. The brutal truth that had just been revealed shocked everyone and took time to process. It was hard to accept the fact that their entire army had been wiped out, save for one man.

At last, Jayfor spoke, his voice heavy, addressing the servant, who was standing awkwardly to the side. "Take him to the barracks. Give him whatever he wants and needs."

The soldier suddenly looked up at Jayfor, terror in his eyes. "Please, sir, please — I can't do this anymore! They are coming, coming for me, my wife and children! They will — they will kill me, then they will come for them! Please, my lord, I can't be a soldier!"

Jayfor looked back at the soldier, and saw the fear in his eyes, and it startled him. He nodded. "O-of course. You have my permission to leave the army. You have already done far more than I expect from any soldier. Take your family far away from here, to the west, where it's safe."

For the first time since he had entered the room, relief filled the soldier's countenance. "Thank you... Thank you, sir!"

Jayfor smiled as best he could. "You deserve it. Good luck."

The terror and fear in the soldier's eyes subsided slightly, and, after bowing low, he walked out the doors of the sanctum, standing a little taller. The servant bowed as well and followed him out. The doors closed, and Trenson and Jayfor were left alone.

After a short moment of silence, Trenson asked gloomily, "What are we going to do now?"

Jayfor sighed dismally. "I don't know, my friend. I don't know.

<u>XII</u>

"Y OU HAVE DONE WELL, Cosgroc." Thrall spoke to his second-in-command, who was standing beside him. "I asked you to wipe out the disgusting remnant of Faldon's forces, and you did. That's more than most of my warriors could do."

Cosgroc grunted. "I simply do your bidding, my lord. It isn't my problem if they can't do the same."

"Indeed," Thrall replied.

Both figures were standing on a hill, overlooking a plain that stretched as far as the eye can see. The hill they were standing on was green and lush. The sky was clear and, coupled with the green grass, made the hill look rather cheerful.

A large bird, flying high in the air, passed over the hill. It was a carrion bird. Its shadow trailed on the green grass below. It cruised over the two figures on the hill and kept going, over the plain that the warriors were looking at. The carrion bird was joined by another one. And another one.

Until the vulture was flying with thousands of others in a giant swarm over the plain. They formed a black cloud in the sky, almost completely blocking out the sun.

They came to feast on the aftermath of the battle, on the millions of bodies that littered the ground and seemed to make up the ground itself.

"A pity I wasn't here to see them exterminated myself. I had orders to deal with a group of Senver spotted up north."

"Anything serious?" Cosgroc asked.

Thrall shook his head. "Only a few in number. We didn't lose a single warrior in the process. They can't say the same."

Cosgroc nodded, then waited for Thrall to continue. He already had a fair guess at what his next orders would be, but he thought it better that the general say them himself, rather than he inquire about it. Thrall didn't like to be asked questions. As he waited, he watched the vultures fight with each other over the carcasses, as if there weren't enough to go around.

"You made sure every one of Faldon's captains are dead?" Thrall asked.

"Yes, my lord. I personally identified each and every captain slain. Faldon now has no more generals."

"What about Randolph? and Norman?"

"Both dead."

"Excellent." Thrall said with twisted glee. "And what of Kylor?"

"That is something I needed to discuss with you, my lord. I did not receive orders on what to do with Kylor after the speech. Since Faldon has labeled him a criminal and is actively searching for him, I thought it best to remove him to the woods, with food and supplies, in case we have any further use for him."

Thrall grunted. "And that we do not. I recently received orders from our lord that Kylor has fulfilled his role. In other words, he has no further use. You may dispose of him whenever you have time.”

Cosgroc nodded casually. “I shall, my lord.”

A brief silence elapsed before Thrall changed the subject. “It must have been a sight to see, the pompous and proud army of Faldon, all reduced to ashes in a few hours!” Thrall chuckled, a guttural sound that was far from human.

“It was indeed,” Cosgroc agreed enthusiastically. “We’ve been chasing after their ragtag force for too long. Now... *finally*... they are no more.”

“Yes, there is only one step remaining until we eliminate them for good.” Thrall let the sentence hang in the air, building suspense. Cosgroc waited patiently.

Thrall couldn’t hold his excitement for long, though. “Faldon’s army is no more. The Senver line that we have worked for decades to destroy is gone. The moment has finally come.”

Cosgroc looked at Thrall’s spiked and horned helmet. If he had a face, he would have been smiling. “I have your permission to launch a full-scale assault on Loronis?”

“Permission?” Thrall laughed. “You need no permission, for I am leading the assault on the capital tonight!”

“You are?” Cosgroc asked, surprised, then, as Thrall’s empty eyeholes turned to stared at him, he wished he never had asked. He had hoped that Thrall would be occupied on other business so that he may lead the assault himself.

“Yes, I am,” Thrall said slowly, challenging Cosgroc to say anything against it. Cosgroc knew better and kept silent. Thrall, pleased, continued. “Nothing will be held back. Our lord has declared that not a single Faldian should die a painless death. Our assault will be primarily with fire. We will burn the drawbridges so they cannot escape, then we will use our trebuchets to throw fire missiles into the city, until all of them burn." A strange light glowed in Thrall's eyes as he said *burn,* a red flicker that subsided almost as quickly as it began.

"I like that plan, my lord. No one will escape." Cosgroc chuckled darkly and held up his hand. "No one!" He clenched it closed, making a fist.

Thrall started laughing, then Cosgroc joined in as well, the hills echoing the sound of their chilling glee over the war-ravaged plain until it startled even the vultures.

In the plains, amid all the carnage, a certain carrion bird landed on a small box, small enough to fit in a hand. The wood on the box was smashed on one corner, allowing the bird to reach in and peck at the contents inside. The bird squawked in displeasure, and quickly flew away in search of something more edible, for inside the box was pink candy.

XIII

THAT NIGHT, LYING STILL in his bed in the cloak of darkness, Jayfor couldn't fall asleep. It wasn't from lack of trying. He had put every effort possible into drifting off to sleep. He was exhausted, just like every day. He rarely had trouble with this since he had become king. Practically every night he would hit the bed and instantaneously fall asleep for what felt like five minutes before waking up again.

Not tonight. Every time he closed his eyes, he saw a battle, two sides fighting, one side losing as the other swarmed and surrounded them. He saw Randolph being pulled off his horse by a black knight, the black knight raise his sword, Randolph scrabbling to get up, but not being able to get away before the blade plunged down on him. He saw Norman riding through the battlefield, his spear swinging left and right, then a warrior coming behind him unnoticed and striking him, Norman crying in pain and falling from his horse...

Jayfor opened his eyes, and the images were replaced with the sight of the rafters, boards crisscrossing to hold the roof up. He sighed. Sleep wasn't his friend tonight, and just when he needed it most, of course.

Why did Va'ar let them lose? Or, better question, why did he let Randolph and Norman die? He searched for an answer, but found none. They were faithful to Faldon and to Va'ar, and had never let Jayfor down. What reason did they have to die? He wished Va'ar would speak to him like he did five years ago, when they were fighting to free Loronis from Xavson. Back then his faith in Va'ar was strong. Now, as a tornado of questions and emotions swirled through his mind, his faith was put to the test.

His thoughts drifted as he lay still. The possibility of what Elara would do next still loomed in his mind, just as it had been all day. Never before had he felt so helpless for his kingdom. A massive force beyond reckoning was coming to annihilate them, and he didn't even have enough soldiers to form a single battalion!

But wait! A thought suddenly appeared in his head. *Va'ar won't let Faldon fall to ruin. This is His kingdom, His people. Elara can't destroy it!*

The thought comforted him for a little while until he realized the truth: All of Faldon rejected Va'ar as their King. These weren't His people anymore. Jayfor's hope sank like a rock, and he was back where he had started.

An even more daunting question lay before him: what would he do now? There was nothing more to do for the kingdom now. Ruin and destruction were the only certainties. How could he tell that to the people? Maybe he could try one last time to lead them back to Va'ar, to plead with them to believe, before it was too late. But he knew in his heart that the time for that was long over. They wouldn't listen, not even when Elara came storming through the gates.

Even as Jayfor was thinking about these things, he felt the exhaustion of the day's work more than ever, and his mind slowly quieted as he slipped into the deep sleep he had searched so long for.

***

"Jayfor!"

Jayfor awoke with a start. His eyes flashed open, and he saw a large figure standing over his bed, arching over him. He let out a gasp of surprise and sat up on his elbows, heart racing.

The figure spoke in a frantic voice. "Hurry! There's not much time!" It backed away a few paces from the bed, allowing room for Jayfor to get out of bed. Jayfor's senses were on overdrive, and he starred dumbly at the figure, not exactly sure what to do. It was too dark to see anything other than the tall outline of the person standing there.

"I said hurry!" The figure spoke sternly, almost harshly. Now Jayfor reacted, quickly throwing off the covers and standing uncertainly in his room, his eyes trying to adjust, not to mention his brain, to the situation that he found himself in.

Then a low rumble shook the room, and a powerful *boom* sounded through the air. The ground shuddered, and Jayfor stumbled to keep his balance. The figure didn't budge an inch, or even seem to react to the shaking at all. Then it stopped, and Jayfor looked around the room, bewildered.

"It has begun," the figure said, in a sad tone. Jayfor's eyes adjusted enough to see that the figure was wearing a long, flowing cloak, with the hood cast over his face. "Gather your equipment," the figure said. "Anything you need, bring. You won't be coming back."

Jayfor didn't need any more prompting. As fast as he could, he raced to his dresser and started donning his gear. He didn't know what he was getting into, but he figured it had to be serious. As a result, he put on his leather-padded armor and boots, clipped his sword in its scabbard to his belt, and grabbed his traveling pack, which was a light satchel that — thankfully — he hadn't unpacked from his last journey. It took only a few minutes, but it felt like forever, especially with the mysterious figure in the room, watching him silently, unmoving.

Finally, after making sure he had everything essential, he looked at the figure. Seeing that the king was ready, his cloaked head nodded once. "Let's go," he said urgently. He strode to the door leading out of the room and walked through it, not waiting for Jayfor. Jayfor hurried to catch up with him.

The hallway was lit with torches on the walls, which made Jayfor squint with the brightness. Jayfor was surprised to see Trenson, ready and armed just as he was, standing beside another figure. This person — or whoever it was — was also wearing a long cloak, and was almost indistinguishable from the man who had helped Jayfor. Unfortunately, the cloak's hood made it impossible to see the men's faces. They were both tall and stoutly built.

"Trenson!" Jayfor asked, "What is going on?"

Trenson shook his head, equally confused. "I don't know, I—"

Suddenly, there was another thundering crash. The ground shook violently. Jayfor fell to the ground. The sound of glass and wood splintering filled his ears. Everything became blinding bright for a few seconds.

"What's happening?" Jayfor screamed. His only reply was more deafening roars of destruction.

The shaking stopped, and he opened his eyes and gasped. A giant stone, encircled in sprawling flames, lay just a hundred yards down the corridor from where they stood. The roof and part of the wall where it had come in was shattered and splintered, piles of wreckage on the floor. The flames from the boulder started to crawl up the wall and towards the piles of wood. Jayfor had thought the torchlight on the walls was bright. Now the entire room was bathed with orange light – hot orange light.

"We haven't much time," the cloaked figure who had woken Jayfor said. Both figures threw back their cloaks, revealing two chiseled faces that both testified, with their scars and their scowls, of warriors who had seen a battle or two.

"We'll explain everything," the other warrior said quickly, "once we get out of here. But for now –"

Another crash sounded, and the ground shook again. Both Trenson and Jayfor stumbled but managed to stay upright by flailing their arms until the shaking stopped.

"—For now," the warrior continued calmly, as if nothing unusual was happening, "All you need to know is I'm Reginold, and this..." he nodded to the other man, "is Erador. We're here to get you out of here safely. Follow us."

Before Jayfor could say a word, the two figures turned and started jogging at a brisk pace down the corridor, away from the smoldering boulder that had just crashed through the wall. Jayfor cast a glance at Trenson, who returned it with a look of confusion. Then both of them shrugged and ran to catch up with the two men.

Crashes and the sounds of destruction filled the air, some distant and quiet, others ear-splitting. Jayfor smelled smoke, and saw it too, a thin hazy smoke that filled the palace and made breathing difficult. They turned the corner. Another hole in the wall, and the culprit, a giant boulder dripping with flaming tar, was stuck halfway in the other wall. The flames licked the walls and the floor, crackling and popping. The warriors stopped briefly to look at the stone, then with a quick glance at his comrade, they started down a different hallway. Trenson and Jayfor quickened their pace to catch up.

Screams from servants and knights were barely audible above the chaos, but they were still heard. Occasionally, Jayfor would see a servant run from across the corridor ahead of them, or hear the sound of armor clanging as a group of guards marched through a nearby hall, but they never ran into any along their way.

Jayfor's mind spun, not just because of the smoke and intense heat. What was happening? Is this a dream? It had to be a dream. This couldn't be happening. A piece of ash floated through the air and landed on his arm. He winced in pain and brushed it off. A dream where he could feel pain, maybe.

The two warriors ahead of them seemed to have no trouble keeping a swift pace. They didn't even look like they were breathing heavy. Jayfor had his doubts. Who were they? What were they doing here? Where were they leading them...

BOOM! Behind them, not twenty yards away, a giant boulder tore through the wall and roof, then smashed through the next wall. Jayfor felt the blast of heat and stumbled, fell forward, then rolled and got back on his feet. Pieces of wood and glass powdered his back and the air. He turned around and looked at the massive hole in the palace, breathing heavy. It was all on fire.

"Come on!" Jayfor felt Trenson grab his arm and pull him. His voice sounded so far away. "We need to keep moving!"

In a daze, Jayfor started running again to keep up with Reginold and Erador. The two men didn't even turn to see if Jayfor and Trenson were following them; they continued running forward through the halls and turning the corners, knowing exactly where they were going.

They turned a corner, and all four of them stopped short. Ahead, the corridor was engulfed in orange flames. Jayfor held his arm up to shield himself from the intense heat, but all that did was scorch his arm. A piece of the roof fell to the ground with a crash and the fire blazed higher.

"This way," Trenson shouted, "to the front gates!"

"No!" Erador exclaimed, "If we go that way you'll never escape alive!" He started running towards another hall. "The gardens are the only way out!"

"The gardens?" Jayfor asked, but Erador didn't respond. He sighed, and started following them, Trenson right beside him.

They ran through the rumbling and shaking palace as fast as they could. Every second the heat was more intense, the smoke hazier, the feeling of doom stronger. They descended a stairway and made towards another stairway that led to the ground floor. Once there, Jayfor mused, it was a straight shot to the gardens — for whatever reason they were being taken there.

But, halfway to the stairway, a sound caught Jayfor's attention, one that made him and the others stop. It was a sickening cracking sound, the sound of too much weight being placed on one thing at a time. And it was coming from above.

"*Run!*" Trenson screamed.

All at once, the roof gave out. A giant flame-surrounded boulder dropped from the ceiling and towards them. Trenson and Jayfor ran and jumped. The stone crashed to ground, then smashed through the floor, leaving a giant hole, and kept going down until it hit the bottom floor. It came inches from crushing Jayfor, who lay prone on the ground from leaping forward. But the floor around the hole was unstable, and before Jayfor could react, the ground gave way under him. He cried in panic and felt himself falling. He flailed his arms and gripped a piece of jutting board from the edge of the floor.

"Jayfor!" he heard Trenson yell. Jayfor's legs dangled in nothingness. He looked down, then wished he hadn't. The high vaulted ceiling of the palace looked great most days, but now Jayfor would have traded anything for the bottom to be closer. He saw the boulder as a small speck at the bottom, wreathed in fire, waiting to catch Jayfor if he fell.

His hands were wet with sweat. Desperately he gripped the board with both hands, but his grip was failing. He saw Trenson above him, looking down on him with a panicked expression. He reached his arm out for Jayfor to grab. Jayfor heaved and stretched his free hand up just enough for Trenson to grab him by the wrist.

Just then, there was another explosion. The palace shuddered and boards and windows crashed. Trenson lost his footing and started to slide into the hole with Jayfor. Jayfor felt a surge of fear as Trenson was pulled into the hole and, with a cry, started to fall headfirst towards the bottom...

Until Reginold reached down and grabbed Trenson legs, suspending the two from their fall. Both Trenson and Jayfor were helpless, on the verge of falling to their deaths. For a second, Jayfor was certain the warrior would lose his grip and they would fall into the blazing inferno beneath. With a grunt, Reginold heaved Trenson and Jayfor out of the hole and onto solid ground.

The two lay sprawled on the floor, gasping for air. Jayfor's head throbbed from exhaustion and adrenaline. He wanted to lay there forever, until things finally cleared, but Reginold grabbed his arm and picked him up. "We can rest later," he said unsympathetically.

Jayfor groaned but stood up. His legs wanted to buckle under him, but he wouldn't allow them. Trenson lagging beside him, Erador and Reginold in front of him, he ran towards the stairway and descended the spiral, going down what felt like an endless flight of stairs before they reached the bottom.

After running down another hall, the door leading to the garden was finally in sight. Without slowing, Reginold ran shoulder-first towards the door and blew it open. They were in the open air now. Jayfor took a deep breath. The smoke here wasn't nearly as suffocating as it was inside, and the air was much cooler.

He looked around. The sky was black, and if it weren't for the fact that the palace was on fire in multiple places, he would have been able to see the countless stars that sparkled in the sky. The air was cooler, and a faint breeze wafted through his sweat-soaked hair. Everything in the garden was illuminated by the fire. Jayfor didn't notice the colorful winter flowers and trees that adorned the garden. His attention was focused on the orbs of fire he saw flying through the air and into the palace. They looked like shooting stars.

"The secret exit," Reginold said calmly, as if commenting about the weather. Trenson and Jayfor finally understood. Now they knew where they were going. Jayfor ran past Reginold and Erador towards the spot where the trapdoor was.

Pansies claimed the ground on which the trapdoor stood — after retaking Loronis, Jayfor tried to conceal the trapdoor's location as much as possible. Jayfor ripped them up and started to dig, throwing dirt in handfuls to the side.

He was only a few handfuls in when the wooden door was unearthed, and Jayfor heaved it open. It was the same trapdoor Trenson and Agrond had used to infiltrate Loronis all those years ago. Now they were using it to escape the kingdom they had saved. It was a bitter irony.

Jayfor threw his legs over into the hole and climbed down the ladder into the murky darkness. He jumped off at the final rung, his feet squishing into the soft mud. His feet were instantly soaked, but he didn't notice. He looked around but couldn't see anything other than the hole in the roof. It was humid and clammy, and filled with a putrid smell, but it was better than suffocating smoke.

He heard a squish behind him, then another and another, as Trenson, Erador and Reginold dropped beside him into the passage. Nobody closed the trapdoor above them; there wasn't any point.

"Anyone have a torch?" Trenson asked.

"Not me," Jayfor replied. He realized he should have brought one with his traveling gear, but oh well. Maybe Reginold or Erador had one.

As it turned out, they had something even better. They threw aside their cloaks, and in the dim light above it was visible that both wore swords at their hips. These they brandished, and held before them. Slowly, the blades started to glow a faint blueish-white. The light filled the passage and made everything visible, including Jayfor's awestruck expression.

"Wow," Jayfor said breathlessly.

Realization hit Trenson. "You're Senver!"

Erador and Reginold didn't respond or even look them in the eye. "We're still far from safe," Erador said, completely ignoring them. "Keep going."

While he wanted to ask even more questions now, Jayfor knew their first priority was getting out of the city. Erador and Reginold took the lead with their glowing swords, revealing the way forward, and the party ran through the secret tunnel as fast as they could.

Jayfor hadn't been in this passage in many years. Trenson had, when they were taking Loronis back from Xavson, but the last time he was here was when he was a young boy. He remembered the passage being bigger — and cleaner. Water droplets fell from the roof on his face, and he relished the cool water, a relief from his hot sweat.

"Do you feel that?" Trenson asked suddenly, breaking the silence.

Jayfor was startled for a second. "Feel what?"

"The ground and walls." Trenson stopped running and pressed his hand against the dirt wall. "They're shaking."

Jayfor slowed to a stop and paused. Now that he was paying attention, he could feel the ground vibrating slightly and hear a noise from above. It was extremely muffled, but it sounded like voices. Screaming voices.

"We must be under the streets," Jayfor concluded. "I think I can hear voices from above."

"So can I." Trenson said. He removed his hand from the wall. "What's going to happen to them, all the people? And the city?" He turned to Jayfor with pain in his eyes. "Is it... Is it all going to be destroyed?"

"I... I don't know." It was the truth. Jayfor had no idea what was going to happen next, or even what was happening right now. "All we can focus on now is getting out of here. Then," He glanced at Reginold and Erador, who continued running through the passageway, not bothering to stop for Trenson and Jayfor, "maybe then we'll have some answers."

Trenson nodded, and they both started to catch up to Reginold and Erador. "I hope so," Trenson mumbled.

After running for who knows how long, Erador and Reginold finally stopped. Jayfor stopped, but Trenson, who was running behind him, was a little late and crashed into Jayfor. Stumbling forward but staying upright, Jayfor cast a dirty look at Trenson. Trenson shrugged apologetically.

There was a ladder that led to a trapdoor above. Reginold sheathed his glowing sword, but Erador's sword still afforded plenty of light. Reginold dexterously climbed the ladder and pushed open the door. Shafts of white moonlight spilled through the opening. Reginold made it through, then motioned for them to follow him.

Erador sheathed his sword as well, not needing its glow in the moonlight. "Go," he said, gesturing for them to go up first.

Jayfor was eager to get out of the clammy and cramped passage. He quickly ascended the ladder and when he poked his head out the opening, he found himself surrounded by trees. Cool air blew across his face, and he sighed contently. He recognized this place: the Ashdin woods. Five years ago they had assembled here and organized a force to free Loronis. The memory of it made Jayfor pause and remember how much had happened since then.

Trenson and Erador soon clambered through the door, and it was shut closed by Reginold.

Although Jayfor felt the urge to soak up the cool air and use this moment of respite, there were questions that needed answering. Jayfor turned to Erador. "You've kept us waiting long enough. What is going on?"

For once, Erador looked him in the eye. Jayfor was surprised to see, behind his stoic countenance, deep sadness. Erador looked at Reginold, who simply nodded once. Erador turned away. "Very well." He started to walk away.

Jayfor was confused. Should he follow him? Reginold walked beside Jayfor, and, sensing his thoughts, nodded before walking after his comrade. Trenson looked at Jayfor, shrugged, and started following behind the Senver. *Guess that answers my question.*

Despite their crunching footsteps on the leaves, Jayfor could hear distant sounds. Straining his hearing, he made out a deep booming sound, one that repeated every few seconds. *Thoom. Thoom. Thoom.* With a sick stomach, Jayfor was almost certain what the noise was. And his suspicions were proven correct when they mounted a steep hill, where the trees cleared and, far away in the distance, they could gaze at the mighty capital of Loronis.

Or what was left of it.

"No..." Jayfor whispered. He closed his eyes tight. More than ever, he wished this was a dream. But when he opened his eyes again, he saw what would be engraved in his mind for the rest of his life.

The city was on fire. Every part of it, the walls, the streets, the houses, it was all in flames, like a giant bonfire in the night. Surrounding the city were trebuchets, giant ones, bigger than Jayfor had ever seen. They formed a circle around the enormous city and were launching fiery missiles, giant boulders wrapped in tar and on fire, into the city. Hundreds of boulders flew into the city at a time, some smashing through the tall walls of the gates, some slamming into the ground of the town streets and rolling through houses and markets, leaving a trail of destruction in their wake.

Jayfor could see the faint silhouettes of trebuchets, hundreds of them, forming a circle around the capital. Mercilessly, they flung more flaming rocks into the capital, over and over and over again. Jayfor recognized the size and build of the trebuchets: Elara.

Screams and shouts for help rose above the chaos, but it was mostly drowned in the sounds of destruction. There was no way out of the city. Loronis was proud of its large moats, larger across than most kingdoms, and the water surface level was much lower than the ground. This only made the capital a death trap, as all the drawbridge gates were smashed to pieces, leaving no way across, even for those who could swim.

The proud, tall palace of Loronis, a beacon of the kingdom's power and unity, was now a giant torch, engulfed in consuming flames.

XIV

"N o," Jayfor whispered. "No!" It suddenly became difficult to remain standing.

"It..." Trenson fumbled for words as he stared at the capital. "It's terrible."

Hot tears welled in Jayfor's eyes. He quickly rubbed them away, which only caused more to form. He gave up and let them run down his face and mix with the cool sweat that soaked his face.

Trenson was in a daze. His mind was still spinning. He was finally starting to grasp the reality of what was happening, or at least he felt like he was, so the spinning was spinning a little less. The realization that hundreds, thousands, millions, were being slaughtered with no hope of escape, slowly dawned on him, the weight of it slowly crushing him.

Then it hit him: why were Reginold and Erador just standing there? They should be helping the people! In fact, why was Va'ar letting this happen in the first place? He turned towards them and burst out, "Why are you letting this happen? Why is *Va'ar* letting this happen?! I thought He would protect us! We sacrificed so much in His name, and this is how he repays us?"

Trenson's fury surprised Jayfor, but he couldn't help but agree. It didn't make sense. He eyed the two Senver, waiting for a reply.

Erador and Reginold exchanged a glance. Then Erador nodded, and Reginold met Jayfor and Trenson's gaze. "The people of Faldon have turned away from Va'ar. They no longer honor Him like they did in the days of old."

"And that's a good reason to kill them all?" Trenson interrupted furiously.

Reginold answered with a cold look. "You don't understand. For hundreds of years, the Senver have fought and died for your kind. Without our intervention, you would all be extinct ages ago." The Senver's tone, smooth but with a trace of frustration, exposed his passion.

Reginold paused, trying to find the patience to continue. He must have found it, because his anger subsided, and he started again slowly. "The people of Faldon have grown more depraved and blind than you realize. You two have no idea what people's thoughts are, or what they're really doing behind the curtains. Even I don't know what is truly going on. But I have seen far more than enough, far more than what I want to see, to know that the people of Loronis were evil. Very evil. More evil than you realize."

Trenson still didn't understand. "Evil enough to do *this*?"

Reginold cast a glare at Trenson. "Everyone mortal has committed enough crimes against Va'ar, mentally and physically, to deserve a much worse fate than this. You truly have no clue how wretched Loronis was. Elara wasn't much worse than what was done here in the shadows."

The words kicked Jayfor in the stomach. Not much worse than Elara? That couldn't be right. "But we fought against Elara!" Jayfor protested. "Countless soldiers died for Va'ar on the battlefield."

Erador nodded and picked up the conversation. "You are right. But that is what they all are now. The last souls that believed wholeheartedly in Va'ar died on the battlefield a week ago. You two are the only ones that still hold to the truth."

"The only ones?" Trenson asked. "But there are thousands of people in Loronis, easily millions! Are you saying that out of a million people, we are only two who still believe?"

Erador looked him in the eye. "Yes," he said simply.

Trenson sighed. He looked back at the raging flames of the palace, hearing the distant *thooms* of more tar-covered boulders flying into houses and streets. "But... why this way?" Trenson whispered.

For once, Erador's countenance softened. This stoic warrior must have a soft spot after all. "I cannot deny the fact that watching thousands of people meet a fate like this... pains me." His voice was slower than usual, and not as hard. "I know that Va'ar had the right to do this at least a hundred times over the centuries, and I always said they deserved it." He sighed. "We gave them many chances to believe, but they rejected every one."

Trenson didn't respond. He was still mad at Reginold and Erador, which made no sense since they had just saved them from a painful death. But he needed someone to point his anger towards, and the Senver seemed the least concerned with what was happening. Jayfor was silent, watching the destruction with tears running down his face.

Reginold sensed Trenson's resentment. "I know you're still mad. I don't blame you for being so. But there is one last thing you should know: Va'ar doesn't do things like this unless it's the best way for it to happen. If the future would have turned out better if this hadn't happened, then it wouldn't have."

A hand rested on Trenson's shoulder. Trenson expected it to be Jayfor, but he was surprised when he saw Reginold standing beside him, looking into his eyes with piercing blue ones. "This was for the best."

The statement was short, but it somehow eased Trenson. He met eyes with the knight, and as a sign of acceptance, he nodded once. "Thank you. Thank you for getting us out of there alive."

Reginold returned the nod. "It was Va'ar's will." He removed his hand from Trenson's shoulder and backed away a few paces. Then he turned and looked at Jayfor. "Jayfor."

The king was distraught. He looked up through teary eyes at the Senver, and the eyes of the warrior seemed to calm the storm in his soul ever so slightly.

"This is not the end," Reginold said. "This is merely the beginning of another chapter in the history of Faldon. What happens next relies on you two." Reginold's gaze became firm again. "You have a mission."

Jayfor was confused. "A mission?" His voice was broken.

"Yes." The corner of Erador's lips raised ever so slightly. "You didn't think Va'ar would let things end this way, did you?"

Jayfor shrugged and waited for him to continue.

Erador continued. "You two must travel north, together. Follow the road that leads north from the capital. Stay on that road, and always head north. Keep going until you reach the Tree of Ramadus. That is when you will reach your journey's end."

There was a period of silence. They waited for there to be more, but Erador's face made it clear he had said it all. "That's it?" Trenson asked.

Erador frowned. "You seem confused."

Trenson huffed. "Well, it's just, I was expecting a little more... information. About where we're going and how to get there."

Erador was even more baffled. "I just told you where you're going, and how to get there. To get to the Tree of Ramadus, follow the north road."

"Well," Trenson fumbled for words, "how will we know when to stop?"

"When you reach the Tree of Ramadus." Trenson could have swore Erador's voice was sarcastic. The Senver gave no sign of it. Instead, he looked at Trenson with one eyebrow raised, not sure what he was getting at. Trenson wondered if Senver were allowed to be sarcastic.

Jayfor cut in. "Is it far away?"

It was Reginold who answered this time. "Yes — and no. 'Far away' is a matter of perspective."

Jayfor sighed. That was helpful. He wanted to ask more questions, to gather more intel about this mission, but the Senver didn't look too keen on handing off more information, so he remained silent.

"You'll need to leave soon if you want to reach it in time," Erador said. "There is one more thing that we will give each of you. It will greatly assist you — if you choose to wield it when the time comes."

Jayfor was surprised. The Senver were giving something to them? It was somewhat amusing how the Senver could be on one topic, then completely change to another, without any explanation and in the same even tone.

The two Senver each reached behind their backs, under their cloaks. Trenson suddenly felt excited. He expected it to be given some sort of immaculate armor, or an immaculate sword, or at least something immaculate-like. Coming from warriors of Va'ar Himself, it had to be, well, immaculate.

Erador and Reginold both pulled out two scabbards of swords, but not just any swords. Trenson was taken aback at the sight of them. He was expecting something grand, but this?

They were the most normal, most plain, most modest, most non-immaculate swords Trenson had ever seen.

The eager looks on Trenson and Jayfor's faces were replaced with disappointment. Before he could stop himself, Jayfor blurted out, "That's it?"

The withering gaze of the two Senver made the king cringe. He made a mental note to not act disappointed around a Senver.

"I know these swords aren't especially... appealing." Reginold knew exactly what they were thinking. "But if you are to survive this quest north, you will need them."

"But we already have swords," Jayfor said. He had clipped his onto his belt at the last minute, and was very glad he had done so. Even his sword's sheath was worth more than most swords, with rubies and emeralds and diamonds all inlaid in a majestic scene that turned eyes and brought attention everywhere he took it. His sword inside it was even more priceless, the hilt a special design for maximum grip and weight distribution. The blade was forged from a special alloy that included Tronkelli, the strongest metal in the world, and the most valuable.

The two swords in Reginold's hands looked like they were made by some green blacksmith yesterday. The scabbard was nothing to boast about; it was a dull brown color and the same as every other scabbard in the world. The hilt protruding from the top was a simple T-shape. A normal handle, and a normal crossguard lacking anything special about it made Jayfor wonder if the Senver were actually serious about giving these to them.

Erador met his eyes, and Jayfor realized with a turn in his stomach that the Senver knew everything he was just thinking. "I am aware that you already bear weapons," Erador said. "But they were made in the world, by mortal hands, with tainted steel. They serve only one purpose: to fight for the world. In the future, you will face things that cannot be conquered by worldly means." He paused, letting the words sink in, before he continued. "These swords I give you were crafted in the Forge, the same place Reginold and mine were made. Likewise, they hold the same, or even greater, power than a Senver blade. They are nothing special to the eye, but they hold the potential to conquer the greatest enemies — if, and only if, you wield them with the dignity they deserve."

Trenson and Jayfor looked at each other in surprise. Reginold raised his hand to signal them to hold their questions, and he picked up where Erador left off. "It is up to you to take these weapons. I cannot force you to take them, only tell you that you will need them in the journey ahead. You will both have to give up your swords to take these, for you cannot walk the path of the world, and the path Va'ar has waiting for you, at the same time."

Jayfor wanted to ask questions, but before he could, Reginold walked up to him and presented the sword to him, pressing on him to decide now. Jayfor was faced with a choice: Keep his sword, which looked like it could splinter this blade easily, or trust the Senver and swap it with his own? It was a hard choice. A blade that held the same power as a Senver's, or even greater, would be a great asset. But he was tempted by the eloquence of his own sword to not take it. His mind yelled, *Keep your sword. This pathetic blade couldn't cut armor, or even butter, by the looks of it. Your sword is the strongest in the world. You will need it. These Senver are letting your kingdom burn! Don't trust them!*

But another, softer but much more powerful, voice spoke in the corner, telling him to take it. Without another thought, Jayfor unclipped the most immaculate sword in Faldon from his belt, and handed it to Reginold. The Senver seemed to smile slightly as he took the sword from Jayfor and held the new sword for him to take. Jayfor took the sword. He expected to feel something, maybe power from the sword, but he felt nothing, only a sting of pain of parting with his most treasured possession. Jayfor clipped the sheath to his belt. He saw Trenson had made the same choice, and a dull-looking, modest sword now hung by his hip, and Erador held Trenson's old sword.

"You have chosen well," Reginold broke the silence. "Those blades have more uses than you know of. If used properly, they will aid you when all else is dark."

Trenson looked longingly at his old sword in Erador's hand. A big part of him wanted to walk over and take it back. His sword had become an extension of his body, and now to take a new one felt strange. But he knew this was the right decision, and that knowledge was the only thing holding him back.

Reginold and Erador exchanged glances before looking again at Jayfor and Trenson. "That is all the aid we can give you. This path has been laid before you, and it is up to you how you shall walk it. Take the north road leading from the northern gate of the capital and follow it until you reach the Tree of Ramadus. You will know it when you reach it." Reginold gave them both an assuring nod. "May Va'ar protect you."

And with that, both Senver turned and walked into the woods without another word, quickly disappearing into the shadows. Jayfor heard the sound of their footsteps in the woods, but it faded away until it too was gone, and silence pervaded. Trenson and Jayfor were left alone.

Trenson and Jayfor's eyes met. Neither of them said a word, but both of their expressions sent a clear message: *What just happened?*

XV

"BEAUTIFUL, IS IT NOT?" Thrall commented to Cosgroc.

Without turning his helmet to look at his general, Cosgroc nodded. "Indeed."

Standing outside Loronis' walls, both warriors had an unmatched view of the capital's destruction. A trebuchet, one of many that surrounded the city, was beside them. Two Krenors were at work maintaining the steady onslaught of boulders from their machine. They heaved the large, tar covered boulders, each hundreds of pounds, into the device like it was nothing, then took a torch to the tar. After the boulder was enshrouded in flames, they pulled the lever, and with a whoosh, the giant arm flew into the air and threw the boulder head over heels into the palace, or the town, or the wall, or somewhere else in the capital. As soon as the arm returned to the ground, they quickly loaded it again, and the process repeated.

Other Krenors were at work as well. Those that weren't firing the siege weapons were covering boulders in tar, using ladders to reach the tops of the rocks, then using buckets to drench it in oozing black tar. The dark knights blended in with the cloak of night so well that it was only when they were near a fiery boulder could they be seen, creatures of shadows working in the shadows.

"You are witnessing history, Cosgroc." Thrall continued. There was an ecstasy in his voice that Cosgroc had never heard before. "Hundreds of years we have been fighting these infidels; hundreds of years we have lost our best men by the hand of Faldon; hundreds of years, these pricks have been a thorn in our side; and now the vainglorious kingdom of Faldon is finished."

Thrall chuckled, a chuckle which turned into a laugh, a laugh which turned into uncontrollable, maniacal, glee-filled hysteria. "We have won!" Thrall yelled, as if talking to the people on the other side of the wall. "Your precious Va'ar has abandoned you! All of you will die! *Die*!" As if there were something funny about it, Thrall burst into another round of laughter. Cosgroc said nothing, only waiting for Thrall's outburst to stop so they could get back to business.

Finally, Thrall contained himself. He turned to look at Cosgroc. "Why the stoic face, Cosgroc? We have just won the greatest war in history!"

"I know," Cosgroc replied slowly. "I think it's too early to be celebrating yet."

Immediately, Thrall's mirth ceased. He gave a sideways look at his second in command. "What do you mean?" he demanded.

"Va'ar's not one to go down without a fight," Cosgroc explained. "I fear this is not the end of the Enemy's schemes. He will likely come up with another plan, perhaps even a lethal one, to attack us while we relish our victory."

Thrall was silent as he let the words sink in, then he nodded. "Good reasoning. We should always make sure our enemy is dead before we claim victory," he said, as if he hadn't just been celebrating. His mood switched from jubilant to serious.

"Do I have orders on how to respond to a potential counterattack? Or prevent one?" Cosgroc asked.

"I doubt we'll need to take such precautions, Cosgroc. You see the same sight as I do before us. The chance of any retaliation is slim, but follow any leads that may present themselves. I don't want to be made a fool after this victory."

"Yes, my lord," Cosgroc replied uniformly.

Thrall turned his gaze on the flaming capital once more. "We will keep up our barrage until morning. How many missiles are at our disposal?"

"Hundreds, my lord. We need not fear of running out of ammunition for our machines. They could continue a steady barrage like this for days."

"Very good," Thrall said. "Like I said, we shall continue our attack until morning. Then, I will send a regiment of soldiers into the capital to make sure there are no survivors, and to make sure that king Jayfor and his lapdog, Trenson, are both dead. We must stamp out any embers of Faldon before they ignite another flame." He looked at Cosgroc. "I want proof that Jayfor and Trenson are dead. I will take nothing less."

"Yes, my lord." Cosgroc replied.

Thrall turned his attention once more to the chaotic city. "Until then, enjoy the show," he said. "We have won a victory worth celebrating. Faldon is dead — all that's left is for it to stop kicking."

XVI

"**T**HIS IS IMPOSSIBLE!" JAYFOR threw the two sticks to the ground in frustration.

Trenson watched the scene with mild interest. "I used to start fires all the time by doing that. Maybe you're just doing it the wrong way."

Jayfor shook his head. "I'm doing it the same way you're telling me to! I think there's something wrong with these sticks. I'm going to get some better ones."

With that, Jayfor stood up and walked briskly into the woods on the edge of the road. Trenson chuckled to himself. The fact that the mighty king of Faldon, revered for his battle prowess and wit, couldn't start a fire without getting angry and breaking kindling in the process amused him.

Jayfor returned in a few minutes with a handful of "better" sticks, ready to try again and certain that this time he would succeed. His spirits were dashed, however, when he saw a small, healthy fire crackling in the center of their camp, with Trenson sitting beside it with his legs crossed, poking it casually with a long branch. "I decided you were taking too long," he said.

Jayfor was miffed. "I almost had it! I guarantee you if you would have let me try again, I would have had it." He tossed the sticks in his hand into the fire. They popped and cracked as they were licked by the flames.

Without looking him in the eye, Trenson nodded. "Oh yes, I'm sure you would have, eventually. But I enjoy my youth, and I would rather start it myself than grow a gray beard waiting."

Jayfor sighed and took a seat on the other side of the fire from Trenson. He was too tired to argue and was secretly glad Trenson had already started the fire. The nights were cool, making the warmth all the more enjoyable.

Fire. Jayfor felt a stab a pain every time he gazed at the orange tongues. The memories of last night, his home and everything he owned turned to ashes, still hurt. Ironic, now, that he was using fire for comfort.

He didn't want to think about it now, so he looked for something else to occupy his mind. He noticed Trenson was fiddling intently with something on his wrist. He soon realized that they were his throwing knife sheaths.

"I see you brought your knives," Jayfor said. The statement was so obvious that Jayfor cringed after saying it, but at least it broke the eerie silence.

Trenson didn't make any sign that he heard Jayfor, other than a mumbled, "Mhm." He didn't look up, instead continuing to slide his knives in and out of their sheaths, one by one, inspecting them.

Based on Trenson's somewhat curt reply, it was clear he had no interest in chitchat. Unfortunately for him, Jayfor was. "Do you think you'll need to use them?"

Trenson turned his head to the side and met Jayfor in the eye with a peeved look. "If I didn't, I wouldn't have brought them."

"Oh," Jayfor said, cringing again at how dumb he sounded. "Of course." Jayfor didn't follow it up with anything. He figured silence was better than more embarrassment.

Which Trenson was just fine with. Unlike some people, he didn't feel the need to fill the dead space with dialogue. In fact, he rather liked it. He was perfectly content checking his knives and listening to the music of fire popping.

Out of the corner of his eye, Trenson saw Jayfor sitting awkwardly across from him, spinning a blade of grass in his fingers. Jayfor looked extremely bored and like he wanted to fill the dead space, but didn't want it to lead to another obvious statement. Trenson tried to ignore him, but the more he tried, the harder it was. He inwardly sighed and stopped messing with his knives. "Do you know where we're even going? I mean, where this road will lead us?"

Jayfor looked ecstatic that Trenson wanted to talk. Quickly, he reached into his satchel and pulled out a large, coiled map. He unrolled it and spread it out on the ground beside him, angled sideways so that both of them could see it. "Nothing much for now. For another few weeks, it'll be nothing but easy plains and a few towns along the way."

Trenson nodded. "That's good with me." Then another thought occurred to him. "Did you bring any money?"

Jayfor stared at him for a few seconds, then realized with a jolt what he was talking about. He grabbed his bag and rummaged through it. After a few minutes of intense searching, he said gloomily, "Of course I don't. I didn't even think about it." He sighed. "I don't guess you have any either."

"Actually, I haven't checked mine yet," Trenson replied, grabbing his bag. He opened it, and immediately his face lit up as he pulled out a small jingling pouch. "I got us covered," he said triumphantly.

Jayfor breathed a sigh of relief. "Thank goodness." Honestly, he was a little embarrassed that he, the king of Faldon who had access to amounts of gold so large, the number of pounds of it wouldn't fit on ordinary scrolls, had to mooch off his right-hand man's purse. Nothing he could do about it now.

"If we use it wisely, we could probably go two months off of it," Trenson said after he counted the coins, all gold and silver. "We have enough rations to go a few weeks. After that, if we stick to bare necessities, we should be fine for at least a few months."

"That is, if this tree is within a few months of travel," Jayfor added, rubbing his chin and looking back at the map. "There's nothing about a great tree anywhere on this map. A few forests along the road, but that's it."

Trenson scanned the map, looking for anything, but found nothing. "Maybe it's farther north than what this map shows."

Jayfor raised an eyebrow. "Even farther north than the Splitting Waters? I hope not. That's at least a six-month journey."

"Well, who knows how far away this 'tree' is? It could be a mile, or a hundred miles away. What did Reginold say? About how we'll know when to stop?"

Jayfor grabbed a stick lying beside him and started to poke the fire absently. He said, "That was Erador. 'You two must travel north together. Follow the road that leads north from the capital. Stay on that road, and always head north. Keep going until you reach the Tree of Ramadus. That is when you will reach your journey's end.'"

It was times like these where Jayfor's almost perfect recall came in handy. "Right," Trenson said. "Not much to go from, really. Wish he would have been more specific."

Jayfor cracked a smile. "I know. I almost laughed at the sideways look on Erador's face when you tried to get more information."

Trenson shrugged. "Senver aren't great when it comes to details."

Jayfor didn't respond, but his smile said it all. He threw the stick he was using as a poke into the fire and stretched his arms above his head, yawning heavily. "I think I'll turn in. My luxurious royal bed awaits."

Trenson grunted. In reality, the "luxurious royal bed" was a smoothed-out area on the ground with a blanket laid on top. It was a far cry from their beds in the palace, and Trenson found himself wishing that he could have brought his bed with him. When he woke up earlier this morning, his back ached and cracked when he stood up, and continued to do so for most of the day. It probably wasn't a good sign that he was having back problems at his age, but unless he planned to go back to the palace and get the remains of his bed, he would have to deal with it.

Jayfor stood and walked to his bed, then started to stretch his arms by holding them out in front of him, then pulled his knees to his chest. This habit annoyed Trenson to no end, though there was no plausible reason why it should. Jayfor always insisted that the best way to get a good night's sleep was to stretch before you got in bed. It was the strangest habit Trenson had ever seen. "Try it," Jayfor had told Trenson. "It really works."

Trenson did try it, and he slept terribly and had back pain the next morning. He blamed it partly on the bed, partly on the stretching. Since then, Trenson had no further motive to join Jayfor in his nighttime flexibility training, and he wasn't afraid to tell Jayfor so.

He decided it was probably a good idea to do the same. Not stretch, but go to sleep. He threw his stick into the fire and walked over to his "bed." He frowned as he imagined how badly he would sleep tonight, and how much more his back would hurt in the morning.

He didn't remember much more of what happened that night, but when he woke up the next morning, he felt refreshed and well-rested, and his back barely hurt at all. Trenson was overjoyed. This could mean only one thing: it *had* to be the stretching.

XVII

A FTER A FEW DAYS of traveling, Jayfor and Trenson both agreed they needed to stop at the next town. Their rations weren't low — not dangerously, but they had no idea how far they were going, and how far apart the towns were spaced. Experience taught them that when you go near a town, you restocked, even if you didn't really need it. Better safe than sorry.

There was also the issue of horses. Trenson and Jayfor were split on whether buying horses would be a good idea or not. Trenson said that it would be wasting their ration money, which they needed for their long travels. Jayfor, on the other hand, argued that horses would allow them to travel much farther every day, making their journey shorter and actually saving money in the end.

"But we don't know how far we're going," Trenson said while they were debating the topic. "We need to save every coin we have. If we run out, what are we going to do then?"

"Buying two horses would actually save us money," Jayfor shot back, "because we would go farther without running out of money."

"It depends on the price. Maybe if we find two cheap palfreys, it would be worth it."

"I'm not looking to get a war horse." Jayfor knew he was gaining ground. "Just something to double our distance traveled. Anything pricy wouldn't be worth it."

So in the end, Trenson consented, but on the condition that any horse they bought was cheap. He was determined to get as much out of his coin as possible. The last thing he wanted was to cut to journey short because of frivolous spending.

One thing they both agreed on was to keep Jayfor's identity a secret. Now that Faldon was in ruin, the title of king was useless, even harmful, because it put a target on his back. An alias was needed.

"An alias?" Trenson asked when Jayfor brought it up.

"It's an alternate name," Jayfor explained, "like a nickname or something."

"Huh. Well, I agree. A different name of some sort would be a good idea."

"Probably. Then again, Jayfor is a somewhat common name. I remember at least two knights in the army whose names were Jayfor."

Trenson still shook his head. "While that might be the case, it's better just to be safe."

Jayfor nodded. "Alright." He thought for a few seconds, evidently trying to come up with a good name, then his expression cleared and he said decisively, "Conrad. I've always liked that name."

Trenson raised an eyebrow. "Conrad?" Obviously, he didn't share Jayfor's opinion. "I mean, it's... fine. But why not choose something more exciting? Like Honorius? Or Duthlac?"

Jayfor gave him a patient look. "I thought the whole point of an alias was to be better hidden."

"Well, Honorius is a normal name, and it sounds cool!" Trenson was defending his conviction to the last.

Jayfor grinned. "I think I'll stick to Conrad."

Trenson threw his hands up in defeat. "If you say so."

There was really no need for Trenson to have an alias. He wasn't a well-known figure outside the capital, so the risk of him being a target was minimum. He would stick to Trenson.

After they had that settled, they checked their map and found they weren't far from Dunbar, a trade center and rather large town. It was as good a place as any to restock and find some cheap horses, so they set their sights on stopping there.

They reached the town by midday. Not surprisingly, there was a cheerful riot of colors and vendors in the streets. A sea of people ebbed and flowed through the streets as merchants called out from their tents along the sides of the street, promising the best fruit in Faldon, or the finest cloth fit for kings... All for a right, or not right, price.

Thankfully, Trenson and Jayfor weren't looking for anything too extravagant. Just a few weeks of provisions and two cheap horses — emphasis on "cheap," Trenson reminded Jayfor.

Once they were fairly into the town, they both stopped. People swarmed around them, going from one place to another, moving around them. "I think we should split up," Trenson said.

"What?" Jayfor yelled, cupping his ear towards Trenson. The sounds of hundreds of footsteps and noises made it difficult to hear.

"I said I think we should split up!" Trenson yelled back. "You could look for horses at the stables while I get some rations for us."

Jayfor was doubtful. "I don't know. We could get separated and not be able to find each other."

"True, but we'd save time. We could meet back in another hour or so in front of that big monument there." Trenson pointed up ahead, where a large stone statue of a horse rearing stood.

Jayfor thought about it. Splitting up could be a bad idea. But they could cover more ground that way, and faster. Eventually, he shrugged. "Alright. I guess I'll start looking for the stables. I'm going to need some money first."

Trenson grunted like this was an act of charity, but he pulled out the jingling bag from his satchel, grabbed a handful of silver coins, and dropped them in Jayfor's hand. "That's fifty crescents' worth, I think. Should be plenty."

Jayfor was doubtful, but knew better than to ask for more. "Hopefully. Meet you there in another hour."

"Sounds good. I'll be at that market." Trenson nodded towards a tightly packed group of tents lining the street, calling — more like screaming — about their wares.

Jayfor said, "Sounds like a plan. See you shortly."

And with that, they split up, each going in another direction.

***

Trenson honestly had no idea how he was going to find what he needed in a crowd this large. He could barely see anything through the sea of people flooding the streets and spilling into every alley-way and road. He had no idea what all the commotion was about. It really made things easy, he thought sarcastically to himself, with this many people out. It was hard to hear himself think with all the noise.

Trying to ignore the thousands of sounds, smells, and sights vying for his attention, he walked closer to the edge of the street, where the vendors stood at their booths. Most booths were covered, a large canvas held up by four poles, under which a table with items stood. A wagon usually stood nearby the tent, the merchant's means of transportation.

Trenson knew that finding customers and standing out was important for business, but he wondered if screaming, *"Fresh grain! Barley, buckwheat, and oats by the pound!"* as loud as possible was the best way to attract attention. It attracted Trenson's attention alright, but not in a good way.

He scanned the tents for anything that looked like it sold rations, like nuts or preserved meat, but apparently, in this giant assortment of merchants, that was hard to come by. Nobody seemed to be selling non-perishable food, which was surprising, because Trenson thought there would be a great market for that, with all the travelers in town. Apparently not.

"Sir!" One of the merchants called out to Trenson. He held a long piece of blue cloth that complimented the merchant's already extravagant outfit. "You look like you could use a new look! Please, come over and see what I have to offer!"

Trenson stared at him suspiciously and shook his head. He kept walking.

The merchant didn't give up. "I'm practically giving my wares away! Please take a look before they're all gone! You'll never know until you come see!" The merchant yelled his last words as Trenson merged into the crowd.

***

Jayfor honestly had no idea how he was going to find not one, but two horses in good condition with fifty crescents. One horse would be hard enough with that budget, but *two*? He inwardly sighed as he pushed his way through the crowd. There was a chance it could happen, but that chance was slim.

He still couldn't believe how crowded the streets were. He usually made a point of visiting towns and provinces every now and then, to find out for himself the people's condition. He had stopped about two years ago because of the increased hostility from the people. He tried to remember if he had been here before, but his mind came up empty, which was surprising because if this place was as busy as it was today as when he had last visited it, surely he would have remembered.

There was probably some festival or something going on that he didn't know about. Merchants always flocked to events to make easy money. Maybe a harvest festival. After all, the end of summer and the beginning of autumn was fast approaching.

Up ahead, he saw a large, square building with two sliding doors on the front, both of which were open. He caught the whiff of hay and manure, and it didn't take an expert to guess where the stables were. His destination in sight, he kept pushing through the crowd and towards the building.

"Hey!" Jayfor heard a voice above the noise of the crowd. "What are you... Hey, get back here! Thief! Thief! Stop him!"

His interest aroused, Jayfor looked for the source and matched it with a rich merchant, evident by his fine clothing and well-fed appearance, who looked rather flustered. He stood behind the table at his booth and waved both arms in the air. "Help! He's getting away!"

Jayfor saw a man sprinting away from the booth, holding a large bag in his hands. When the man turned his head to look behind him, Jayfor saw the thief was wearing a bandana over his face. There was absolutely nothing about this man that didn't scream: *Criminal!*

Jayfor stopped in his tracks. His sense of justice pulled him towards chasing the man down. On the other hand, he knew he needed to stick to getting the horses. He looked around, hoping someone else would give chase, but everyone just stared and moved out of the way as the bandit dashed away from the yelling merchant.

Jayfor sighed. *Guess the horses will have to wait.* He broke into a full sprint after the man, pushing aside people and clearing a way towards the retreating figure. *But hopefully, not for long.*

XVIII

"YOU WANT SOMETHING?" THE merchant with the foreign accent asked Trenson as he was looking through the booth.

Trenson met eyes with the merchant, a small, thin woman with strange white paint under both eyes. It was some sort of tradition where she was from, probably. "Just some provisions and food for traveling. Things that won't go bad quickly."

The lady nodded once, and quickly. "Yes. Me have much of that. See," she pointed to a pile of salted pork sitting on the table. "Salt pork. Very good. See," she pointed to a stack of colorful fruit. "Zara fruit. Last long. Very good. See," she pointed to a pile of hand-sized, golden-brown cakes. "My special cakes. Last very long. Very, very good."

Trenson couldn't help but raise an eyebrow. The merchant's particular way of talking made everything she sold seem... less appealing. He didn't have a choice, though — in this vast variety of vendors, this was the only one he found that sold what he was looking for. He would just have to ignore creepy accents.

"Yes, it all looks... very good." He agreed. He picked up one of the cakes. It had the texture of a brick and weighed about the same. Definitely not something he was wasting his money on. He set it back, and the lady, who had eyed him while he picked it up, looked relieved, like she was grateful that he wasn't taking her precious cakes.

Instead, he grabbed eight of the cured slabs of pork and stuck it into his satchel, making sure the merchant was watching, and three loaves of bread. He figured this should get them far enough to the next city. To his delight, he also found a bundle of torches wrapped in cloth set in a basket on the ground. He didn't think that a ration vendor would carry any, but he wasn't complaining. He grabbed two. "I think this will do it for me today. How much for all of it?"

"Eighty-nine celts," the woman replied promptly.

Trenson furrowed his brow. Celts? He had never heard of it. "I... Alright." He wondered if it was the same thing as crescents, which was the standard currency of Faldon. It sounded the same. He pulled out coins worth eighty-nine crescents and placed them on the table in front of the lady.

Almost immediately, the merchant's face contorted with anger. "No! This not celts! This bad money, bad money! You try to cheat me!"

Trenson stepped back in surprise. "What? There's nothing wrong with the money! Everyone uses crescents!"

The lady shook her head violently. "Not me. Me only take celts, good money! Me no take these, 'crescents!' It bad money, bad money! Give me celts!"

Trenson was aware of the difficult situation he was in. "I don't have celts."

"Then you get no food! You give me no celts, I give you no food."

"Hey, let's be reasonable here." Trenson really didn't want to search for another vendor. "Everybody takes crescents! You could buy anything with them. They have gold and silver in them, I promise you."

"Me no care about gold or silver," the lady retorted. "Me want celts."

"I just said I don't have any celts."

"Then you get no food!"

Trenson sighed. "Do you only take celts?"

"Yes," the lady replied abruptly.

"What about a trade?"

The merchant raised an eyebrow. "A trade?" She didn't seem opposed to the idea.

Now Trenson had a foot in the door. "Yes, a trade. Maybe something like..." He rummaged through his satchel, looking for something that might appeal to this finicky lady. He was surprised at how much junk he found. He had a bad habit of using his satchel to put trash in. "Like this!" Trenson held up a small, handheld candlestick. He had no idea why it was in his bag, but he was thankful for it now. It was only about the length of his forearm, but it did the job nonetheless, although currently it was holding no candle. It had traces of silver in it, making Trenson figure it was a good trade.

The merchant, however, looked at the candlestick with disgust, like Trenson just offered her a handful of dirt. "I no take this." She clearly had no idea what it was.

Trenson mumbled under his breath and shoved the candlestick back into his satchel. He searched around some more and pulled out a porcelain drinking bowl. Likewise, this also had traces of silver in it, with patterns of flowing wisps encircling the bowl. It was worth maybe a little too much for a few provisions, but it was the best he could find.

Unfortunately, the merchant seemed even less liable towards the bowl than with the candlestick. "No," she said quickly. Trenson could tell she was getting impatient.

With a sigh, Trenson started looking for something else in his satchel. He pulled out a handful of items and held them up to search deeper. He found things that he had no idea were in his bag. Everything he found, however, was either worth too much or too little for a few provisions.

Suddenly, the merchant pointed to something in Trenson's hand. "That!" she said excitedly.

Trenson stopped and looked at his hand, where he was holding items he had taken out to search deeper, and couldn't help but raise an eyebrow when he saw that all he was holding was a small feather. "This?"

The merchant nodded enthusiastically. "Yes, yes! I take that!"

Trenson took a second to register surprise. It was a brown feather the size of his finger. It was a piece of trash to him. Trenson shrugged. "Sure." He held it out to the merchant. She snatched it from his hand and held it in both hands, holding it close to her face like a precious artifact.

"This will cover everything?" Trenson asked, making sure this wasn't some trick.

The lady didn't move her gaze from the feather, "Yes, this plenty."

Not wanting to disturb the merchant from her moment, and already having the goods in his satchel, he walked away from the booth and into the street, feeling both pleasure and a little confusion. Guess one man's junk is another man's treasure, he thought.

***

Finally, Jayfor was gaining on the thief. Chasing after criminals while decked in heavy equipment wasn't the easiest thing in the world, but he was naturally fast anyway, and used to bearing burdens. Still, it would have been easier without all the gear.

The crowd parted for the criminal as he dashed ahead, the bag of coins held awkwardly in both hands. Much to Jayfor's frustration, no one seemed to want to stop him. They simply stared and moved out of the way. He wanted to yell for people to help him, to stop the man, but he was out of breath. So instead, he pushed forward and tried to urge his tiring legs to go faster.

Evidently, this wasn't the first time the thief had been chased. He weaved left and right, throwing Jayfor off a few times before he caught sight of him and began chasing once more. If the thief thought he was going to discourage Jayfor, he was mistaken, as the harder the pursuit was, the more Jayfor was committed to catching him.

The thief disappeared around a corner. Jayfor followed right behind him, almost close enough to attempt to tackle him. But it was a cruel trick. The thief had stopped on the edge of the corner, dropping the bag, and pulling out a dagger. When Jayfor came running around the edge of the building, the criminal tackled Jayfor to the ground.

Jayfor was knocked almost breathless in surprise. He fell hard to the ground, the thief on top of him. He saw the silver glint of a knife held high in the air, ready to begin its journey downward. Jayfor quickly punched the man hard in the stomach, and heard him groan in pain, giving him the time to push him off himself and scramble to his feet. The criminal rose to his feet as well, brandishing the knife in his hand.

Both men stared at each other, breathing hard. The criminal spoke first, his voice muffled by the bandana that covered his lower face. "You messed with the wrong people."

Jayfor had the feeling that if he could see the man's face, it would be smiling. He heard footsteps behind him. Jayfor turned and saw two more disguised figures approaching, both with swords drawn and roguish in appearance. Neither of them wore bandanas, showing the smile on their square faces, but the rest of their attire was identical to the original thief.

Jayfor felt a pang of fear. He was outsmarted and outnumbered. What had started as chasing a street thief had turned into a life-or-death situation, with death being much more likely than life, and his adversaries knew it. To deflect three weapons at the same time, especially with a sword, was a hopeless endeavor.

Suddenly, he remembered: his sword. It was given to him by Senver. Hope welled inside him, and he pulled his sword out of its sheath with the hiss of metal and held it in a ready stance that testified of mastery. Maybe it was just him, but there was an inert feeling of confidence as he held the weapon, a feeling of security.

While nothing special about it on the outside, holding it himself, Jayfor felt newfound power. Time to see if this sword could stand the test of battle.

The thieves hesitated slightly, smart enough to see by this man's ready position that they weren't dealing with some brazen do-gooder. They formed a triangle around Jayfor. The disadvantaged position Jayfor was in did nothing to sooth Jayfor's resolve.

One of the thieves behind Jayfor attacked first. Swinging his sword sideways towards Jayfor's back, he lunged forward, preparing to end his life in one fell swoop. Effortlessly, instinctively, without even knowing what he was doing, Jayfor flipped the sword upside down in his hand and held it behind him, effectively guarding his back. It was an extremely risky move, for the momentum of the swing was so powerful that, holding the blade upside down, it was almost impossible to hold the guard.

The blades slammed together with a crash. Jayfor waited, but, amazingly, he felt nothing. His arm didn't rattle, and his sword didn't move an inch. Before he could even comprehend what he was doing, he spun around and, the blade still in an upside-down grip, slashed at the bandit who attacked his back. The speed of the maneuver was unstoppable; there was nothing to be done. The bandit flew backwards from impact and fell to the ground, unmoving.

Jayfor returned to his ready position and stared at both bandits, daring them to come at him. He was insurmountable now. A gasp escaped the two remaining criminals, and they glanced at each other, each beginning to grasp just how skilled their opponent really was.

One of the thieves seemed to shrug and ran at Jayfor with his sword raised above his head, clearly intending an overhead slash. Once again, the sword seemed to take control of Jayfor. In what seemed like slow motion, Jayfor leaned to the side, and the blade passed beside him and hit the ground hard. Without missing a beat, Jayfor brought the bottom of the handle to the side and into the bandit's head. The bandit's eyes rolled back, and he sank to his knees.

Only one thief left — the one who stole the money in the first place. Jayfor stared at the bandit, a fire in his eye, power in his figure. The thief didn't think twice. Not even batting an eye at the sack of coins he was leaving behind, the criminal broke into a mad dash away from Jayfor, looking back over his shoulder at Jayfor, who was calmly watching him. This was too much for him; a few coins weren't worth this. Soon he disappeared around another street corner.

With his foes either unconscious or having fled, Jayfor's fire slowly diminished. He looked at his sword with wonder. What was that? Nothing visible had taken place — at least, nothing physically extraordinary had happened with the sword. Yet when he used it in battle, he didn't even have to think about his next action. It just seemed to happen. His view on the modest sword changed dramatically.

He took the bag of money from the corner and started walking back towards the stand. Now he could get back to getting two horses.

***

Trenson felt like he had waited forever for Jayfor. He leaned against the horse statue, wondering if it had been close to an hour. Probably not. He had finished his part of the deal quickly, which was good, because now they had the supplies they needed, but it left Trenson with extra downtime.

Maybe he could go looking for Jayfor and meet up with him. If the stables were nearby, it would save them time. Deciding that was the best course of action, he stood and started walking down the street that he had last seen Jayfor going down.

After roughly fifteen minutes of uneventful weaving through the crowds of people, Trenson spotted the stables up ahead. But he caught sight of Jayfor standing by a vendor in front of the stables, chatting with the merchant. What puzzled Trenson the most was that Jayfor didn't have any horses with him. He sighed. Jayfor was always one to talk and probably spent this whole time in a conversation instead of looking for horses.

Trenson almost called out Jayfor's name, then remembered that Jayfor was using a different name, so instead called, "Conrad!"

Thankfully, Jayfor remembered his alternate name. He stopped talking and scanned the crowd until he saw Trenson, then sent a quick nod Trenson's way. Jayfor wrapped up the conversation with the merchant, during which the merchant shook his hand with a big smile. After concluding remarks, Jayfor started towards Trenson, a smile on his face.

The same could not be said of Trenson. "What are you doing?" Trenson wanted to know.

"I was just talking to that merchant," Jayfor said, as if it weren't already obvious.

"I know that! I thought you were looking for horses to get."

"I was! But..." Jayfor voice trailed off, and his heart sank when he looked over Trenson's shoulder. It was a group of bandits, pushing aside people and scanning the crowd, looking for someone... him. His fight with the thieves hadn't gone unnoticed. "I'll explain later. Right now we need to get out of here."

Trenson didn't know what he was getting at. "What?"

Jayfor spoke urgently, keeping his eyes on the advancing group of masked men. "I said I'll explain later! We need to the leave the town — right now!"

Trenson was still taken aback. "But what about the horses?"

"The horses will have to wait for another time!" Jayfor started to run in the opposite direction.

"Hey, wait up, Ja—Conrad!"

XXIX

T RENSON WAS A LITTLE annoyed at first with the fact they had to leave town without horses. But when Jayfor related the story about chasing down the thief and the fight that followed, along with the inexplainable feeling of power and reflex he felt in the fight, Trenson's annoyance abated. "You certainly had a more interesting time than me," Trenson said.

Jayfor smiled. "I'm not so sure. Haggling with foreign merchants sounds like quite the task."

Trenson nodded. "That's for sure."

Overall, though, Trenson was fine with the fact they were still traveling on foot. He was against the idea of getting horses in the first place anyway, so not having a steed to ride didn't bother him a bit. Besides, not getting horses saved them a lot of money. He considered the trip to Dunbar a success because they got everything they needed and only had to spend a feather.

After hearing the description of Jayfor using his sword and the power it gave him, Trenson couldn't wait until there was a fight or something so as to try his sword out for himself. By the way Jayfor described it, it sounded amazing. Trading his original sword with this mediocre one might prove to be the right decision, after all.

According to the map, it was smooth traveling for the next week or so, the road north taking them through plains and crossing a few rivers along the way. With their new provisions, coupled with the old ones, they could probably go a little over a month without stopping for more. Trenson wished he had bought more provisions, not just because they would run out sooner than he thought, but because of the bargain that they came at. He wondered if all merchants in the area were particular about their payment. He hoped so. If he found a few more feathers, he could purchase a wagon's worth of rations, with some to spare.

The road was easy to follow, and even when it forked out to multiple places, the original path leading north wasn't hard to find. Trenson hoped this tree wasn't far away. He didn't dislike traveling, but unlike some people, he was keener to his destination than the journey.

One day, they walked down the road in silence. Stretches of farmland blanketed the hillside as far as the eye could see, most of the crops being wheat or some type of grain. Harvest season now upon them. Many people were out in the field, cutting the grain with sickles. It gave a peaceful picture of the world and almost made them forget of the turmoil they had been through and the future turmoil that was sure to be in store for them. Almost.

"I wonder what Elara plans to do now," Jayfor thought out loud.

Trenson looked at his comrade. "What do you mean?"

Jayfor stared forward as they walked. "Well, they've claimed victory over Faldon, and thoroughly crushed any hope of rebuilding it. Now that the war is over, what will they do?"

Trenson pondered the question. He had never really thought about it. "Maybe they'll start fighting Kallary. After all, the two were never friends, and it's the last thing on their way from world domination."

Jayfor was skeptical. "I'm not so sure. In southern Faldon, where the two kingdoms have met after destroying our forces, they never fought each other, or at least not that I heard. It seemed to me that Elara formed an unspoken pact with Kallary, that both of them would focus their efforts on their common enemy — us — before dealing with each other."

"Right," Trenson agreed, "But now their common enemy is vanquished."

"Exactly. Although it's quite possible that Elara will resume fighting with Kallary — in which case Elara would easily win — I doubt that will happen. I've had some reports from Kallary, and from what I can tell, it's a region not so different from Elara. The two have similar ethics, which are basically no ethics at all, so I'm thinking maybe more of a mutual alliance, or even them joining under one flag."

Trenson shuddered inwardly at the thought. "You're right. They could conquer a third of the world without shedding a drop of blood." A short silence followed, during which Trenson contemplated how easily Elara could finish what they started and rule the world. "Let's hope it doesn't come to that," he concluded.

Jayfor cast him an uncertain glance that said it all: *there's almost no chance it won't.*

***

A few days later, in the early afternoon, as the two were walking past fields, they saw a horse-drawn wagon behind them, slowly gaining on them. Although they didn't need anything, they agreed that they should hail the driver and ask if he would mind giving them a ride, since they were going in the same direction.

Before long, the wagon, drawn by two large horses, caught up to them, and the driver, a friendly-looking man with a curled mustache that protruded on either side of his face, hailed them. "Greeting! Fortune be in my favor for finding two travelers like me on the road."

Jayfor smiled, "Yes, fortune indeed! It's always nice to see another of our kind."

The merchant nodded, still wearing a giant smile. It was almost as wide as his mustache. "True, true! It is a lonely occupation, it is, the many days gone from home, but I am heading back home now to see my wife and children, and to enjoy my home for a time before going back into the world."

"Oh, really?" Trenson joined in the conversation, "Then I wish you safe travels!"

"Thank ye kindly!" The man tipped his hat, which was triangular in shape, towards them.

Jayfor knew if he was going to ask for a ride, it was now or never. "Say, since we're going the same way, would you mind us riding with you a little while?"

"Of course, of course!" The merchant slid over to the opposite side of the long bench seat, making room for the two. "Please, come sit! You must be weary from your journey."

Trenson and Jayfor exchanged a pleased glance before climbing up into the seat. Although they hadn't been traveling long enough to feel tired, it was nice getting off their legs and relaxing while still making progress. The clopping of the horses' hooves on the dirt road and the jostling of the wagon behind them sounded like music to their ears.

"If you don't mind me asking, where is it that two young men like yourselves are going?" The merchant asked.

Trenson and Jayfor looked at each other, a little panicked. They never thought about making a cover story about where they were going. Jayfor spoke quickly, "We're going north to visit some of our kin."

"Is that right?" The merchant never lost his grin. "Well, good for you! It seems we're both on family business then, after all!"

Jayfor nodded, relieved that he didn't compromise his mission. Although he doubted that letting this man know their real intentions would do any harm, it was better to be on the safe side. Elara might catch wind that they were still alive, and that would make things much more difficult, to say the least.

"Where are you two from?" the merchant asked.

Trenson supplied an answer. "Dunbar. We only set out a little over a week ago."

"Ah! I see. It seems that you just got on the road."

Trenson nodded. Never too keen on conversation, he didn't start another topic, instead waiting for the merchant or Jayfor to bring one up.

And the merchant did. "Me, I have been traveling for quite some time. I haven't even stopped to sell wares for a few weeks, on account of me wanting to get home sooner. Va'ar willing, I'll make it there soon."

Jayfor perked up. *Va'ar willing* was a term that indicated this merchant might, in fact, be a follower. To test the theory, Jayfor added, "You have had His protection this far, and all you can do is ask that it continues."

"Yes, it's all we can do. He protects the ones that honor him, and me and my family are believers. I can only ask that He has kept them safe in my absence."

Jayfor nodded, smiling from the knowledge they finally found someone who was on their side. "We are believers as well," he nodded towards Trenson, who nodded his reply.

The ever-present grin of the merchant widened. "Well, Va'ar must really be looking out for me to send two friendly souls in the hardship of my travels! Where are my manners, I haven't even told you my name! I am Phantas, at your service."

"Conrad," Jayfor said, referring to himself, "And this is Trenson." He looked over at Trenson, who gave Phantas a nod. "Nice to meet you," he said simply.

Phantas nodded at each of them. "It's my pleasure! Whoa, whoa." The last two words were for the horses pulling the wagon. In talking, Phantas had slowly forgotten about the reins and was pulling one side harder while letting the other side go limp. As a result, the horses were just a few steps from going into the ditch and taking the wagon with them. After ordering them to stop, the merchant directed them back towards the road, and they soon returned to their casual pace.

"My apologies," Phantas said. "Sometimes I forget what I'm doing when I'm talking."

"It's alright," Jayfor replied, "I would probably do the same."

No one said anything for a brief period. The clip-clop of horse hooves and the low sound of wagon wheels turning make a peaceful tune that everyone was content listening to. Even Jayfor was silent, which was a first.

At length, the merchant broke the silence. "If you two are coming from the south, no doubt you have heard about Loronis."

The statement was directed towards Trenson. Trenson shot a quick glance at Jayfor. News traveled quicker than they had expected. They had hoped to stay ahead of the reports, but it was clear that it had traveled faster than anticipated. "I have," Trenson said.

Phantas, his good humor replaced with gloom, shook his head with a sigh. "It's terrible. I never thought it would happen, and yet here we are. I still can't believe that Elara could ever do this. We've stood for so long, it just seemed impossible to lose." He shook his head. "Those days are over now, though. Jayfor was a good king from what I've heard, but I guess even he never saw it coming."

Jayfor and Trenson both solemnly nodded. They knew staying silent was a little rude — or Jayfor did, Trenson never seemed to mind — but both knew that there was a chance, if they started talking about it, they could accidentally give away their whole mission. It was better to be rude than risk their whole endeavor.

After another period of silence, adequate to change the subject, Jayfor asked, "So where are you traveling from?"

Phantas' smile diminished even more. "Havilah," he replied. His voice remained doleful.

"I see," Jayfor responded. "If I'm not mistaken, that city-state is in Kallary, right?"

Phantas didn't look him in the eye. "Yes... or it was."

Was? What does that mean? Jayfor sensed this was an uncomfortable topic and decided to wrap it up. "In any case, I'm sure it's a fine place for trading."

Phantas didn't respond for a few seconds, then he turned and looked at Jayfor. "You haven't heard what happened there?"

Jayfor shook his head, a little confused. "No. What happened?"

Phantas chuckled, but it was a dry chuckle. "That, my friend, is a long story. But it is one that must be passed on, so that our children's children will not make the same mistake they did. If you like, I will tell it to you."

Jayfor got more comfortable in his seat. "Yes, please." He always liked a good story, and this one seemed like an especially good one. Trenson also looked interested — for once since they joined Phantas on his cart — and leaned forward in anticipation.

And so Phantas began.

XX

K ing Ragnar — or lord Ragnar, as he preferred to be called — was a man that no one dared cross, and those who did never lived to tell others. He was a capable warrior, strong enough to cleave knights in half with one swing of his axe and ruthless enough to not think twice about doing so. His reputation spread fear throughout the lands, but while he was a cruel man, the people respected and honored him, not just out of fear, but because in Kallary, strength and brutality were considered a virtue. The people didn't hate him; rather, they hailed him as their great lord, and no one thought of him as evil and cruel.

Despite his position, Ragnar had not one drop of royal blood in his veins. He was born and bred a nomad, his father being chief of a ragtag group of doughty and vicious warriors. Ragnar inherited his father's position, and the want of destruction that came with it. He led his warriors through towns to ravage, pillage and burn anything, including people, that stood in his way. After gaining a fearsome reputation, he set his sights on a more ambitious prize: the large city-state of Havilah.

On the contrary, the king of Havilah was meek and far from a warrior. From his size, it seemed he didn't lift anything heavier than the cups of wine he was fond of drinking. He was scheming and adept in matters of business, but the people didn't like that. They wanted a powerful king, one who struck fear into hearts and could wield any weapon with prowess. And Ragnar was the perfect candidate.

In an attack that almost seemed too easy, Ragnar and his warriors burst into the city of Havilah, slaughtering guards and commonfolk alike as they made their way through the streets towards the king's palace. The city was unprepared for the attack, and its soldiers were lazy. They paid for it.

Ragnar and his band stormed into the palace and, in the span of a few hours, killed the king of Havilah and seized control of the city-state. Ragnar took the title of king as his own, and his reign of absolute authority began.

Ragnar considered compassion a flaw and mercy a weakness. It was easier to just kill them rather than risk them making another mistake. His brutality was unprecedented, and he swept through every town close to Havilah. He was determined to gain as much power as possible, to crowd as many cities as possible under one banner. Many lords in Kallary had tried this to little effect, but Ragnar liked a challenge. And with each city that fell into his hands, more opportunities for more territory came into play. And he wasn't one to turn down an opportunity.

But it wasn't enough. As his status and authority increased, so too did his greed. He swooped into unsuspecting towns and settlements, ravaging the inhabitants and claiming what was left as his own. Soon, word began to spread of this man's might, until cities openly came to him to join his side, rather than be destroyed in the process. Ragnar always agreed, and soon the city-state became a domain, and from a domain to a country.

And it still wasn't enough. Even though his name was spreading throughout Kallary as one of the few rulers who had unified a large part of the disjointed region, it still wasn't enough. There was always one more town that needed raiding, one more foe that needed to be slain, one more political adversary that had to be removed. And after he dealt with that, there was another.

Ragnar wanted to do something that would solidify his name in history, something that future generations would look back on and marvel at his power. Although he had conquered more lands than any previous Havilah king had, and even more than most kingdoms in Kallary, he felt he would be forgotten in the future. This drove him to raid even more towns and storm more domains, but every time he looked at his ever-changing map borders, it was never enough for him.

What he needed was a monument. Something physical that his inheritors could see and look at and remember him by. It would have to be bigger than anything ever done before, bigger than the dainty little statues that the domains around him called towers. No, this one would be much bigger. It would be the largest monument ever in Havilah, in Kallary, in the world. That would make him be remembered. And so that was what he decided to do.

The task daunted his architects. They told him it was impossible. Ragnar wouldn't let them tell him it was. Either build it, he told them, or I'll get rid of you until I find someone who can. Of course, everyone knew just what Ragnar meant by "get rid of," and so they put their head down and started to work.

The pace was slow. It took the architects a long time to agree on how they should go about building this monument, and even longer to procure the resources and workers to begin construction, causing it to take over a year to begin the actual building. Ragnar was impatient, but even he understood a project of this magnitude would take time. He busied himself laying waste to nearby cities not yet in his control.

They finally began work laying the foundations. Ragnar ordered that the statue be made to look exactly like him, and often corrected the plans of the builders to add a detail here or there that he didn't mention earlier. Because of this, the architects sometimes had to backtrack or redo some things to add the changes, which was frustrating, but the alternative was complaining to the king that he was changing too many things — and everyone knew the result of doing that.

It still felt like it was taking too long. At the snail's pace everything seemed to take, Ragnar started to worry that this statue may not be finished in his lifetime. He started taking all able-bodied men from his raids as slaves and set them to work on the statue. The method was effective in increasing the labor force, but even though thousands of people spent all their time working on this monument, it was still slow work.

But there was still progress. Every year the monument grew higher, and the region of Havilah grew larger. Ragnar's notoriety had become legendary, and that in itself was enough to please him. His fame and progress was enough, his advisers told him, that he would be cemented in history regardless, but the monument would certainly help. So construction continued, and in the meantime, Ragnar kept conquering regions around him.

About halfway through the construction of the monument, an old man came to the palace steps and requested an audience with the king. Ragnar wasn't one to do audiences, and would have shooed this man away just like he did everyone else who wanted to talk to him, if not for the fact that this old man claimed to bear words of warning for the king. Again, death threats were common in his household, but he was in need of something amusing that day, and so he admitted the man inside and brought him before his throne.

What Ragnar heard was the last thing he wanted to hear. This hunched-over man told him that his rule would soon be over, that his "wicked ambitions and acts" would be avenged; that the true king of the world, a being called Va'ar, saw Ragnar's pride and would bring his kingdom crashing to the ground in judgement; that Va'ar would make a spectacle out of Ragnar and his monument, that future generation would hear the story about Ragnar's fall and see that pride destroys all things.

To say that Ragnar was enraged was an understatement. His face turned bright red, and he trembled with hatred, so consumed with wrath he couldn't speak. Slowly, he rose from his throne, his hands clenched so tight that they started to bleed where his fingernails cut into his skin. With a scream, Ragnar rushed at the old man, making to throttle him dead. But right when he was about to grab him, the old man disappeared. He vanished, and Ragnar only gripped thin air.

Everyone in the room gasped. One second, the old man was there, calmly denouncing the most powerful king in Kallary. The next, he was gone, vanished. Ragnar ordered a search to be conducted for the old man, in case he was using some sort of trickery, but after a week, everyone gave up. No one could find the slightest trace of him. Ragnar swore everyone who had been in the throne room that day to secrecy, to not tell anyone of what they had seen, on pain of death. Everyone readily agreed, and the event was pushed to the side, never spoken about again.

After a staggering thirty years, the giant statue was finally finished. It was a sight to behold. So large it was that the shadow cast by it would shade the entire city, and even more so after that. The top of the head, which resembled Ragnar's as close as possible, was twice as tall as the giant palace he built himself. Ragnar was proud of it, and could honestly say it was worth the wait. Now no one would forget him. Now everyone would worship him as lord.

The day after the statue was complete, Ragnar hosted a giant celebration festival. Food and drink were given freely to everyone, and the entire place was an uproar of activity. People from all over, even those not in Havilah's region, came to hear about this fabled statue, supposedly the largest in the world. And when they saw it, they had to believe it.

When the appointed time came, Ragnar stepped onto the podium that had been placed at the feet of the statue just for the purpose. Everyone cheered at the husky warrior who had achieved so much in his lifetime. Ragnar smiled, pride welling inside of him. It was all his, every part of it.

He told the people, now in a hushed silence, about how he would continue his domain until it stretched to the ends of the world. His statue stood as proof that he could do the impossible, and that his reign would never end, that none could stand against him. He was the ruler of the lands. A deafening cheer rose from the crowd. Ragnar smiled smugly.

"I am the greatest warrior in the world!" he said. Another cheer. "I am the most powerful man in the world!" An even louder cheer. "I am the only person who can rule the world! *I am the lord!*"

Another cheer started, but at that moment, something happened. A loud cracking noise filled the air. The ground started to rumble and quiver. Everyone forgot about Ragnar's speech, even Ragnar himself.

Then, the ground split open. Four cracks appeared on the ground, one on each side of the great statue, creating a giant X under the structure. The ground continued to shake, making it difficult to stand. Panicked screams erupted from the crowd, almost as loud as the cracking ground. The hole made by the cracks was deep, too deep to see the bottom. And it would swallow anything in its way.

Each of the four splits in the ground continued to widen, each one now as wide as a street. People ran as fast as they could away from the opening ground, but many of them found it wasn't fast enough. Buildings fractured and fell in splintering shambles into the cracks. The holes continued to yawn even more, chasing down everyone trying to escape.

Ragnar stood as well as he could on the stage, struggling to keep his balance. He looked around him as the natural disaster devoured homes and people whole, easily destroying everything he had conquered. Anger rose in him, anger at this earthquake for ruining everything. He looked up at the sky and screamed in vehement anger, cursing the earth for ruining his moment.

His outburst didn't last long. The four cracks met under the giant statue, and as they widened, the X where they met got larger and larger and larger, the hole getting bigger and bigger, until, with a deafening crack, the ground completely gave way under the statue. The huge monument fell straight down into the chasm. The ground exploded into the air as the edges of the monument smashed into the sides of the hole. As it fell, the giant nose of the statue, sticking out more than the rest, slammed into the podium Ragnar was standing on, smashing Ragnar and the entire woodwork to pieces on its way down. In a few seconds, the entire monument was gone, disappearing into the endless pit.

And it was so that the old man who had warned Ragnar was right; the proud capital of Havilah, once a powerful empire, fell and shattered.

XXI

"**T**HAT'S IT?" TRENSON ASKED.

Phantas shrugged. "I'm still trying to figure out a good place to end the story, so when I tell it to other people it doesn't seem like a drag."

"I don't think I'd call that a drag," Trenson replied. "It was pretty interesting from start to finish. But what happened after that?"

Phantas took a deep breath. "Even after the statue fell into the hole and Ragnar was killed, the cracks kept getting larger and large, until four valleys, at least a mile across, were formed, and then the earthquake finally stopped. The distance between each of the four squares of land was so great no one could get to the other side even if they tried, and the valleys ran for so long we couldn't keep walking and meet back together. Entire families were separated. In the end, everyone on each part of the land went their own way. I was one of them, and luckily, my cart and goods were still intact. And here I am now."

Trenson nodded. "That's a much better place to end it, in my opinion."

Phantas smiled and nodded. "I'll keep that in mind."

Jayfor said, "That was... probably the craziest thing I have ever heard."

"It was the craziest thing I have ever lived through," Phantas agreed, "but I promise you, everything I said was true. You can even see the valley for yourself if you're in northern Kallary. There's a pile of rubble in the middle of the valley, and that is what's left of the statue."

"I see," Jayfor said. He mused over the story, for it gave him a lot to think about. He was surprised at how much it sounded like his own experience with the destruction of Loronis. It was for the same reason, too — bringing justice to people who had turned away from Va'ar and whose pride was beyond measure. "How did you know about the old man that approached Ragnar? I thought you said Ragnar swore everyone who saw it to secrecy."

"Oh, he did, but after Ragnar died, no one felt the need to keep his promises anymore. I heard it from a guard of the palace that saw it himself and managed to escape the earthquake. He's a changed man now, and a follower too."

Jayfor nodded. That made sense. He couldn't spot any holes — besides four literal ones, of course — in the merchant's story, neither did he detect that he was pulling their leg. He had lived through something like that as well, and maybe it was just empathy, but he believed it.

For a time, they rode in silence — well, almost silence. The occasional horse snort and the creaking of wagon wheels were the only noises, but they had grown so used to them now they hardly heard them. A cool gentle breeze wafted through the air and reminded them that fall was fast approaching, the days becoming shorter and the nights growing longer.

A forest lay ahead, the road they were on plodding on through the trees that started densely along the edge, almost like a wall. Trenson was glad at the sight of it — some shade would be welcome, especially after being in the sun all day.

Phantas drove the cart towards the woods, like he planned on going right through. But when he reached the border where the trees started, he pulled on the reins and brought the cart to a sudden stop.

Trenson looked at him quizzically. The merchant was looking left and right, and peering deep into the woods, like he was looking for something. There was a worried expression on his face. "What is it?" Trenson asked.

Phantas didn't respond immediately, but checked around him one more time. Then he looked Trenson in the eye. "Listen," he said in a hushed voice, "I need your help."

Trenson raised an eyebrow, more confused than ever.

Phantas once more peered into the woods. "I grew up around these woods. They are famous for a band of thieves who live entirely by pillaging merchant caravans like my own. This is the only road through the woods; to go around would take weeks." He looked at Jayfor, waiting for him to finish the sentence.

Jayfor caught on. "So you want us to help defend the caravan if it comes to blows?"

Phantas nodded. "Precisely. I'm going to try to get us through as fast as I can. From what I heard, they like to chase down the caravan on horses from behind, then jump on the wagon." He nodded to the back. "There are a few bows and a bundle of arrows back there. Grab them, and shoot if anyone starts chasing us."

Trenson peered over his shoulder, and sure enough, spotted a neat stack of shortbows balanced on a bundle of boxes, with a few quivers filled with razor-tipped shafts beside it. He grabbed a bow and tested the string by pulling it gently. He didn't consider himself very good with a bow, it never being a very important skill to him. Still, he could hit a target. A very close target, but a target nonetheless. He considered Jayfor the expert in bows.

Jayfor grabbed a bow as well and tugged the string a couple of times. He didn't consider himself very good with bows either. He preferred sword drills to target practice any day, and while he could still hit a target with a bow, it had to be a very close one. He considered Trenson the expert in bows.

"I'm not very skilled with a bow," Jayfor admitted to Phantas.

"Me neither," Trenson piped.

"Well, I don't see anyone else who can shoot a bow while I drive, so it's up to you two." He checked the hitch that connected the horses to the cart, and satisfied that it was secure, looked both of them in the eye, one at a time. "Are you ready?"

Trenson shot a look at Jayfor that asked, *should we really be doing this?* Jayfor shrugged and returned with one that said, *why not?* "We're ready," Jayfor answered for them both.

Phantas returned the nod and flicked the reins with a spirited, "Hiya!" The horses started forward at a brisk pace into the cloud of trees. Trenson and Jayfor each grabbed a quiver and nocked an arrow into the string, ready to fire at a moment's notice.

XXII

MAYBE IT WAS JUST paranoia, but the forest seemed more eerie than Trenson expected. The canopy was dense, but directly above the road it was clear, allowing light to shine straight down on the road. However, besides the road, the thick overgrowth of trees prevented most light from shining through. The result was the forest was dark everywhere but the road, with thick vines and gnarled trees reaching towards the road, as if to grab travelers. It gave Trenson the heebie-jeebies.

It was the perfect place to ambush a caravan, Trenson mused. The narrow road and lush undergrowth allowed ambushers to lie and wait, and even shoot at their target without being spotted.

The rickety creak of wagon wheels turning only added to his uneasiness. He gripped the bow and string so tightly that the wood started to creak beneath his fingers. He thought he spied movement beside the road and hastily drew his bow and aimed at the spot where he saw the trees move. A squirrel poked its head around the tree and started barking at Trenson.

Trenson released the pent-up breath he didn't realize he was holding in and relaxed his bow. He turned and saw both Phantas and Jayfor staring at him.

"What?" Trenson whispered. "It could have been a bandit!"

Jayfor shook his head with a half grin. Phantas returned to looking at the road and silently urged the horses to go faster, but not too fast that they were loud.

"How long will it take to get out the other side?" Jayfor whispered.

Phantas didn't avert his eyes from the road ahead. "About twenty minutes at most." His answer was quick, and Jayfor didn't say anything else, preferring to let Phantas drive. He watched the road behind them. If anyone were to come up on them, he reasoned, it would be from behind. While he hadn't seen anything that suggested people were in the woods, there was no reason thieves couldn't explode from the underbrush at any moment and take the convoy. With three men defending, and only two of them armed, a small group could take the cart without breaking a sweat — unlike Trenson and Jayfor, who were breaking many a sweat just sitting there waiting for something to happen.

After they were about ten minutes in the woods, Trenson started to relax. His early apprehension started to wear off. Maybe they wouldn't be attacked by bandits after all. The forest wasn't really that dark and broody — in fact, the scenery was actually nice. He spotted a bird chirping in a nearby branch. He wondered what type of bird it was. Maybe a—

Thunk! The hollow sound of an arrow striking the wagon cracked through the air. Everyone jumped. All thought of the pretty bird vanished from Trenson's mind as he whipped around. His heart dropped when he saw a man, about fifty yards behind them, holding a poised bow in the air. The man wore a strange mask that covered his face, a zigzag symbol on it. He lowered the bow and grabbed a horn that was on his belt. Before Trenson could say anything, the man pulled up the mask just enough to put his lips on the mouthpiece and blew a loud, piercing bugle into the air.

There was a brief pause. Then another bugle answered it farther away, then another, then another. Trenson, Jayfor and Phantas all looked at each other in fear. Then Jayfor said, *"Go, go!"*

Phantas whipped the reins hard. "Hiya!" The two horses took off, and the cart and its passengers rocketed forward.

Three more bandits, this time mounted on horses and all wearing the same strange mask, appeared out of the woods next to the man who had blown the bugle. The man with the horn jumped into the saddle beside his comrade, and together they all took off chasing the wagon.

Phantas looked behind him and saw the bandits gaining on them. "Shoot, shoot!" he said frantically.

Trenson and Jayfor were already on it. They drew their bows and tried to take aim amid the shaking wagon and the moving bandits. Trenson centered the mark on the closest one and fired. The arrow sailed high into the air, far above the man's head. Trenson groaned in anger and grabbed another arrow. Jayfor saw Trenson miss high, and so tried to aim lower. His arrow sailed straight and true... into the ground.

The bandits were unfazed by the arrows and continue to draw closer and closer. They all drew bows of their own and started firing at Jayfor and Trenson with unsettling accuracy. Firing while riding a horse was an impressive skill that took years of practice.

Even though they were trying to kill him, Jayfor had to marvel at the skill it took to ride a horse and shoot a bow at the same time.

After an arrow landed a foot from his face and quivered in the wood of the cart, however, he started to marvel it less.

After two more shots, Trenson finally hit the closest bandit in the chest, who was now less than twenty feet away. The impact of the shot knocked the man backwards out of the saddle, and he fell lifeless to the ground. His horse reared to a stop a few seconds later. Trenson let out a cheer. One down, two more to go.

Just then, four more horsemen burst from the woods behind them and joined the group in pursuit. Six more to go, he corrected bitterly.

Jayfor got lucky too. Another bandit went flying out of the saddle with an arrow in his chest, leaving another horse stopped in its tracks. Jayfor cheered, then ducked as an arrow whooshed over his head.

"How many are there?" Phantas asked, yelling over the sounds of horses galloping.

"Five more," Trenson responded, taking aim at another one. He missed wide, but just barely. "Are we almost through?"

Phantas shook his head. "No, we still have..." He stopped in mid-sentence as his eyes widened in terror. He pointed ahead. "Look! Three of them, ahead! They have spears! They're going to kill our horses!"

It was all too true. Three bandits, all wearing identical masks, emerged from the woods about a hundred yards away, all mounted and brandishing long spears. They charged towards them with the points lowered and aimed towards the horses.

Trenson and Jayfor's focus immediately riveted on the three men ahead that came closer and closer with every second. Trenson fired too quickly, and his arrow fell short. They came closer. Jayfor shot and managed to hit one in the arm, knocking him out of the saddle. They came closer — twenty yards now. Trenson brought another one down. The final man was less than ten yards away.

There was no time to shoot. All they could do was watch as the man drew back his spear and, as he passed by the cart, thrust the weapon into the horse on their left.

The horse screamed with pain and convulsed. The cart rocked to the side. The bandit, either by choice or not, let go of the spear. The animal ran a few more feet, then tripped and fell down. The cart rocked violently to one side, then there was a snap as all the harnesses that connected the horse to the wagon broke. The wagon stumbled back upright, and the horse passed under the cart. Trenson and Jayfor held on for dear life as they were jostled and almost sent flying from the wagon.

The bandits behind them cheered. The one who had speared the horse joined the group and pulled out a bow of his own.

Phantas said, "This isn't good!" As if it weren't obvious. Luckily, all the things connected to the horse broke loose when it fell, including the reins, which Phantas was holding, one side tight while the other hung limp. The dead animal passed under the cart, and they didn't run over it. The bandits swerved or jumped over the fallen animal.

Still, the one horse left pulling the cart faithfully kept on. Sweat dripped down its side, and now he was carrying double the load, but he kept going.

Their speed was greatly reduced now, and the bandits grew closer. Trenson brought another one down, and Jayfor had an arrow nocked, but before he could fire, the closest horseman pulled in close to the side of the wagon, stood in the saddle, and jumped onto the cart. He stood over Jayfor triumphantly, waving a small sword in the air, like he had already won.

Jayfor simply pulled back the string of the bow and let go. The arrow flew through the bandit and out the other side. The man stood uncertainly, then fell sideways like a statue off the cart.

The other bandits, undaunted by how bad it went for the first one, had the same idea and put aside their bows, two more starting to pull up beside the cart. Trenson put his bow to the side and climbed out of his seat into the top of the wagon, drawing his sword. "Trenson!" Jayfor called behind him, but Trenson ignored him. In exasperation, Jayfor dropped his bow and clambered beside him. For some reason it came as a surprise to Jayfor that standing on top of a jostling cart moving as fast as possible was hard. Luckily, because of his skilled balance — or luck — he didn't go flying off the cart's edge.

Two bandits jumped from their horses onto the cart, drawing short swords. Trenson engaged one, and Jayfor the other. Trenson didn't have much room to fight or move around, but he launched a feign attack by holding his sword up high in the air, like he was preparing on overhead slash. The bandit instinctively raised his sword, but instead of bringing his sword down, Trenson brought his boot hard into his foe's abdomen. The bandit stumbled backwards, lost his footing, and tumbled backwards off the cart and onto the ground.

Jayfor's opponent was more resilient, blocking blow after blow Jayfor aimed at him. Apparently seeing an opening, the bandit thrust towards Jayfor's chest. Jayfor saw it coming and parried, then countered with a thrust of his own. The bandit didn't parry, and another one bit the dust as the sword went in and out.

Another bandit drew close to jump on the cart, but Trenson saw it, and in a flash, he pulled a knife out of his wrist sheath and sent it flying to the bandit. The bandit was standing up in the saddle to jump across when the knife hit him in the throat, and he sank back into the saddle and slumped forward. The horse, sensing the rider was dead, trotted to a stop.

That left two more. Both riders pulled up on either side of the wagon and jumped on, waving their swords viciously. Trenson and Jayfor made ready to engage them, but before they could, Phantas' voice rose through the air.

"Hard turn!" The merchant yelled. Everyone, including the two bandits, looked ahead and saw that the road made a right-angle turn to the left. Trenson and Jayfor looked at each other, then at the bandits. Then they shrugged and jumped back into their seats besides Phantas and held on tight to the seat.

The bandits were confused, and looked at each other questioningly. Then they realized just how bad the situation was. Before they could do anything, the hard turn came, the wagon swung out to the right, and with a cry of anger, the two bandits flew off the wagon and into the woods. They hit the ground hard, and the breath was knocked out of them. They watched the wagon disappearing into the distance, and muttered curses under their breaths.

The way out of the woods was just ahead. The relief Trenson and Jayfor felt at seeing it was inexpressible. As the final tree passed over their heads and they emerged from the woods into the open fields once again, Trenson said jubilantly, "We made it!"

XXIII

"I'm not entirely sure staying the night at Phantas' house was a good idea," Jayfor said wistfully as they trod down the road north once again.

Trenson gave him a sideways look. "Really? I had a great time. Got to eat as much as I wanted, the company was good, I finally had a decent night's sleep, and we're full on provisions, not to mention the very generous amount of coin he forced us to take. I'd say stopping there was the best thing that's happened during our journey."

"I can't deny that," Jayfor agreed, "but after sleeping in nice beds like that and being treated like royalty again, it's tough to get back onto the road again. Well, not really tough, just, less enjoyable, I guess."

Trenson thought about it for a few seconds, trying to figure out if he felt the same. After deciding he didn't, he shrugged. "If you say so. Next time we're offered hospitality, I'll let you sleep in the cold."

Jayfor laughed dryly. "Thanks for your consideration."

Trenson didn't understand Jayfor. After living on stringy meat and stale bread for a few weeks, the sight of Phantas' dinner table seemed almost as great as the feast they had back at the palace in Loronis.

Phantas' family, which included his wife and two young girls, both about seven years old, greeted him ecstatically. Phantas' wife, after he explained how the two young men who were with him saved his life, had begged them to eat dinner with them and spend the night. Trenson and Jayfor declined, but Phantas practically forced them into his house, and so they eventually accepted.

In celebration of Phantas' homecoming, a whole pig was butchered for the occasion, and the slabs of meat were roasted over an open fire, along with potatoes slathered in butter. Coupled with warm bread and a flagon of mead, that supper was the best Trenson had in a long time. Even though technically they hadn't been on the road for that long, to say it was delicious was an understatement.

That night, while Jayfor and Trenson let the girls play with their compasses, they sat by the fire with the last of their mead and talked about traveling. Jayfor brought up a new topic. "What can you tell me about the road north?"

Phantas considered the question for a few seconds before answering, fingering his mustache as he spoke. "That depends on exactly where north you're going. Northwest, obviously, will take you into Kallary, which is not a very friendly place. Straight north will take you to the Endless Mountains, which are barren and cold, I can tell you from experience. I have never been northeast before, but the Splitting Waters are there, and from what I've heard there's a lot of trade that goes on." He shrugged. "Most of my travels were west, or northwest."

Jayfor nodded. "I see." His sipped his mead appreciatively, relishing it because they couldn't take it on the road. He let a few seconds drag on, staring at the cackling fire, before speaking again. "Is there anything... noticeable, up north?"

Phantas raised an eyebrow. "Noticeable?"

"Yes. Like — say, anything special? Maybe a certain place or thing?"

Phantas chuckled. "I had no idea you two were in the business of sightseeing."

"Well, no, I'm just curious." Secretly, Jayfor was trying to figure out where this great tree was that they had to get to, without giving away the full of their mission.

Phantas eyed Jayfor. "You're going to have to be a little more specific."

Jayfor didn't meet his eye, but kept looking into the fire. "I don't know... perhaps... a tree?"

"A tree?" Phantas repeated incredulously. "Here I thought you were visiting kin, and now you tell me you're after some special tree!"

"Well," Jayfor fumbled for words, "we are. I mean, we are still visiting kin! It's just a question!" He couldn't think of a better reply, and cringed at how awkward this was getting.

Phantas stopped chuckling. "Alright, alright. Let me think. There are forests up north with some pretty large trees, but no one particular tree." He looked at Jayfor apologetically. "Don't know if that helps. I don't pay that much attention to trees."

Jayfor held up his hand. "It's alright." After that, he quickly changed the subject to something more trivial and never spoke about it again.

Now, the day after, as Jayfor walked down the road, he thought about that conversation. If this tree — what did Reginold say it was called? Ramadus? — was famous, then why didn't Phantas know about it? Or maybe he just missed it. Either way, it was likely that this tree wasn't something very distinguished. Or maybe — the thought made Jayfor shudder — they had already passed it.

Earlier today, a few hours before they left the merchant's house, Trenson said, "I see what you're talking about. With the sword."

"What?" Jayfor asked. "Oh, about it controlling your movements? I meant to ask you about it sometime, to see if you felt the same thing."

Trenson nodded. "I did. It was strange, it's only now, looking back on it, that I can really see how it happened. When I was in the heat of the battle, it was just like you said; I didn't have to plan my attacks or do anything. It just happened. The sword seemed to take over. I swear I could sense what was going to happen before it did." Trenson shrugged. "I was actually a little disappointed that the fight didn't last longer, so I could experience that feeling more."

Jayfor smiled. "Don't worry, I'm sure there will be plenty more fights in the future that will give you chances."

So it wasn't just him, Jayfor mused. Trenson felt it too, how the sword guided the fight. Of course, Jayfor had heard expressions from his training instructors about how to let the sword do its work and to "let it go as it will." They seemed to allude to the sword taking over. And to be honest, there were a few times when fighting that Jayfor felt something akin to this. But that was more instincts. This was something entirely different. Swapping his kingly sword for this one was worth it, by far. He wondered what would have happened if he chose to keep his royal sword, if he would still be alive, or what Erador and Reginold would have done.

"I think," Trenson interrupted Jayfor's deep thoughts, "if I manage it right, I can make this cake last for a week."

Jayfor smiled. "They gave a slice to each of us. It's meant to be eaten in one or two sittings."

"I know that. But why waste it all at once when we can make it last for *a week?* Who knows when we'll get the chance to eat something like this again. We better make it last."

"*You* can," Jayfor replied. "I am going to eat it in one sitting, probably tonight."

"Tonight?" Trenson was shocked. "But you just had some yesterday at Phantas' house!"

Jayfor looked at his friend with an amused countenance. "I know that. Your point is?"

"My point is you're not trying very hard to get the maximum enjoyment out of this." Trenson seemed offended that Jayfor would treat a piece of cake like it was simply food. "Wait a minute," Trenson said to himself, "if I only eat a small sliver every other day, I can get this to last *two* weeks!"

Jayfor sighed with a smile on his face. "Have fun with that. I'm eating all mine tonight."

Trenson shot a doleful look at Jayfor. "In two weeks, when I'm eating my last delicious piece of cake and you aren't, I'm not sharing."

"Since when did you do that anyway?" Jayfor wanted to know. Unfortunately, Trenson didn't answer.

XXIV

As usual, Thrall's audience chamber was dull and dark. And that suited Thrall just fine. He liked dull and dark places, and his audience chamber at his dark castle in Elara was a testament of that.

As he sat on his throne, looking around the room with critique, he wondered if maybe he should redo the interior. The only thing giving light to the room were two small windows, high on the wall, which cast rays of dismal light onto the door of the sanctum and in front of the throne, where petitioners were designated to stand.

There was no furniture or statues, no rug leading to the throne, no... anything. Besides the throne on the other side of the room, the sanctum was completely empty. It was a long, rectangular room with barely enough light to see in, and was entirely made of stone, except for the throne, which was made of obsidian.

In other words, it fit Thrall perfectly. He decided against redecorating, concluding that anything extra would take away from the atmosphere he was trying to produce in the room.

The large doors on the other end of the room opened, and a guard poked his head through. "My lord, Cosgroc requests an audience."

"Admit him," Thrall replied. There was something he wanted to discuss with his subordinate, and this provided the perfect opportunity.

The guard nodded and opened the door fully, allowing the husky form of Cosgroc to come striding through. The guard closed the door behind him. Cosgroc's footsteps were the only sound, and they echoed loudly across the room, one by one, until they stopped when he stood before the throne. He bowed low. "My lord, thank you for allowing me into your presence."

"Oh, skip the formalities, Cosgroc," Thrall snapped. "You're here for a reason, and the sooner you're out hunting followers, the better. So get on with it."

Cosgroc's attitude of respect turned to one of fear. He thought about replying, *Yes, my lord,* but wondered if that was considered a formality. Either way, he decided to trash it. "I came with a report about Loronis." He paused, wondering how he should continue. Thrall's impatience increased every second as the eyeless eyeholes in his helmet stared at him.

"It concerns your command to find the body of Jayfor and Trenson. We haven't been able to find them yet."

"What?" Thrall demanded. This was what he had wanted to discuss with his aide anyway, but he was not expecting this news. "You mean you haven't found them?"

"Well, no, sir. But my men are continuing the search as we speak." Cosgroc added quickly.

Thrall shook his head, disgusted. He had promised the Master that Jayfor and Trenson were dead. And he was almost completely sure that they were. But there was a chance, if their bodies weren't found, that they could be alive. "Sir," Cosgroc ventured cautiously, "It — it's possible that they were buried under the destruction. Or maybe they burned," he suggested. "They were likely in the palace, after all. We did reduce the entire structure to a pile of rubble."

Thrall considered the idea. It *was* likely, the more he thought about it, that their bodies were completely destroyed. "Still," he concluded out loud, "I would rather have proof than not at all. Continue the search for another week. If they aren't found, we can assume that they perished completely."

Cosgroc nodded once. "Yes, sir." He didn't leave, but instead kept standing, shifting his weight uncertainly. He had something else to say, but wasn't sure how to begin — in fact, he didn't want to begin at all. It was bad news, and Thrall wasn't the greatest at receiving bad news.

He stood uncertainly for too long and made Thrall angry, anyway. "Do you find my sanctum particularly intriguing, Cosgroc?"

Cosgroc snapped to attention. "No, sir."

"Maybe you've forgotten how to walk. Are you waiting for me to carry you out?"

"No sir!" said Cosgroc with fear and took an involuntary step back. He cringed when he realized this probably wasn't the best response.

Thrall nodded. "I see you can walk." He spoke with a voice like thin ice, cold and ready to burst at any moment. "Then would you mind doing me a favor? Either say something, or get your sorry self out of my sanctum. Please." Thrall added the last word with an unmistakable tone of sarcasm, and Cosgroc felt the sting of irony. Thrall was obviously seething with anger at this moment, and

Thrall knew that Cosgroc knew it. Cosgroc started to wish that he would instead just start yelling instead of keeping this charade of politeness any longer.

At last, Cosgroc found words. "Yes — yes, my lord. Only one more thing. It has ties to the fact that we haven't yet found Trenson and Jayfor's bodies. Last week, one of our division commanders to the north of Loronis — or where Loronis was — received a report from a bandit that caught my attention. These brigands make their living by raiding merchant caravans passing through the woods. Last week, however, these bandits were reduced to less than half their original number after attempting an attack on another merchant caravan that ultimately failed. The reason for this failure is credited to two young men — both of whom match Jayfor and Trenson's appearance surprisingly well — who were defending the caravan."

Thrall didn't move, or show the slightest reaction. Cosgroc was quick to add, "Of course, this is only rumors. The chance that it is them is extremely unlikely, but it is still worth taking note of. But like I said, my men are looking for their—"

"I get the picture, Cosgroc!" Thrall cut in petulantly. Subordinates these days, he thought. One moment they're standing there tongue-tied and bashful, the next they're chatty and give a second opinion on everything. "These 'rumors' are nothing more than gossip, at most, and all probably fabricated or just a product of their imagination. Remember how we were conducting a search for Reginold and Erador?"

"Yes sir," Cosgroc replied. Reginold and Erador were two commanders of two very large divisions of Senver warriors, and they had been searching for them for quite some time. It was a common tactic of Elara to go after an individual, rather than a whole army, and the two had been on the list for a long time.

"Well," Thrall continued, "after we issued the order to seek them out, I received almost twenty reports from our scouts who thought they might have seen something that looked like one of the two. All twenty scouts, simultaneously, from the far north to the desert south, all claimed they had seen 'something' that 'may have been' Erador and Reginold." He shook his head. "Disgusting. We can't even get reliable reports anymore. It's all 'maybe's' and 'I think I saw's'."

Thrall sighed and leaned back on his obsidian throne. "Unless you get concrete, guaranteed, solid, face-to-face, multiple witnesses type of evidence, don't ruin my day following me around pestering me with rumors."

"Yes, my lord," Cosgroc said enthusiastically. The prospect was actually appealing to him. The less he had to report, the less he had to be in Thrall's presence, and the less he was in Thrall's presence, the greater his chance of not being killed by the brutality of the general. Such events weren't uncommon.

"We have enough on our hands solidifying our new reign in Faldon and dealing with the recent outbreak of Senver attacks. Trenson and Jayfor are two people, two people who no longer have any authority in Ralladin. If they are alive, then their threat to us is minimum, at most."

Cosgroc nodded. "Yes sir." He started to edge towards the exit of the sanctum in relief that he had survived another briefing when Thrall's voice once again cut through the air and addressed him.

"However, if Trenson and Jayfor are found to be alive, don't hesitate to kill them, or better yet, bring them here to be imprisoned and tortured; suffer for what a pain they caused us in the past."

"Yes sir," Cosgroc replied again, edging closer to the exit, farther away from the Thrall. He technically couldn't leave until Thrall dismissed him. Which is why he was elated when he heard these words from the general.

"Now get out of here before I feel the need to kill someone."

XXV

A FTER A WEEK, JUST as Trenson promised, he still had half of his cake left.

"I honestly didn't think you'd stick with it," Jayfor admitted one night as Trenson was taking another miniature bite of the slice.

Trenson looked at him in mock anger. "In case you're wondering, I give lessons on self-discipline. I'll give some to you for a discounted price," he said around the cake in his mouth.

Jayfor rolled his eyes. "No thanks. I have plenty of discipline."

Trenson raised an eyebrow. "Hm," he said, in a tone that made it clear he didn't believe him. "But you ate all your cake in one sitting, the day after you got it," he pointed out.

"That took discipline," Jayfor replied with a grin.

Again, Trenson raised his eyebrow, but this time, he kept his mouth shut and enjoyed his extremely small bite of cake.

According to the map, they were a few days away from a mountain range. Neither of them were looking forward to it. The nights were already chilly, and the days were becoming no different. In addition, the mountains were probably covered in snow at this point, and neither of them liked traveling through snow either, let alone sleep in it.

"Maybe we'll find this tree right before we get to the mountains," Trenson suggested. "It's still a few days until we reach it. There are probably hundreds of trees from here to there."

Jayfor wasn't convinced. "Probably. But in all of Ralladin there's only one tree that we're looking for, and that tree could be a hundred miles from here."

Trenson shuddered, either from the chill of the night or at the thought, Jayfor couldn't tell. He guessed both. "Let's hope not."

At any rate, they hadn't found it yet, and with no idea how far they had to go to reach it, they assumed they would end up going over the mountains, anyway. It wasn't the worst thing that could happen. Then again, it wasn't the best thing that could happen either.

The road was easy going. They met nobody on the path, besides an occasional merchant, and the weather was sunny most days, so there wasn't anything to complain about. Actually, there were a few things Trenson wanted to complain about, like the fact that his feet were starting to blister for no reason, and the fact that he had nine knives instead of ten because he wasted one on the bandits. But there was no use in voicing those complaints, and he was sure Jayfor had his own share of discomforts, so he kept silent.

Actually, Jayfor didn't feel like he had any discomforts at all. He woke up every day cheerful, spent the day cheerful, and went to sleep cheerful. Trenson swore he even dreamed cheerful.

Trenson preferred to call himself a realist, seeing things the way they were, not really thinking negative or positive — although he tended to drift towards the negative, but he didn't consider this a bad thing. Jayfor considered himself a realist too, but both had very different dispositions, with the former king always in a good mood and seeing everything from the best possible angle. Jayfor liked to talk, Trenson preferred silence; Jayfor found everything interesting, Trenson looked at it as another thing to remember; Jayfor rudely ate his cake all at once, Trenson saved it for two weeks. It would have come as a surprise to anyone that they got along so well for their differences.

"We should be getting close," Trenson declared one day, out of the blue.

Jayfor gave Trenson a sideways look, confused. "What makes you think that?"

Trenson shrugged. "Intuition."

"Intuition. Well, seeing as I put a tremendous amount of faith in your 'intuition,' I believe we won't have to worry about crossing the mountains after all."

Trenson was unfazed by Jayfor's sarcasm and kept a stoic look. "We might still have to cross the mountains. 'Close' is a pretty relevant term."

"Just how relevant of a term?"

Trenson shrugged again. "I don't know. My intuition isn't very specific."

Jayfor made a mock frown. "I see. That's truly unfortunate. What else does your intuition tell you?"

Trenson didn't miss a beat and kept a straight face and looked ahead. "That we should drop this whole conversation about my intuition."

Jayfor nodded, pretending to be enlightened. "Ah. I guess it's only polite to consent to your intuition's wishes."

"That would be appreciated," Trenson agreed readily.

Jayfor set his eyes back on the road ahead, but he couldn't help but grin. He looked over at Trenson, and thought he perceived the faintest touch of a smile on his lips, but it was almost completely masked by his normal broody expression.

He sure has a strange sense of humor, Jayfor thought.

Trenson was thinking the same thing.

Not for the first time, or the dozenth time for that matter, Trenson wished they had packed warmer clothes. They were only halfway up the mountain, and Trenson's toes already felt like icicles. He had heard before that if your toes or fingers got frostbite bad enough, they could fall off. Since he couldn't feel his toes — he kept his fingers warm by tucking them under his armpits all day — he couldn't tell if he still had toes or not. Wouldn't that be nice, he thought grimly, to take off his boots and all his toes fall off. It would be just his luck.

The road started to get harder to follow. Before the mountains it was easy, the path was wide and hard to lose track off. They never lost their way once. The closer they got to the mountains, the narrower it became. And it became more made of pebbles and rocks rather than dirt. Then a thin layer of snow covered it, which didn't stay thin for long before they were trudging through two feet of the fluffy white foam.

At least it wasn't hard snow, Trenson told himself. Walking through two feet of that would be impossible, he knew from experience. Actually, he reminded himself, it was easier because you didn't have to walk through it at all — you just walked on top of it. Then Trenson started wondering if it would be better if it was colder so that the snow would get harder.

He was thinking about this when he realized Jayfor was talking to him. "I wish we brought snowshoes."

Trenson looked to his left to see Jayfor up to almost his waist in snow, taking giant steps forward to push through the wall. Trenson reasoned that the snow must have gotten deeper for Jayfor to be up to his waist. Or maybe he had just gotten smaller. Either or, Trenson decided. Trenson noticed that the snow was deeper to walk through for himself as well, so it must be the former.

Jayfor's face was red with exertion, and sweat built across his forehead, which quickly formed into a layer of ice in his eyebrows and hair. "Yes," Trenson said simply, then added, "or sleds."

Jayfor raised a frost-covered eyebrow. "Sleds?"

Trenson didn't realize he had said the last part out loud. He shrugged. "Why not? We could have carried them with us on our backs. It would make going downhill much easier." He was going to add *and more fun* but stopped himself.

Jayfor shook his head. "We're going uphill, not down. Sleds would just get in the way."

"Well, that's basically what snowshoes are anyway, right? Just two small sleds attached to your feet." He had no idea why he was suddenly defending the dignity of sleds, but he was bored, and it was something to do.

"Basically," Jayfor corrected, "snowshoes are made for walking, not sliding." He was starting to catch on to the fact that Trenson was only arguing to annoy him, but he didn't say anything. In fact, he needed something to focus on besides snow, which was a little difficult at the moment, so he kept the conversation going.

"Hm," Trenson said. By the way he said it, it sounded like this was a new discovery to him. He let the silence drag on a few more seconds before saying, "That's actually not a bad idea."

Jayfor looked at him again. "What isn't?"

"A sled attached to your feet." Trenson had his head pointed down and was fingering his chin thoughtfully, like a genius at work. "You stand sideways on it and strap your feet on. Then you lean forward or backward or left or right to turn whichever direction you want. And when you're done," his voice got louder the more excited he became, "you can carry it on your back using the same straps you put on your feet!" He looked at Jayfor like he had just received a revelation. He waited for praise, or at least agreement that it was a good idea.

Jayfor, however, was cruel. "I... don't think so."

Trenson's face fell. "Why not?"

Jayfor's eyes didn't alter from the ever-higher slope in front of them. "If that was a good idea, someone else would have thought of it by now."

"That's a terrible reason!" Trenson exploded. He threw his hands in the air to add to his point. "Just because someone hasn't thought of it before doesn't mean I can't think of it and that it's not a good idea!"

Jayfor shrugged and cracked a smile. He was starting to enjoy this now. "I guess that's true."

"You guess?" Trenson repeated accusingly, "You know. I know what you're up to. Secretly, you think my sled attached to the feet

— I need to name it — is a great idea. So great, in fact, that you'll pretend to not like it and convince me not to make them, while you turn around and start a monopoly on sled making. Soon hundreds are clamoring in your shop and asking you to put foot attachments to their sleds. After a few years you'll build an empire on it, and I'll be the poor beggar on the street corner, claiming I started the whole thing first."

Trenson stared daggers at Jayfor, as if he had already gone and stolen his lifetime dream. Jayfor returned the look with one of faint amusement, and, playing along, he twirled a fake mustache while chuckling evilly. This made both men burst into laughter and stop walking altogether. Even Trenson was laughing, although it didn't really sound like laughing as it was a husky, dry sound.

After a few minutes of standing there laughing, Jayfor finally said in between gasps for air, "Alright, alright, I'll admit, it's a decent idea. You can keep it."

Trenson held his chin high in triumph. "I knew you would agree."

"Indeed," Jayfor said with a nod. He had already drawn the breath to say something else when he spotted something ahead. "What in the world?"

Trenson saw it and was no less surprised. As they turned a bend in the road, the road suddenly came to an end as it hit the wall of the mountain — except for a giant cave mouth that yawned and seemed to swallow the road they were on. There was a sign beside the cave. One part of the sign pointed towards the cave and said, "Do not enter." A little below it were more words, where the words were written even bolder, "West detour — exits mountain."

Another path leading steadily down the mountain was beside it, obviously the detour it described.

Jayfor walked up to the sign — the snow wasn't quite as deep here — and read it carefully multiple times. He pondered the problems the situation brought up. "I guess the north road keeps going through the cave and eventually out the other side. But there's a detour that takes us around and will get us to the same place." Somehow the fact that Trenson could read and had already read the whole thing multiple times didn't stop Jayfor from saying it out loud.

Jayfor backed up a few paces and looked down the detour path, which snaked down the mountainside and looked much safer. "Guess we know which one we're going down," Jayfor concluded, and he started picking his steps carefully going down the West detour.

He didn't hear Trenson's footsteps or the jingling of equipment he carried, so he stopped and turned around. Sure enough, Trenson was standing firmly at the split in the road, eyes squinting into the darkness of the cave.

"Trenson," Jayfor said, "we can't go there. It says so right there," he pointed towards the sign.

Trenson met Jayfor's eyes with a sideways look of his own. "I can read, but I also have memory, and if it serves me clearly it says that we are supposed to stay on this road at all costs."

Jayfor sighed and walked back up to the break in the road where Trenson was standing. He assessed the cave. The entrance into it was at least ten feet tall and maybe fifteen feet wide. A few jagged rocks hung down from the roof, pointed at the bottom and giving it the appearance of teeth. The sun was angled on the opposite side of the mountain, and so no light shone into the inky blackness. Jayfor had no desire to go in there and told Trenson as much. "That doesn't look promising at all. Come on, the detour will take us to the same place!"

Trenson didn't budge. "But he said, specifically, we shouldn't deviate from the path! This road is the only one that will get us where we need to go. And how do you know that the detour will take us to the same place?" Trenson challenged.

Jayfor knew he was backed into a corner, but wasn't about to admit it. "You know it's never a good idea to go into a cave!" he ignored Trenson's last question. "There are countless things that could go wrong, like we could get turned around and lose our way, or fall down and break our necks, or be eaten by the bear that's probably sleeping in there waiting for us!"

Trenson shrugged. "I was going to let you go in first, anyway."

Jayfor heaved what sounded like a combination between a sigh and a groan. He was about to declare he was going down the detour no matter what when a memory filtered into his mind. It was a flashback of Loronis after they escaped and were talking to the Senver. Erador's words echoed in his head: *You two must travel north, together. Follow the road that leads north from the capital. Stay on that road, and always head north. Keep going until you reach the Tree of Ramadus. That is when you will reach your journey's end.*

He looked at the path that went west. Easier and much safer, no uncertainties or risks. The cave was a stark contrast from that. But if he took the west road, would it really be alright? Would they eventually join back with the north road and go on like nothing happened? There was no way to be sure. And Erador must have had a good reason to tell them specifically never to leave the road. Maybe he was right.

Still, he felt the presence of doubt pushing him towards the detour. It was the logical choice, he told himself. Logical? Was any of this he had been through logical? He was the last king of Faldon, a kingdom which no longer existed, heading blindly north to a tree that would supposedly help them, a sword that could control his instincts, and were running from an ancient evil order that wanted them all dead. None of that made logical sense in his mind, and yet no one in his place would doubt it was true.

If Va'ar had gotten him this far, why not trust Him at least one more time? Why not?

"I guess you're right," Jayfor said after a long period of silence.

Trenson looked at him skeptically, "About what, you going first?"

"What? No! About this being the right way. Erador said to stay on this path no matter what. I should have listened the first time."

Trenson raised an eyebrow incredulously. He couldn't remember the last time Jayfor apologized. He usually didn't have to; he was usually right about everything, and Trenson always had to make amends. Now the tables were turned, and Trenson smiled. Maybe it should be like this more often, he thought to himself. "No hard feelings. At least now we're finally on the right path."

Jayfor looked up at Trenson, caught sight of the warm eyes and returned with a smile. "Yes, I guess you're right."

"So!" Trenson clapped his hands together in anticipation and looked into the darkness of the eerie cave. "You go first."

There were two things that both of them didn't know that would have both comforted and worried them.

One was that the detour to the west, after snaking down the mountain a little way, ran through a gulley that was high on each side. This road was traveled many times over the course of the year, and because of that, packs of wolves had gathered and laid claim to the gulley. They would ambush travelers from above and surround them for an easy meal, and their numbers had swelled over time so much that even large, guarded caravans had fallen prey to the hunters. This fact would have comforted them that they didn't take that way.

The fact that would worry them was that a long time ago, there was no detour, but the cave was a mining area many, many years ago. It was a highly maintained mine and was the source of ore, lots of ore. The miners set torches to mark the way for travelers to go through the mine safely and quickly and out the other side without having to go around the mountain, and so everyone was content with using the mine as their way of traveling through the mountains.

Until one day, decades ago, all the lights in the mine went dark, and no one inside made it out alive. And no one going in has since.

XXVI

"It smells funny in here," Trenson commented after Jayfor handed him a torch. They were only using one torch between the both of them to save their supply. Who knew how long they would be down here?

"Sulfur," Jayfor replied, catching a whiff of the familiar smell and wrinkling his nose in response. "I don't know why it smells so bad, but it's common in caves and underground waterways. There must be a stream that runs through here." He made the last comment to himself. His canteen was about two-thirds full, still plenty, but experience told him that whenever there's water, you top off. Even if it smelled and tasted like rotten eggs.

"I know about the sulfur part," Trenson said, looking around the spacious cave. "I was just remarking on a fact."

"Hm. Well, on that note, I think it smells bad too," Jayfor agreed. He turned and looked around him in wonder at the cave.

It was obvious that this used to be a well-used area, but that time had long passed. The entire cave was large enough for a caravan to travel through easily, the roof being high and the path smooth. Torches stuck out at intervals along the walls, but these were covered in cobwebs and were past the point of burnable.

"I didn't think this was possible," Trenson said softly to himself. "Whoever heard of a road underground that was well kept? This could be a great idea to replicate more often. Instead of going over a mountain, just go through it!" He felt the walls. They were chalky and left a thin layer of dust on his hands. He wiped it off on his garb. "I wonder why it's not still kept in shape."

Jayfor shrugged. "It took a lot of work. People probably stopped keeping it clean once they didn't need it. But when they did, it was probably easier to just take the detour than walk through it."

Trenson nodded. That was usually how it went. People enjoyed a luxury, but when it needed to be taken care of, they ignored it until it couldn't be used anymore, then just used a different one. He used to see it all the time at Loronis. Buildings renovated were much easier than building a whole new one.

In any case, the cave clearly hadn't been used in years.

There were places where openings in the walls allowed separate rooms to be on either side of the road. Trenson wanted to nose around and see if there was anything worth taking in them, but he felt that Jayfor wouldn't like the idea. They started walking down the main road, led by the pool of light cast by the torch.

The funny thing was, they didn't notice that their sword sheaths were glowing. If either of them looked down, or waited a few minutes before lighting the torch, they would have noticed that around the spot where the hilt met the sheath, a faint glow could be seen. Had they seen it, they would have drawn the sword and found that the entire blade was glowing. It was glowing a faint blueish-white, exactly the same as Erador and Reginold's swords during the escape from Loronis. Maybe they could have remembered this and pulled out their swords.

But they didn't. And so, while their swords were shining and ready to be used, Trenson and Jayfor kept them covered and didn't notice.

The path wound left and right through the heart of the mountains, steadily going downward, but not steeply. The turns were always easy and wide, the road never having more than a few stones in the way. The only problem was the smell, which only got worse the farther they went.

"We *are* still in the dominion of Faldon, right?" Trenson asked as they rounded another corner.

Jayfor nodded. "We are. We're closer to Kallary territory now, but yes, these are still our mountains. Or they were," he corrected bitterly.

"Huh," Trenson replied. "Then these are technically our roads. We're not *that* far from Loronis. I wonder why I've never heard of this place."

Jayfor was wondering the same thing. "By the looks of it, it's been out of business for a long time, maybe longer than me or my father. I..." His attention was suddenly taken by something lying against the wall. He squinted to try and see it better, which made no sense, as he needed more light to see. Trenson saw it too and walked towards it, holding his torch.

"What in the world?" Trenson said. It was a skeleton, lying peacefully against the wall, like it had laid down to take a nap and never woke up. Its jaw hung down, and a few moths fluttered out of the eyeholes as they approached it. A few pieces of threadbare clothing still covered the torso and legs, but most of the owner's clothing were completely rotted. This skeleton had been here a long time.

Trenson kneeled beside it. "It's broken," he said. Jayfor didn't understand until Trenson pointed to the bones of the ribs. Some were cracked at least partially, most of them completely, in two. "He was hit hard by something," Trenson said, "and fell against the wall."

He spied something to the side and pulled it with his free hand. It was a pickaxe, a standard mining tool. The wood was smashed inward in several places, but what made Trenson furrow his brow in confusion was the fact that the metal spike was broken and bent, a piece of the tip lying a few feet away on the ground.

He held it up for Jayfor to see. "This couldn't have been done by digging."

Jayfor looked at the fractured pieces and frowned. He didn't have an explanation either. He was suddenly nervous, all his feeling of awe towards the mine replaced with an uneasy anxiety. "We should probably get going," he said readily.

Trenson felt the need to agree. He looked at the pickaxe for a few more seconds, then tossed it to the ground beside the skeleton. The bones didn't seem to mind. Trenson got to his feet and turned away from the scene, his pace quicker than it was before. The gaunt eyeholes of the bones watched them as the light of the torch faded into darkness.

***

They took turns carrying the torch. It was Jayfor's turn now, and he accepted the torch without complaint. The road continued the same way as it had before their run-in with the skeleton, except they both inadvertently walked faster and noticed little sounds and movements they didn't before. The cave showed no sign of ending.

"I wonder how far this goes on," Jayfor remarked. "My guess wouldn't be long, as we've already been walking for at least thirty minutes."

"Maybe. It feels more like forty to me," Trenson responded with about as much enthusiasm as he felt — which wasn't much. He was tired of the pungent stench and damp air. Additionally, he wasn't fond of closed-in places, even if there was plenty of room in the cave.

Jayfor grunted. Truth be told, he felt like it had been an hour, but he deduced half because he figured that was more accurate. Like Trenson, he didn't like this cave very much either. He was ready to get out, and not *just* because of the skeleton — although that certainly added a big reason.

He wasn't paying close attention to the path. All of a sudden, the ground turned downward sharply, and he almost fell down. He stumbled backwards. After regaining his footing, he saw the ground suddenly went straight down about eight feet before leveling out for a few yards, then shot back up six feet, and the road kept going smoothly after that. There were tunnels to the left and right of the pit — big, rounded tunnels that ran even with the sunken ground. It looked like something big plowed through the tunnel and took a section of the road with it.

In the torchlight, Jayfor saw Trenson's eyes widen as he surveyed the drop in the road and the two tunnels on either side. "First the skeleton, now this! I'm starting to see why this road is abandoned."

Jayfor simply nodded. He couldn't make sense of it either. It was obvious that no human had made the tunnels or the dip in the road, and the fact only added to his apprehension. He said promptly, "If we toss the torch to one another while we're climbing, we shouldn't have any issue."

Trenson agreed and took the torch from Jayfor, a gesture showing that he should go first. Jayfor climbed down the rocky edge with little difficulty, then Trenson passed the torch down and clambered beside him. He and Jayfor both took a moment to look around at the pit they climbed into.

Looking back on the situation later, Trenson swore he saw it before it struck. He swore he heard a noise in the darkness of one of the tunnels and turned and saw the two long antennae staring at him for a split second before it jumped out and attacked. Whether he saw it or not made no difference to what happened next.

It was a giant centipede. It had been there for a long time, waiting patiently in the darkness. Being at least thirty yards long and with legs the size and thickness of a person, it had a hard time finding food large enough to sustain it. He had no eyes, but two long antennae that were even better in the darkness, that could sense the surroundings and detect the scent of an edible creature. Which is what had happened, and why he was waiting for the right second to come out and subdue the two scavengers who wandered into his cave.

Opportunities to eat were few and far between. He was a species that kept getting larger and larger as time went on, and his size was a clear indicator that he had managed to survive a long, long time. Seeing that he ate all his kin, and that the mine was empty after he had ravaged it and eaten everyone, it was hard coming by new prey. Sunlight burned his hard exoskeleton, keeping him in the dark and forcing him to burrow more caves in search of food. Usually, he had to bait traps to his caves with pieces of other prey to attract things big enough for him to eat. He ate the wolves that scoured the mountainside by baiting them in this way, and sometimes even bears that sauntered in to hibernate in the caves.

For not one, but two unsuspecting creatures to come this deep into the cave and to his nest was an opportunity that never happened. He must act fast to get his meal. He locked on to the closest of the two — which happened to be Jayfor — and when they were both halfway between the two edges of the pit, he made his move.

Trenson could barely catch sight of the centipede as it rushed out of the tunnel and came at them. It skittered towards them with such skill and dexterity that before Trenson or, more importantly, Jayfor knew it, it was on them. Once within range, it reached out with its long front legs to grab Jayfor and, suspending him in midair, stabbed its venom-injecting pincers into his back.

Jayfor screamed with pain and terror. Trenson stumbled backwards and hastily dropped the torch and drew his sword and pointed it at the giant insect. He was too panic-stricken to notice that his blade was glowing a faint hue of white and blue. All he thought about was freeing Jayfor. With a cry of defiance, the sword in his hands seemed to take over, and he rushed towards the centipede and brought an overhead slash down on one side of its head.

The blade went down deep and stuck in the hard exoskeleton. The creature made a high-pitched screech and involuntarily dropped Jayfor to the ground, turning its head to grab this threat with its long front legs. Trenson saw it coming and jumped backwards just in time as the legs swung in front of him. Jayfor stumbled to his feet, a little delirious from the brief injection of venom, but still standing and ready to fight. The former king drew his sword. Trenson quickly stood by his side, and for the first time noticed that both of their swords were faintly glowing. He was too high from adrenaline to say anything, though.

The centipede let out another screech of indignation. Now it was facing two armed and dangerous creatures, one of whom had already given it a head wound to remember. In most cases, he would have backed off from such enemies. But his hunger drove him forward, and he rushed at Trenson with the intent of running him over.

His size made him several hundred pounds in weight, and the pointed ends at each end of his many legs made being run over the equivalent of being jabbed with dozens of spears with hundreds of pounds of force behind each blow. Trenson didn't see the move coming, and tried to jump backwards and out of the way, thinking that it was trying to grab him, but instead it came head-first towards him. He was knocked flat on his back.

He closed his eyes and expected to be trampled on, but he was saved by sheer luck. He was lying on his back directly under the middle of the centipede, and since the insect didn't turn, the legs passed harmlessly on either side of him. For weeks afterward, Trenson would hear the skittering noise of the feet churning and the whoosh of air as the creature passed above him. But he escaped unscathed, and in a few seconds, the thing passed above him.

The centipede turned after going over Trenson and skittered up the edges of the pit to make a wide turn. It made another rush at Trenson, but Jayfor, who was standing ready to the side, slashed at its legs. The sweep completely split three of them in half. The centipede stopped its attack on Trenson immediately and let out a long screech. Then it suddenly turned its body and, Jayfor being closer to the back of it, swung the two long spikes at its tail at him. Jayfor couldn't see them coming in time, and they slammed against him hard. He was knocked hard against the wall of the pit, gasping for air. His sword flew out of his grasp and clattered to the side, still glowing prominently.

Trenson ran forward and struck at the creature in the head, landing another piercing blow right between the two antennae where the eyes would have been. The blow went deep, but still wasn't enough to kill it, the hard exoskeleton protecting it. The centipede used Trenson's close blow to grab him and hold him hostage in the air. Trenson yelled in fear as he was hoisted high. He squirmed and tried to get his sword arm free, but the two legs held him so tight he had to gasp for air.

He saw the two venom-injecting pincers hovering in the air, preparing to strike. In a last attempt, he kicked at the face of the centipede, but his reach wasn't long enough. He watched helplessly as the pincers swung up in the air in anticipation of a downward strike...

Only it never came. After Jayfor had been knocked to the side, he found his sword and saw that Trenson was being held captive. Using the fact that he was unnoticed, he clambered up the edges of the pit and stood an extra eight feet high. While he still wasn't as tall as the centipede at full height, it was high enough. He spotted a pile of debris, and using it as a boost to reach several more feet, he got a running start and jumped off and landed on the back of the creature near the head.

His feet were almost swept away beneath him as the creature jerked at the sudden weight. Without wasting a second, he held his sword high in the air and thrust down, burying the light-imbued blade almost to the hilt into the head of the creature. The exoskeleton of the head was weakened from Trenson's previous blows, and the blade pierced deep.

The convulsion that followed was enough to throw Jayfor off the creature and onto the ground. The centipede dropped Trenson to the ground and screamed, its arms trying to pull out the sword stuck in its head. Its body swung left and right wildly in a frenzy. In a few seconds, the screams got weaker, and the crazed convulsing stopped. In one last act, the creature raised its head high up in the air, higher, higher, higher — then dropped with a smash to the ground, dead. Its antennae fell limp on the floor.

Trenson stood dumbly, his breathing still heavy, as he starred at the dead centipede. He didn't notice that the light from his sword had faded after the creature was killed, and now the light was gone. Instead, he noticed that Jayfor didn't rise after being thrown to the floor. He was lying still on the ground, curled in a ball. Trenson ran towards him.

"Jayfor!" He quickly rolled his friend onto his back and saw, in the little torchlight that came from the torch lying on the floor, that Jayfor's eyes were glazed over. Jayfor groaned and looked at Trenson like he was a million miles away. "It... It got me," he said, almost unperceivably. Trenson didn't understand at first, but then saw two red blotches on the back of Jayfor's garb and realized with a sick feeling that Jayfor had been poisoned.

"It's alright, it's alright, you'll be fine," Trenson said with not much certainty. He was telling himself this as much as he was telling Jayfor.

Jayfor chuckled at nothing in particular — the poison was starting to set in — and looked over at the centipede. "My sword... my sword..." He kept saying those two words over and over again, reaching his arm out as if to try to grab it.

Trenson jumped to his feet and ran to the head of the dead centipede. In one swift motion, he yanked the sword out of the head. The blade was covered in insect brains and far from clean, but that was the last thing on Trenson's mind. He ran over to Jayfor and leaned down to hand it to him.

But Jayfor was out of it. His eyes were still open, but he was limp and incoherent, still looking towards the centipede, his arm reaching out and grabbing nothing. His breathing came in shallow, ragged spasms. Now that he could see better, Trenson saw the two wounds from the poison-injecting pincers were still bleeding, leaving a pool of red on the ground, staining the rest of Jayfor's garb.

Trenson felt sick to his stomach. He had never understood the expression, *out of the frying pan and into the fire,* but now, standing helplessly beside his unconscious friend, he had a pretty good idea.

XXVII

IT ONLY GOT WORSE as time went on. Jayfor was only conscious half of the time, and when he was, he rambled on and on about random things, then dropped off into sleep again. Trenson was left to carry his friend, which wasn't convenient at all, and slowed their pace considerably.

After their run-in with the centipede, Trenson climbed out of the pit with Jayfor on his back. Thankfully, the exit wasn't but a hundred yards and around a few turns from where they fought, and Trenson welcomed the fresh, cold, stinging mountain air.

After that, Trenson had to carry his still-unconscious comrade through the knee-high snow, while already carrying lots of weight from his supplies. He had to stop a few times later that day and set Jayfor down to take a break. No offense to his friend, but he wasn't the easiest to carry.

Most of the times when they stopped, Jayfor was still passed out, his eyes flickering under the closed eyelids, like they were about to open, but they didn't. Except one time that day. Trenson was sitting beside him when his eyes suddenly shot open and he looked around, confused. "What happened?" he asked, his voice slurred.

Trenson wasn't sure how much he should say. "You're hurt," he replied simply.

"Hurt," Jayfor repeated under his breath. Then he turned his head slightly and looked at Trenson with a sideways look. "Who are you?"

Even though he knew he knew that Jayfor was delirious, the words still hit Trenson hard, a phantom punch in the gut. He was amazed at how fast the poison was working. This wasn't a good sign at all. "I'm a friend," he replied, slowly. "I'm going to get you to safety, and get you help."

Jayfor nodded once, then leaned his head back and fell into another slumber. Once he was certain Jayfor was asleep, Trenson pondered the situation. Within a few hours, he mused, Jayfor had forgotten where he was and who his friends were. He wasn't an expert on poisons, but for it to take effect so quickly could mean only one thing: that the final effect – death – would come quick too.

He needed to get Jayfor treated, and fast. He may be no medicine expert, but maybe there was an apothecary nearby. He checked his map. After finding his position, he spotted a village on the map, probably about a day's travel away.

That would be the fastest and most likely chance of finding an apothecary. He shouldered his pack once more and heaved Jayfor over his shoulder, and set off.

The next morning, Trenson was glad that the snow lessened and the air grew warmer. The farther down the mountains he went, the more of these two things he saw. The cold didn't decrease as much as he would have liked, though. There was still a nip in the air, and with winter approaching, this was warm compared to what laid in store for the future.

There was plenty of time to think about what happened in the cave. So that was why the path wasn't used anymore, because someone — or something, rather — had laid claim to it. That explained the bones. But now that the creature was dead, maybe they could reclaim it. That would be a good idea, Trenson thought to himself. When he got back to Loronis, he would direct an order to have the path rebuilt. They needed to improve trade routes, anyway.

When I get back to Loronis? What are you thinking, there is no Loronis. There is no Faldon. It hit him hard, the realization that it was no more. He sometimes reverted to the habit of thinking back on it like it still existed. It didn't, he reminded himself.

He had something else to think about, though, that would take his mind off it: the swords. Trenson recounted that they glowed while in the cave. As soon as he left the cave, he checked it again, but the glowing stopped. When he first thought about it, he was surprised, but the more he pondered, the more it made sense. Erador — or was it Reginold? He couldn't remember — said that these blades were as powerful as Senver swords, if not more. And when they were escaping Loronis, the two warriors lit the way with their swords. So it made sense that their swords glowed.

It made Trenson excited thinking about it. What else could these swords do? Maybe they could even fly and carry them to this "Tree of Ramadus." Wouldn't that be nice? Unfortunately, he couldn't find a way to make his sword do it. He made a mental note to ask about this next time he ran into a Senver.

***

The next day, when he was about halfway down the mountain, he spotted a few columns of smoke rising together through the treetops. He breathed a sigh of relief. This must be the town he saw on his map. Columns of smoke meant a town, and a town meant an apothecary, and an apothecary meant someone who could heal Jayfor. Hopefully. At any rate, the sight of it bolstered Trenson's morale, and he walked a little faster now.

Jayfor didn't wake up after his confusion about where they were and who Trenson was. He slept all day and night, but judging by the way Jayfor groaned and shifted, it had to be a fitful sleep at that. The closer they got to town, the more convulsing and groans came from Jayfor. And the more Jayfor convulsed and groaned, the faster Trenson walked and the more agitated he became.

After another hour of walking and carrying Jayfor, the town was finally visible through the trees. Trenson was overjoyed and started towards it, but then something else caught his attention. A little out of the way, nestled in the woods right before it cleared into the town area, was a house. A path led to it from the road, and by the path stood a simple wooden sign. It was a picture of an herb with leaves — the universal symbol of apothecaries.

Even more elated at the sight, Trenson hurried down the path and came to a small cabin. It was plain and simple, with a wooden hatch window that was open beside a swinging door. The house was clearly built a long time ago, the wood a dark brown color, the result of weathering from the elements. Beside the house was a small garden, with a few plants in it, but they were all brown and shriveled from the cold. He walked up a few feet from the rickety front door.

The limp form of Jayfor in his arms, he didn't have a free arm to knock on the door, and he didn't want to set Jayfor down until he was sure this was the right place, so he lifted his head and called at the door, "Hello! Please, I have someone who needs help!"

Silence. There was no reply, except for the fact that nearby birds quit chirping, and the usual forest sounds seemed to hush. Maybe the owner couldn't hear him. "Excuse me! Please, my friend needs help!"

No response. He had taken in another breath to speak again when he felt something sharp poke into his back. "Don't move," a menacing voice warned behind him.

XXVIII

Despite the warning, Trenson did move. He whirled around as fast as he could and stepped a few paces back, holding Jayfor tight in his arm. He realized he wasn't in a great position to attack or defend, but he could run, and so he set his feet ready to sprint at any moment.

Although it didn't look like he would have to run fast to escape his adversary. An old man, hunched over and bearing a head of white hair, stood before him, pointing the end of a three-pronged pitchfork at him. His lips were curled inward, like he had eaten a lemon, and this was probably because he was missing most of his teeth, but he was scowling none the less. His hair looked like a square pile of snow balancing perfectly on his head.

"What are you doing here?" The old man demanded, moving the pitchfork forward and backward menacingly. "Come to steal more of me coin, eh? Don't act so dumb! As if you haven't robbed me dry already. Well, you can try to take it, but I ain't letting you have it!"

The old man looked like he was about to run Trenson through that very second. Trenson shook his head, confused, and said quickly, "No sir, you don't understand! I don't want to take your money!"

The old man raised one bushy eyebrow. "Then what are you doing here?"

Trenson held forward the unconscious Jayfor. "He's been poisoned. I saw the apothecary sign, and—"

"Good grief!" After catching a glance at the limp figure in Trenson's arms, the old man's wolfish look was replaced with one of caring and urgency. "He looks terrible! Bring him inside, quickly!" He straightened himself — though it wasn't by much — and flipped the pitchfork into the other hand like he wasn't just threatening Trenson with it. He hurried past Trenson and quickly opened the door of the cabin, not looking behind him or motioning for him to follow. Trenson slowly walked into the cabin, not exactly trusting the old man after almost being stabbed to death by him, but knowing he didn't have any other options.

The cabin was one large room, and a large messy one at that. There were a few tables spread out, and these were all covered from one end to the other in random things – papers, boxes, bowls, cups, plants, and other small things, all strewn about not just on the tables, but across the floor as well.

"What a mess," the old man muttered under his breath. He walked over to one of the tables and, in one swift motion, swept his arm across it from front to back. Everything on the table, mostly papers and jars, waterfalled off the edge and clattered to the ground. The floor was now an even bigger mess, but at least one table was clean.

The old man motioned for him to set Jayfor down, and Trenson gently placed him on the table, which was just big enough to fit him. Jayfor groaned and shuttered, and his eyelids flickered like they were about to open, but Trenson knew they wouldn't.

The old man started rummaging about through a cabinet by the wall, evidently in search of something. "I apologize for my unseemly behavior. I thought you were one of those peacekeeper rats, coming to steal more of my things." He chuckled, but it was the driest chuckle Trenson had ever heard. "Can't they let an old man live in peace?'

Trenson's interest was piqued. "The peacekeepers steal things now?"

"Aye, and have been for months." Not finding what he was looking for in the drawer, the old man moved to the one below it.

Trenson asked, "But why? They've always protected the people in times of trouble, and although they're a little arrogant, some-times, why are they raiding the people who they're trying to pro-tect?"

"Ha!" the old man snorted. "That's the reason. After Loronis burned to a crisp, the peacekeepers saw themselves as the new authority and started terrorizing everyone. They feel they're owed money because they're *not* robbin' everyone dry — although, fun-ny thing is, they are." The old man let out a breath of relief as he held up a small box with a wooden hinge lid. He brought it over and set it on a smaller table beside the one Jayfor was lying on, which was there to hold everything he needed.

The old man stopped like he just remembered something and turned to Trenson. "The name's Benedict."

Trenson nodded and held out his hand. "Trenson."

Benedict gave the outstretched hand a sideways look, then ignored it and started organizing the things on his small work table. Slightly stung, Trenson slowly retracted his hand.

"His name is Conrad," Trenson added, referring to Jayfor. He figured he might as well insert Jayfor's alias before things got too far, just in case Jayfor woke up or he slipped and called him Jayfor by accident.

Benedict showed no signs of listening as he continued to set things in order on the small table. He set a few bowls to one side, a masher to grind the herbs to another, and a few herbs from the box to another. After being satisfied, he wiped his hands together in a way that said, *let's get to work.* "What happened to him? Kicked by a mule? That's the usual."

"No, nothing so easy like that." Trenson pointed to the sides of Jayfor's garb. Although Jayfor was stabbed twice in the back, he bled enough that, lying on his back, the red stains could be seen from either side. "He was stung and poisoned by a giant centipede."

"He was *what?*" Benedict said with both bushy eyebrows raised.

"Poisoned. By a giant centipede." Trenson was being very matter-of-fact, but he didn't know how else to say it. He simply stated the facts as he remembered them. "We were traveling through a cave a few days ago, and this enormous centipede, bigger than this cabin, rushes out and attacks us. Me and Jay—Conrad, I mean, we killed it, but not before it got him." Memory rushed into Trenson's mind before he could stop it, memories of Jayfor being grabbed and held helpless in midair and screaming while the centipede pierced him with its poison injectors. He cringed, then shook the memory off like water.

Benedict didn't look like he understood in the slightest, but he nodded slowly. "I see." He looked back at the limp figure of Jayfor and scratched his chin. "Well, I don't know what I can do about that, Trenson. My business usually concerns farm accidents and sprained ankles, not anything like this." He shot an apologetic glance at Trenson. "I doubt there's anything I could do."

Trenson wasn't mollified. He had carried Jayfor all this way; he wasn't about to let him die just because of some uncertain old man. "But can't you do *something?* Surely there's some remedy, or at least some way to let him live. He looks like he will die any second!"

At that moment, Jayfor groaned louder and rolled over to lay on his side, facing the two men. His face was pale, and a thin line of sweated beaded on his forehead.

Benedict shrugged helplessly. "And he probably will. Listen, I don't know much about poisons! I wouldn't even know where to start. Besides, every poison is different. There's no 'one size fits all' approach. I didn't even know giant centipedes existed, or even if they do! I wouldn't have any notes that would be ... well... actually..."

Trenson glanced at the old man and saw him deep in thought. "What? What is it?" Trenson asked.

Benedict held up one finger, then walked to another part of the wall where a shelf stood. Lots of scrolls were rolled up and stacked on top of each other, most of them looking like towers about to fall at any moment, only held up by the edges of the shelf, which in itself was old and looked like it could fall at any moment. Benedict mumbled to himself as he pulled some scrolls out, unrolled them, then shoved them back on the shelf. The lines on his forehead grew even deeper as he searched for the one scroll that eluded him.

Trenson couldn't help himself. "What are you looking for?"

Benedict shoved another scroll back into the shelf after being dissatisfied with that one, too. "I had a bunch of old scrolls that had cures for all sorts of crazy ailments. 'Being poisoned by a giant centipede' certainly counts as — aha!" Benedict held up one scroll that looked even older than the others, and Trenson was silently surprised that it didn't crumble to pieces in his hands.

Beaming with triumph, Benedict brought the scroll to the table and smoothed it out, leaning over it so much it almost touched his nose. Trenson tried to look around him to read the writing, but it was extremely small, and Benedict's nose was taking up most of the room, so he gave up and waited patiently for him to say something.

It took a long time for Benedict to suddenly raise his head and grin. "Well, slap my bottom like I was born! There's really something in here for giant centipedes!"

"Really?" Trenson asked in a voice brimming with hope.

"Darnest thing I ever did see. Maybe you're not as crazy as I took you to be. Let's see, it says... it says here that once bitten, the victim will forget where he is and who people are around him within a few hours."

Trenson nodded. "That happened all right."

"It also says that the victim will sleep for long periods of time without waking, sometimes days."

"Check."

"And it says that after a few days, the victim will die." The simple, matter-of-fact way Benedict said it made Trenson's blood run cold.

"Well, we can't let that happen! What do I need to do?"

Once again, Benedict held up a finger for Trenson to be silent as he read more, sticking his nose back into the page. "Alright, that's good... I have that, and that, and I think I still have some of that in the garden... Confound it all!" Benedict hit the table with his hand. "Of course, today! The one day I need it!"

"Need what?" Trenson asked.

"There's a special mushroom I need. I didn't think it had any worth besides curing headaches, but it's one of the main ingredients in this cure they have written here. I used to have some in one of my boxes here, but those dratted peacekeepers stole it earlier today after they barged into my house and took half of everything!"

Trenson looked around the room. A wry thought occurred to him about pointing out that they didn't take half of everything – after all, there wasn't half a table or half a cabin left. But his trustworthy intuition told him now was not the time. And after the realization that without this ingredient, Jayfor couldn't be cured, his humor vanished. "You don't have more?"

Benedict shook his head, still in a fury at the peacekeepers. "Not a single one. Drat those measly, stuck-up pigs!"

Before Benedict could go on with his rant, Trenson interjected. "But say this box was returned with the mushrooms inside."

"Ah yes, then it would be a simple matter." The old man looked at Trenson questioningly. Trenson returned the look with a cunning grin, and realization soon dawned on Benedict's face. "An easy matter too, getting it back. Them peacekeepers are yellow cowards and about as lethal as a kitten. If you're any good with that," he nodded towards the sword at Trenson's hip, "then you should be fine."

Trenson shrugged. "I've had my share of uncomfortable situations. Now, where might a yellow coward take a box of herbs?"

Benedict chuckled at the play on words. "I've seen them flock together like birds in the main square, acting all high and mighty and strutting about like roosters. Maybe you can hear something about my box there."

Trenson nodded. "I'll be right back." He started walking towards the door. "Keep him alive, will you?" he called, referring to Jayfor.

Benedict huffed and looked over at the pale, groaning, convulsing man on the table. "Easier said than done."

XXIX

T HE SHINY, POLISHED ARMOR of the peacekeepers stood out sharply against the rest of the people in the main square. They matched Benedict's description perfectly: strutting about like high and mighty roosters. Their armor was spotless, their faces clean-shaven and their noses held high in the air with dignity, their flashy swords glinting in the sun.

In short, they looked about as lethal as a kitten, just as Benedict had said.

Trenson stopped at a distance to assess the group. There were three of them, all wearing identical armor and talking loudly among themselves. If he wanted to hear any information, he would have to get closer.

Taking care to look casual, Trenson walked towards the group and blended in with a group of people shopping at one of the stands, about a stone's throw from the knights. He pretended to be scrutinizing some fruit while his ear was turned to the group.

"And then the old man comes at us with a pitchfork! If I didn't move out of the way, he would have run me through!"

"And saved us the trouble of cleaning up the mess you started!" Another peacekeeper chuckled loudly. He was different from the other two. On the edges of his vambraces — forearm armor — was a golden line. Trenson guessed this was the mark of a leader. "There was nothing worth taking in that old geezer's shack, anyway. Why you even made off with some of his stuff is beyond me."

The other peacekeeper held his hands up in a shrug. "We have to enforce the law equally, don't we? Wouldn't be fair if we picked favorites."

The leader rolled his eyes. "Some sense of justice you have."

The third peacekeeper walked between the two and put his arms out as if to stop a fight. "Alright, you two," he said with a grin, "let's not get messy. I'd hate to hear Hadrian cry."

The leader huffed with a smile. "Oh, I'd be crying with pity after how bad I'd beat you."

"You took the words from my mouth," the first peacekeeper said easily.

"Now, now, settle down," the third peacekeeper broke in again.

All three men laughed loud enough for the whole world to hear. Trenson eyed them from the side. The two other peacekeepers looked like they had never held a sword in their life. Taking them on would be easy enough. The leader was bulkier and had a look of some experience, but only a little.

He knew from experience never to judge a fighter by their looks, though. He had been beaten before by people who looked weaker than these.

"Let's head back," Hadrian said, "We can talk more over a pint. Or in Dune's case, a gallon."

Dune, who was the first peacekeeper, grinned even wider. "I'm not the one who knows how to drink! Ask Collins here if he's giving lessons." He nudged the other peacekeeper with his elbow.

Collins returned the nudge with a shove. "As if we don't already know you've drained every brewery in the area!"

With another chorus of laughter, the three started walking away. Trenson knew he needed to act fast and follow them until he knew more about this box. Keeping close enough that he could still hear their conversation, Trenson left his position behind the booth and followed them. He considered pulling his hood over his head, but he reasoned that would make him even more suspicious, and so he kept it down.

Either way, he was in a tight spot. There weren't very many people on the streets beside a few people groups here and there, so he stood out like a sore thumb. It was also obvious that he wasn't a local, being covered with supplies and throwing knives. He would have to play this carefully.

"Tell me, Dune, was it really worth it applying the law to that crazy old man?" Collins asked casually.

Dune shrugged. "Eh, not really. There wasn't much in that shack of his. I found a few boxes that I thought might have some loot, but when I brought 'em back to the place, it was just a bunch of weeds and plants! Useless. He could at least have some coin to spare for simple folk like us!"

After a few chuckles all around, the leader, Hadrian, said, "That apothecary's been around since the dawn of time, but I doubt he's had any come to him since them! Everyone thinks he's some sort of magician or something, catching little children to cook in a giant cauldron."

Dune sniffed. "He probably spears them with that pitchfork of his."

"Aye," Collins added, "like he almost did with you!"

"He did not! He got close, but there's no way he could have caught a spry person like me."

Collins and Hadrian exchanged a knowing glance but said nothing.

Trenson was caught in listening to the conversation, and wasn't watching where he was going very closely. As a result, he didn't see the man carrying a large box walking towards him, and apparently, the man carrying the box didn't either. With a crash, the two men collided. The wooden box fell to the ground. Apples spilled out of it like water and rolled across the ground, scattering in every direction.

"You cur!" the man denounced Trenson with a face turning almost as red as the apples. "Watch where you're going!"

Trenson shrugged sheepishly, but was more concerned when he saw the three peacekeepers stop and turn around, all three pairs of eyes looking at him questioningly. Trenson tried not to focus on the peacekeepers and started bending over to pick up the fruit. The man was still cursing Trenson's name as he picked up the fruit from the ground and set it back in the box, not bothering to help.

After a few seconds, the peacekeepers shrugged and started walking again. At the sight of his targets leaving, Trenson stopped picking up apples and rose from the ground and started jogging towards them. The man called after him. "Hey! You start a mess and you don't—" he stopped when Trenson threw a golden crescent over his shoulder, which the man caught. "Good day!" the man's tone completely changed.

That being solved, Trenson walked at a brisk pace to get within earshot of the peacekeepers once again. He eventually came close enough that the conversation drifted back into his hearing.

"—Want to know where we've been. You know he doesn't like us 'applying the law' unless we can get some real reward out of it. A few boxes of weeds is hardly worth it."

Dune huffed. "There was no way of knowing what was in there. For all we knew, there could have been hordes of gold and silver piled inside."

"But there wasn't," Hadrian added.

Dune shot him a rueful look. "And now we know!"

They turned a corner. Trenson lost sight of them behind a house and quickly covered the distance to the corner. He turned it, then jolted to a stop and jumped back behind the corner. The peacekeepers were stopped just a few yards from the corner and were entering a door on the same building the corner was on. Trenson hoped he wasn't spotted, and wouldn't risk a glance to find out. He heard the creaking of a door opening, and, after a few seconds passed, the sound of a door closing. The voices of the three men ceased.

Now he chanced a look around the corner. There was no sign of the three men. Trenson breathed a sigh of relief. Then, a thought hitting him, he backed away from the building to get a better look of the whole.

Judging by its design, the peacekeeper base was formerly a tavern. A stocky two-story building, with lots of windows and even a post sticking awkwardly out over the door where a sign would go all gave evidence to this. Also, judging by the shambled appearance, it stopped being a tavern some time ago. The peacekeepers probably evicted the owners, Trenson guessed.

Getting in would be tricky. If these men were like any thieves — and they certainly seemed to meet the criteria — then they stockpiled all their loot at their home base. So if the box with the herbs was anywhere, it would be here. There was no way to know how many peacekeepers were inside — which is never a good thing when raiding a place — and he didn't see a way in beside the front door.

Although... Trenson peered around one side of the base. Unlike the buildings that bordered it, the tavern was two stories. This meant that the windows of the second story were level with the roof of the one-story houses beside it. Trenson mused that if he were to climb the house beside the tavern, he could easily walk across the roof and jump in the window and into the tavern.

It was worth a shot, at least.

But that only brought up another problem: how to get on top of the one-story house beside it. He looked for a way to climb up, then realized that if he ran fast enough, he could get enough momentum to just run up the wall and grab the roof. He didn't see any other way.

He took a few extra steps back for good measure. Then, after finding his rhythm, he dashed forward, covered the distance to the wall, placed a foot on the windowsill, and used it to burst upward with just enough height to grab the edge of the roof.

His hands immediately wanted to let go, but he held on tight. Using what little momentum that was left of his jump, he hauled himself up onto the roof, not without a large grunt. And he was on.

XXX

OW THAT THAT PROBLEM was solved, he balanced his way the little distance to the window of the tavern. To his relief, it was a simple window with two cloths to keep it closed. These could be moved easily, which he did, pushing them to the side and peering into the room.

From what he could see, the inside was even more in shambles than the outside. The window opened into a small room, the only light coming through the window, that evidently used to be a bedroom, although that purpose had long since been changed. There was no furniture in the room. The only thing worth telling of was a pile of objects in the corner that caught his eye.

Just as Trenson had guessed, the peacekeepers threw their loot together in a pile, disregarding worth or value. This pile of objects turned out to be just that. A random assortment of trinkets created a large heap, and on top of it, apparently just thrown on recently, were a few boxes that looked exactly like the ones in Benedict's house.

Trenson felt another surge of relief. He had found it. Now all he had to do was grab it and make out. Grabbing the edge, he threw one leg over the window, then the other, as he dropped onto the floor of the tavern.

The boards immediately creaked and groaned beneath him, so much so that he cringed. He looked down and saw that he was standing on the weakest part of the room. The floor was visibly stronger in some places than in others, the "others" being where he was standing now. The boards bent down slightly beneath his weight, and the space between each board was so large that Trenson could see a little of the first floor, but not enough to make out anything.

After pausing a few seconds to make sure that he wasn't heard, he carefully walked to the pile on the other side of the room. Each step brought another creak, but the door was closed, and evidently it wasn't loud enough for the peacekeepers downstairs to hear. After reaching the mound, Trenson grabbed the three boxes that looked like Benedict's and checked their contents; it was herbs and mushrooms every time. He shoved all three into his satchel.

Satisfied and his mission complete, Trenson eased his way back to the window. He had made it to the sill and was about to make his exit when he heard voices. "Be quiet, the lot of you! Now then, I call this meeting to order."

It came from downstairs, through the spaces between the boards. Trenson knew he needed to get back to Jayfor, but his curiosity got the best of him. He swung back into the room, walked to the weak spot on the floor, kneeled, and put his face close to one of these cracks. He could see a long table surrounded in a circle by peacekeepers, at least a dozen in all. All of them had at least one tankard in their hands. They formed a semicircle around one side of the table, while at the head, standing alone, was a man who Trenson guessed was the leader. Trenson suddenly realized with a surprise that this was the same leader he had seen with the three men he was following — Hadrian, he remembered.

Everybody was silent and stared expectantly at the leader, who meanwhile seemed to be relishing the attention, and let the seconds drag on before he spoke. "Normally we start the meeting formally, with each man telling of his concerns or problems before addressing the larger issues. But, unlike our usual monthly meetings, I have called this one together for one reason and one reason only. Because of that, I will skip the usual formalities and get straight to the point."

There were a few glances exchanged among the peacekeepers. Apparently, this didn't normally happen. Everyone's attention was riveted even more at Hadrian, who let the seconds hang in the air once more as he enjoyed the attention.

Trenson knew he should get back. These herbs needed to be delivered to Benedict, and soon, before it was too late. But he hadn't been gone from the cabin for long, or at least it didn't feel like long. He could spare a few more minutes. Who knows, these peacekeepers might say something that would help them on their journey. He kept his eye pressed to the crack and listened.

"It happened just a few days ago. A stranger in a hood suddenly came to me and asked me to come with him. Cautiously, I followed him into a dark alley, suspicious. After making sure that no one else was listening, he asked me if I was the peacekeeper leader of the town. I told him yes. He asked me if it was true that the captain of the peacekeepers had more authority than the prefect of the town. Once again, I told him yes, although I had a strange feeling he already knew the answer to the question.

"'Then,' he said, 'I have a proposition for you.' He told me that he was a member of a secret organization, one that strove toward world peace and unity. I asked how that was any different from every other organization or kingdom. He said the goal was the same, but their means were different. 'What means?' I asked. 'Effective ones' was the only answer he gave.

"Before I could ask what he meant, he moved on. He said Faldon was always destined to be brought to ruin, and that ever since Jayfor took the throne, they knew that our kingdom wouldn't stand a chance. He said that they were going to rebuild Faldon, but in a different way. Already, many towns and cities have sworn allegiance to their cause, and he said he hoped ours would be the next to join them."

A low murmur rippled across the room. This was the last thing any of them were expecting. "What does he mean, rebuild Faldon?" Trenson recognized the speaker as Collins.

Hadrian held up his hand. "I asked him the same thing. He said it was quite simple: Faldon was reaching the peak of it's intellect and progress when it was destroyed, and the reason it was destroyed was because the kings, notably Jayfor, were too arrogant to understand this, and brought ruin on it with their own hand. This group's leader claimed this group of his will lead us to a new age of reason, and wants us to be a part of it."

Another murmur filtered across the group, but Hadrian continued before another question could be asked.

"He asked me what my decision was, and I told him I needed time to think and ask my comrades. He gave me five days to decide and told me to find him in the same alleyway that we met at. He also warned that if I didn't meet him before nightfall on the fifth day, they would consider our choice made. And before I could ask another question, he walked out of the alley."

Hadrian now finished with his speech, there was a brief silence to see if Hadrian was finished. But once they found out he was, a dozen voices all spoke at once, all of them asking questions and demanding answers. Tankards were raised in the air in protest. This was the most unusual meeting any of them had ever heard. Hadrian calmly crossed his arms and waited for the uproar to cease.

One voice rose above the others. "Did this fellow look trustworthy?" The other voices hushed, as they were all thinking the same thing.

Hadrian shrugged. "Not really. His face was shaded by that cloak he wore. He wasn't a very tall fellow, either, but that's all I could see about him."

Another voice rose. "That sounds suspicious! Why should we trust him?" A growl of consent came from a few other throats.

Yet another man spoke up. "I don't know. If this man was telling the truth, and if they really have the influence he said they had, then we might be better off their friends than enemies."

"And throw our lot in with a suspicious stranger? I think not!" The other man said.

It looked like a fight might break out, but Hadrian's piercing voice brought the scene into order. "Order, order!" He slammed a fist onto the table to add emphasis. It must have worked, as everyone was suddenly silent.

"Now listen: the deadline for our decision is two days away. We don't have very much time, but I say we make the most of it and see if we can't find any more information about this man or this 'secret organization.' It's better to be safe than sorry, so I think that looking more into this would be a good idea. I don't like surprises," he added.

Trenson suddenly realized that he had stayed way too long. He cursed himself for staying. Jayfor was dying, and he was here eavesdropping! In a hurry, he jumped to his feet.

Which was a bad idea. The boards under his feet were less stable than he thought. There was a sickening crack, and with a cry of surprise, Trenson fell straight down through the floor.

He couldn't see much in his descent, other than dust and pieces of wood falling with him. He felt the table hit his feet with a jolt, and heard the pieces of wood hitting the floor and felt dust and wood splinters rain on his head.

He slowly opened his eyes, and saw the stunned faces of a dozen peacekeepers staring at him. Trenson looked over at Hadrian and replied to his shocked expression with a shrug. "Surprise," Trenson said sheepishly.

XXXI

T RENSON JUMPED.

He knew he didn't have a second to lose. He was vastly outnumbered, in enemy territory, and the center of attention; all dozen pairs of eyes were locked on him. In a few seconds, the peacekeepers would gather their senses and grab him. So he scanned the place for the door, spotted it, got a running start, and jumped.

The idea was to sail over the peacekeepers' heads before landing gracefully on the ground. His jump wasn't quite high enough, though. After clearing two peacekeepers, his foot landed on the shoulder of the last peacekeeper to clear. Without wasting a second, he jumped again, this time using the soldier's shoulders as a springboard.

Hands reached into the air to grab his churning legs as he flew overhead once more, but out of pure luck, none of them caught him. The peacekeeper he launched off of fell to the ground. Trenson descended quickly, hit the floor hard, performed a roll-over to keep his momentum going, then, eyes locked on the door, sprinted across the floor.

By this time, the peacekeepers were starting to gather their senses. Trenson didn't look behind him, but he heard a choir of hissing metal as they drew their swords, and heard Hadrian's voice shout, "Get him!" He heard footsteps as they all ran after him to do so.

Trenson directed his attention to the door. Within a few seconds, he reached it. He hoped that it was a simple swinging door. He put his head down and set his shoulder forward. Lucky for him, it was a simple swinging door, one that swung open and slammed into the other wall as Trenson barged through.

Sunlight immediately exploded into his face. The cool air was refreshing, but he didn't notice. Now to decide where to run. He glanced over his shoulder and saw all dozen peacekeepers in hot pursuit, pouring out of the open door and charging after him with swords in hand. Trenson decided to run to the left, and ignoring his protesting legs, he sprinted as fast as he could.

To get a feel at how fast his pursuers were, Trenson kept a straight course down the middle of the street. Onlookers stopped and stared with wide eyes as the suspicious man ran away from a dozen peacekeepers. Fortunately, there weren't many people on the road, so no crowd to stop Trenson or hinder his escape.

He checked behind his shoulder and frowned. They were gaining on him, ever so slightly. Although generally faster than most people, Trenson still had all his traveling gear, weapons, and satchel, weighing him down considerably. The peacekeepers wore armor, but a light armor at that. If this were to go on much longer, Trenson knew, then he would be caught before long.

He changed tactics. Spotting an alley between two houses, he averted his course and made for it. He heard the sound of armor clanging becoming louder, which meant they, too, had changed direction. The alley opened into another street. He turned left, then found another alley to the left, and dashed down it too. He was gaining ground, but just barely. Now, however, he was out of the peacekeepers line of sight.

Trenson spotted an open door to the side of the alleyway. An idea struck him. While the peacekeeper's eyes were off him, he ran through the doorway and into the house. He found himself in a simple room, a kitchen. He hid around the doorway and waited a few seconds until he saw the figures of the peacekeepers passing by.

He counted them as they ran past the doorway. One by one, he saw the backs of the peacekeepers as they plowed through the alleyway. None of them batted an eye toward the open doorway. After a time, he counted all dozen of them pass. He waited a few seconds for the sound of their footsteps to die away. Then he heard a scream.

His head whipped around and caught sight of a woman staring at him, openmouthed, inside the house. Her face turned ashen at his unruly appearance and dangerous attire. Trenson offered a smile. "Thanks for the hospitality!" he said as he ran back out the doorway.

He turned left after leaving the staring lady's house, and into the street. He had lost the peacekeepers, but not for long. He caught sight of the road leading to Benedict's cabin and ran towards it. He needed to get to the apothecary. He had wasted enough time already, and had to get these herbs to Jayfor soon — if it wasn't already too late.

***

Benedict was pacing back and forth, glancing at Jayfor's still form with anxiety when Trenson barged in the door, face red and breathing hard.

Benedict was immediately on him. "Why in pity's sake were you gone so long? I could have gotten those herbs myself with how long you rambled on!"

Trenson, panting uncontrollably, reached into the satchel and handed the boxes to Benedict. "I... they... had to run..."

"Bah!" Benedict said, waving him off with a gesture of the hand. Without a thank you, he snatched the boxes from Trenson's hand. He brought the boxes to the table beside Jayfor, set them out, then opened them to check their contents. Satisfied, he grabbed a small bowl and starting chunking different herbs into it, mainly using the mushrooms from one of the boxes.

"I was given a fright a few minutes ago with your friend here. He was just sleeping peacefully, minding his own business, when all of a sudden he started screaming and shaking, yelling something about it being too late over and over again."

Trenson's heart dropped. "Really?" He was still struggling to catch his breath.

Benedict nodded without looking at him. "I've never seen anything like it. I had no idea what to do. So I just stood back and waited to see what else would happen. Thankfully, after a few minutes, he stopped, and has been sleeping peacefully ever since. A little too peacefully," he added.

Trenson, now breathing normal, came to the old man's side and looked at Jayfor's tranquil face. "What do you mean?"

Benedict, having put all the ingredients needed into the bowl, now started crushing them together with a masher. "Well, his breathing is almost unperceivable. Better put, he's hardly breathing at all. Not only that, but his heartbeat has faded to almost nothing." Still crushing the contents, he took the bowl over to the side of the room and did some other things to it. "Honestly, at this point, I don't even know if it will be possible to bring him back. From what I know about poisons, there's a certain stage where nothing will work."

"Then hurry and get it ready!" Trenson said urgently. He put his hand under Jayfor's nose and felt a small amount of air moving to and from, but very slowly, and barely any at all. Trenson felt sick to his stomach. He wanted to do something, anything, to help, but he knew there was nothing. Time was the only enemy at this point, an enemy Trenson couldn't fight.

Benedict grunted something about already going as fast as he could, and returned with a small cup of steaming tea. "Hold him up a little so he can drink this," Benedict ordered.

Trenson placed his arms under Jayfor's back and propped him up at a thirty-degree angle. Jayfor didn't stir or react in any way. Benedict held the tea to Jayfor's lips and slowly tilted it forward. Jayfor coughed and wheezed as some made it down his throat, and some of it dribbled down his chin. Benedict patiently stopped the flow and waited for Jayfor's breathing to return to normal, then tilted to tea into his mouth again. This time, he drank it without response.

Over the next ten minutes, they slowly gave Jayfor more and more of the tea. Benedict said they must do it slowly for it to have full effect, so Trenson didn't complain, even if his arm did start feeling uncomfortable after ten minutes of holding Jayfor up. Jayfor didn't show any response while they administered the tea, other than swallowing when they tipped the liquid into his mouth.

After they finished and set Jayfor back down, Trenson waited to see if any change occurred in Jayfor, but there was no sign of anything different. He was as still as ever.

"It'll take a while to find out if we saved him," Benedict explained. "My guess will be tomorrow, in the morning probably. Cures like these usually take a while to set in."

"Tomorrow morning? That's a long time. What if it doesn't work?"

Benedict shrugged. "Then he'll be dead."

For some reason, this didn't make Trenson feel any better.

"Anyway, you and your friend here are welcome to stay the night. You can sleep on the floor right here. Don't expect any hospitality from me, though. As soon as the sun's up, you and your friend — dead or alive — are out of my hair. Got it?"

Trenson nodded and couldn't help but look at the square pile of snow-white hair on Benedict's head. "Of course."

So come nightfall, which wasn't long, Trenson stretched out on the floor beside the table Jayfor was sleeping on. There were many things he could think about, like the peacekeeper's meeting and their talk about the stranger, or his escape from the city, but he was more tired than he realized. He fell asleep almost as soon as his head hit the hard floor.

***

Jayfor drifted slowly out of sleep. At first, he thought he was in his warm bed in the palace. He wondered why his bed was suddenly so hard. And why he was cold.

He opened his eyes slowly. He found himself looking at old wooden rafters. That was odd. His room in Loronis had a high roof, not low. When had they been changed?

Wait... He couldn't be in Loronis. It was destroyed. Then it hit him like a hammer. His mission! Of course! He and Trenson had to reach the tree — wherever that was. They had helped a merchant, he remembered, and went through a cave. Something had happened to them while they were in it. What was it... oh right! A giant centipede attacked them. He and Trenson fought it off, and he had jumped on its back and stabbed it in the head to kill it.

But what had happened after that? His memory was cut short at that point. He felt like a lot had happened since then. But there was nothing after that.

Where was he, anyway? He rolled over to stand up — and rolled right off the table he was lying on. He let out an exclamation of surprise. He fell to the ground and landed on something that was definitely not the floor, something that went, "Oof!" and squirmed when he landed on it.

"Trenson?" Jayfor asked, surprised.

The groaning figure beneath him replied, "What's left of him. Now get off my back before I knock you to sleep again."

XXXII

"So, what happened after that?" Jayfor asked.

"I ran back to Benedict's place," Trenson replied, "and gave him the boxes of herbs. He made this special tea with it, and we slowly gave you it, little by little. After you drank it all, Benedict offered that we could stay the night, an offer I took."

Jayfor nodded. "I think I can guess the rest from there. I woke up in the middle of the night and fell on top of you, right?"

Trenson grunted. "Regrettably."

Jayfor couldn't help but grin. "Sorry about that."

Another grunt from Trenson, one that was equally amused as the first one.

"The thing is, I don't remember any of it," Jayfor said, "Well, the falling on top of you, how could I forget? But everything before I woke up is just empty. I remember jumping on the giant centipede's head, stabbing with my sword, being thrown off, the centipede dying, then — it's all blank."

"Oh, I remember it clearly. Painstakingly clearly. Especially carrying you for miles while you slept like a baby, and didn't even remember who I was!" Trenson huffed.

Jayfor shrugged, not looking too concerned. "At least one of us was enjoying themselves."

Trenson shot Jayfor a dubious look, which Jayfor responded to with a grin. With a winning eye roll, Trenson sighed. He should win an award for putting up with Jayfor's unbearably cheerful self, he mused. It would be a start.

They had left Benedict's house earlier that morning. True to his word, the old man kicked them out the second the sun was up, not offering them breakfast — which was fine with Trenson, as everything edible in the cabin looked like it had gone bad a few generations ago. Despite the fact that Benedict was a little unfriendly, they were greatly in his debt for curing Jayfor and helping them. When Jayfor tried to thank him and offer him some money in return, the old man waved it away.

"You getting out of here is payment enough," was all he said in return. Trenson had a feeling — his infallible intuition told him — that Benedict wasn't as tough as he seemed. Without him, Jayfor probably wouldn't be breathing right now, and for that Trenson was grateful.

Now that that fiasco had been dealt with, they could focus on their mission again: get to the great Tree of Ramadus. After leaving Benedict's, they went through the town. Trenson kept his head low and his hood over his face, which was a good idea, Jayfor thought. He was a wanted man in this town now, and the last thing they needed was to be stuck in prison.

Luckily, they made it through without any trouble. The woods opened into wide farmlands, with suntanned barley stalks swaying in the wind, being harvested little by little by farmers and hired labor. Large scythes and sickles were swung left and right through the grass, cutting it down to lay in piles on the ground. It was a peaceful scene, and both Trenson and Jayfor hoped that this part of their journey would be less eventful.

Trenson kept the story about hearing the peacekeeper's meeting to himself. He told Jayfor about falling through the floor and the chase that followed, of course, but he said that he had fallen through after grabbing the box and heading back to the window, and left out the part about hearing the conversation below. He didn't know why exactly he didn't tell Jayfor. It was interesting, and maybe Jayfor had something to say about it. But he was a little ashamed that he had wasted precious time eavesdropping instead of helping Jayfor. For whatever reason, he kept it to himself.

Trenson's thoughts returned to the present when Jayfor said, "I still can't believe we fought a centipede in that cave. A *centipede.*" Jayfor shook his head. "And it almost killed me!"

"If it had, it would have saved me the trouble of carrying you down the mountain," Trenson pointed out.

Jayfor, however, ignored the comment and continued as if Trenson hadn't spoken. "I used to squish those things all the time in the palace garden. They would get into the tomato leaves, and ugh!" He shuddered at the memory of flicking those creepy-crawlies off the plants. "I always thought they were gross. But I used to step on them all the time!

Trenson thought about this for a second. "Well then, why didn't you just step on this one? It was only a little bigger."

Jayfor glared at Trenson out of the corner of his eye. "It was more than a little."

"I don't know," Trenson said, "you do have big feet."

Jayfor glared even harder at Trenson. He tried to think of a good comeback, but it eluded him. He gave up and decided to drop the subject altogether. Instead, he pulled his map out of his satchel.

"We just left a small forest," Jayfor said informatively, holding the map up as he walked. "We have a lot of open fields to go through for a long while, but in time we'll get to a forest that's just south of the Splitting Waters."

Trenson nodded, then after a short paused commented, "I've never noticed until now how many forests there are in Faldon."

Jayfor looked at him sideways for a second, then his expression cleared. "Oh. Well, you're right, there are."

After the somewhat clumsy reply, there was another, much longer period of silence. The only sound was their footsteps on the dusty ground. Trenson liked it; he enjoyed the peace and quiet and the simple sounds of the world. People filled the world with irritating noise, always yelling or doing something loud. He preferred the stillness of the air to the sound of certain people jabbering on, trying to fill the dead space. Thankfully, one such person wasn't doing that right now, so Trenson was happy.

When the sun started to hover only a few feet above the ground from their point of view, they called it a night. As usual, Trenson started the fire and Jayfor watched wishing he knew how to start one. It was embarrassing that Trenson could whip a fire together in a few minutes, while Jayfor labored away and couldn't get one going in half an hour.

"Fire just doesn't like you," was Trenson's explanation.

Jayfor huffed, his arms crossed. "It would seem so," he said without humor. "Or maybe fire likes you."

Trenson shook his head as he twisted the stick on top of the other, creating friction which would eventually make sparks. "If that were the case, then I would be the only person in the world who could start a fire."

"Well, I've never seen anyone else start a fire that way," Jayfor countered.

"How do you think I learned how to do this?"

"You probably just figured it out."

"I was taught. Everyone does this. It's literally the easiest way to start a fire without flint and steel."

"Now that I have to disagree with."

The shavings from the stick spinning in the same place began to smolder and raise small banners of smoke. The chips soon caught alight and started to lick the bigger logs placed next to it. Trenson stood back and smiled. "I know this is the best way. Want to know how?"

Jayfor knew exactly how. "Intuition," he said dolefully.

Trenson tapped his head with a proud smile on his face. "Intuition."

Deep in the cover of the woods, shrouded in the night, a solitary figured watched the two men. His eyes reflected the campfire light as he stared silently at them, unmoving. He blended in with the vegetation and darkness around the camp. The two men had no idea of his presence there. He waited and watched for a few more seconds. Then he turned and disappeared into the underbrush without a sound. His mission was fulfilled.

The next day brought rain. They woke up to see gray clouds blanketing the sky in front of them, and foreboding, black clouds behind them. This dampened — literally — both Jayfor and Trenson's spirits, as rain was never enjoyable traveling through.

It wasn't long after they woke up that the black clouds behind them started to get closer. They both started to walk faster, hoping to outdistance the rain. It proved of no use. A few drops fell from the sky and onto their faces. Then a few more. Then all at once, the sky pulled out all the stops and unleashed a torrent of water down on them. Throwing their hoods over their faces, they looked down at the ground as they walked to keep the rain out of their face.

And here I thought we might get through our journey without dealing with rain, Trenson thought as his entire outfit rapidly turned wet and heavy. The dusty ground turned into hard sticky ground that latched on to the bottom of his boots and made walking more difficult than it should. *Guess that's another hope out of the window.*

It wasn't as bad as it could have been, Trenson had to remind himself. He had traveled through worse. The storm that he walked through in Tarsen, the town he had burned the inn down at when he was traveling to Loronis to deliver the message, was much worse. And it was colder then. Although now it was becoming cooler every day, it was still fairly warm out. So, in the end, Trenson couldn't complain.

Actually, he *could* complain, and complain he did in his mind.

Jayfor didn't mind it as much. It seemed to Trenson that he didn't mind anything very much; he just shrugged and seemed to say, *oh well, that's life.* Trenson, a hard-core pessimist, didn't understand it. It was another difference that made people wonder how they were such close friends.

The day passed by without anything worth telling of. The rain didn't let up, so they picked trees with as many leaves as possible to sleep under, to try and prevent water from dripping on them – although that didn't stop a few rogue drops from landing on them. They didn't start a fire, as in this weather, there was no point.

The following days passed the same way. It was raining when they woke up, raining when they finished breakfast and started walking again, raining throughout the entire day, raining when they stopped for the night and ate supper, and raining when they went to sleep. There was no end in sight.

One evening, as Trenson and Jayfor were sitting under a grove of trees, trying to dry out their belongings as best as possible, Jayfor was lost deep in thought. He was wondering about Agrond and Xavson. He wondered what they were doing, if they were still alive.

"Who?" Trenson asked abruptly.

Jayfor snapped out of his musing. "What?"

"You said, 'I wonder how they're doing.' Wonder how who's doing?"

Jayfor realized he must have said what he was thinking out loud without realizing it. "Agrond and Xavson," he said. He didn't look at Trenson when he spoke, for that would require raising his head, which in turn would cause rain to hit his face.

Trenson furrowed his eyebrows. It had been a long time since he had heard those names, but it only took him a few seconds to remember the faces that went with them. "Oh," he replied.

Jayfor waited to see if Trenson was going to say anything else. He didn't. So Jayfor said, "Do you ever wonder what they're doing? Or where they are?"

Trenson thought about it. "Not really. They haven't crossed my mind in a while. After all, it's two very different people we're talking about here."

Jayfor nodded, but that caused water from his hood to splash down on his nose. His nose twitched, and he wanted to wipe it away with his hand, but that was covered in water too and would only make things worse. He inwardly sighed at the dilemma, then decided to just let the cold water run down his face.

To take his mind off his miserable condition, Jayfor spoke again. "What do you think they're doing now?"

Trenson would have shrugged, but unlike Jayfor, he managed to resist the impulse. "I don't know. Agrond's probably fighting Krenors somewhere, and Xavson — I have no idea. Probably causing trouble somewhere in the world."

"That'd be my guess. If I know Xavson, he'll be disrupting as many peoples' lives as possible. Or maybe he's changed. Maybe he's realized how terrible the things were that he's done and resolved to live a better life."

Trenson shot Jayfor an incredulous look that said, *are you serious?* "I wouldn't place too much faith in that. I've only met Xavson once, and once is enough for me. I can't see Xavson changing anytime soon."

"One can hope," Jayfor replied.

"And only one will hope," Trenson countered. "You."

Jayfor grunted a reply. He decided that most conversations with Trenson were a lost cause. He wished Trenson would lighten up some. It would make traveling together so much easier.

XXXIII

T HRALL WAS DISAPPOINTED. VERY disappointed. "And you know this as a fact?"

Cosgroc nodded. "One of our subordinates saw it himself. And given that their bodies were never found in the ruins of Loronis, I was considering the possibility."

"You were, were you?" Thrall echoed in a smooth tone, dangerously smooth. He was sorely disappointed. He had already ruled out the possibility of their being alive long ago, and now come to find the two targets were still alive? It was worse than infuriating. It was insulting.

And Cosgroc knew it. He knew that Thrall was liable to explode at any moment when it came to bad news. Which is why he was standing a few extra paces back then he usually stood so he could reach the door out of the sanctum faster. "Your orders, sir?"

And just like that, Thrall snapped. "Either put your sword in your chest, or deal with them! Those two men are the most dangerous men in the world right now. They *cannot* be allowed to roam free!"

Previously, Thrall had placed little importance on whether Trenson and Jayfor were alive. Even if they were, he thought, they couldn't be a huge harm, but he would still capture them if they were. But his Master told him he was wrong. A few days ago in a briefing, the Master said that Trenson and Jayfor were the two most dangerous men in the world and would need to be dealt with accordingly if they were found alive. The Master would take nothing less than their death. And it was Thrall's job to ensure it.

Cosgroc instinctively began walking backward to the door. He knew he had to get out of here. Fast. "Yes, my lord."

Thrall rose from his throne. "Do I need to accompany you personally and hold your hand to ensure that you don't fail me *again?!*" Thrall was screaming now. All the stops were pulled out, and the commander's raw anger lashed out like lightning in a hurricane.

Cosgroc lost his nerve, and rather than reply, he turned around and ran for the door. Before he pulled it open and closed it behind him, he heard Thrall's voice behind him. "Run! Run as fast as you can, because the only thing that will guarantee your survival from me is their heads! Bring them to me or bring me your own!"

XXXIV

AFTER WHAT FELT LIKE months but was really a few weeks, the rain stopped. It was spontaneous; they went to sleep with the rain pouring down from the sky like always, and woke up to a blue sky without a single cloud.

"Finally!" Jayfor exclaimed after waking up. "I'm tired of being wet."

Trenson, who had just woken up, grunted his agreement. He wasn't a morning person — at all — and was unusually grumpy at this time of day. Jayfor was used to dealing with it, and knew that Trenson needed a few more hours without anyone talking to him.

Accordingly, after another hour, Trenson spoke for the first time that day. "I sure am glad the rain stopped. I don't know how much wetter I could get."

Jayfor shot him a sideways look. "Wetter?"

Trenson looked at Jayfor, wondering what he was questioning him for. "Yes, wetter."

A few seconds dragged on. Then, hesitantly, as if he wasn't sure of it himself, Jayfor said, "I don't think 'wetter' is a word."

"Really?" Trenson asked, surprised.

"'More wet' is a word, for sure, but I don't think 'wetter' is."

"Huh. Who knew?"

"I did."

"Technically speaking, wetter is a word, because I just used it."

Jayfor raised an eyebrow. "I mean, I guess. But it's not a proper word."

Trenson thought about it for a few moments. "What does it take to make a word a 'proper' word?"

"I don't know," Jayfor said, a little tired of this conversation. "Maybe there's someone who has the legal right over all words, and he decides if they're proper or not."

"The legal right?" Trenson asked, "Did you just make that up?"

Jayfor shrugged. "Maybe. But who knows, it may be true. I've never heard any evidence against it."

Trenson thought about this new idea for a time. Jayfor thought they had dropped the conversation when Trenson spoke again. "I wonder if people can submit their words for consideration by this person."

"Seriously?" Jayfor asked. He was thinking to himself that he may have taken this conversation too far.

"Of course I'm serious. 'Wetter' is a great word that doesn't deserve to be left out in the cold."

Now he thinks words have feelings, Jayfor thought. *Great.* "But there's already a word that means the same thing: 'more wet.'"

"That's two words!" Trenson pointed out jubilantly, like he had just scored a point. "Wetter is one word. And think about how much time you could save by saying 'wetter,' one word, than 'more wet,' two words."

Jayfor threw his hands in the air in defeat. "If you say so. I was just saying."

Trenson grinned at his victory. Secretly, he had no opinion towards 'wetter' or 'more wet,' but he figured that defending the non-existent word would get under Jayfor's skin. Which it did, so he considered his mission accomplished.

Now that the conversation was finished, Trenson's attention drifted towards the scenery around the road. They were traveling now in what seemed like half-woods, half-plains. There weren't enough trees to call it a forest, but it also wasn't flat or open enough to be plains. Trenson wondered if there was a name for something like this, but dismissed the thought almost immediately. With winter starting to approach and the air slowly growing crisper, the foliage changed. Leaves fell in droves whenever wind swept through, flowers folding on themselves to create fruit, different birds chirping different tunes, and a dead man was lying in the road.

Wait...

Jayfor saw it at the same time Trenson did. They both shot a look at each other, then jogged towards the still body. As they got closer, they heard groans coming from the man, so maybe he wasn't dead after all. Soon they were at the man's side.

By his appearance and garb, he was an ordinary traveler with bad luck. He lay on his back, and his eyes winced with pain as he held his ankle, which was evidently the source of his pain. He looked up at Trenson and Jayfor as they approached, and hope sparked in his eyes.

"Care to give an honest traveler some help?" he asked when they stopped beside him. "My foot... it's broken, I think. I can't walk. Please?"

There was no need for Jayfor and Trenson to think about it. Quickly, they stooped down, grabbed the man by under the shoulder, and stood him up, one man on either side of him supporting him. They took a few slow steps forward, and the man hobbled on one leg uncertainly, but soon he got the rhythm down and started moving with consistency. The pace was slow, but they were moving.

The man breathed a sigh of relief. "Thank you two. Don't know how long I would have stayed there had you not arrived."

"It's no problem," Jayfor replied. "You would have done the same had it been one of us."

"Probably," the man admitted, "though maybe not very readily."

"How did you break it?" Trenson asked.

"Oh, because I'm a fumble foot, that's why. I wasn't paying attention, and there was a dip in the road. I stepped in it without realizing it, and next thing I know I set my foot down the wrong way and it's done for." He looked at Trenson, then Jayfor. "I didn't catch your names."

"Conrad," Jayfor responded, "at your service. And this is—"

"Trenson," Trenson filled in quickly. "At your service."

The man nodded, and Trenson thought he saw a flash of something in the man's countenance — recognition, maybe — but it disappeared immediately. "Well, as much as I wish it wasn't the case, you two are in my service now," he said jokingly.

Trenson shook his head. "It's no problem at all. Is there anywhere we can take you that you'll be safe?"

The man nodded. "Yes. Just across this bridge there's a house. Me and the owner are friends. I will be fine once I'm there."

Looking ahead, Trenson saw a large bridge over a river in front of them. A steady current pulled the water under the stone-arched bridge. The river being wide, the bridge was fairly long and weathered with age, but still stood proudly.

They mounted the upward climb of the bridge, but slowly to allow the man time to walk. The man grunted with pain but managed to stay upright with Trenson and Jayfor's help.

"If I may ask, what business do you two have on the same road as me?" the man asked.

Trenson supplied an answer. "Visiting kin in the north."

"Ah. As it just so happens, I am doing the same."

"Good luck to both of us then on our journeys," Jayfor said lightheartedly.

The man smiled. "Hear hear!"

The bridge went upwards over the river, then leveled out across it until it dropped back down on the other side. They were on this level part now. It was easier to keep the man upright here.

Trenson looked ahead, expecting to see a house by the road on the other side of the bridge. But, surprisingly, there was none. He looked farther ahead down the path, as far as his eye could see — but there was no house.

"I don't see any house," Trenson said absently. They were about halfway across the bridge now.

Then, to Jayfor and Trenson's surprise, the man started laughing. It started off a simple chuckle, but it soon grew into a loud, maniacal laugh. The man stopped hobbling on one leg, placing his "hurt" foot back on the ground, and the hands that were using their shoulders as support suddenly gripped them and threw Jayfor and Trenson forward. The two were completely unprepared and stumbled across the stone, off balance.

"That's because there is none!" The man said jubilantly. Standing upright on both feet, he drew a short sword that neither of them had noticed before. He called in a loud voice, "Now! They're here!"

After regaining their footing, Trenson and Jayfor shot each other a look that said the exact same thing: *oh no*.

XXXV

OUR MEN APPEARED ON either side of the bridge. Their worn attire looked surprisingly similar to the bandits who attacked Phantas' caravan in the woods, only they wore no masks. They started heading towards them. There was only one thing these people could be: brigands.

There was no time for assessing. With two *shings,* Trenson and Jayfor yanked their swords free of their scabbards and held them ready. They stood back-to-back, Trenson facing one side of the bridge, Jayfor facing the other. The bandits walked towards them slowly, trying to intimidate them as they swung their cudgels and weapons around in anticipation. It didn't work.

The man who had been "injured" was on Jayfor's side, and holding his short sword in the air, he ran at Jayfor with a battle cry. Jayfor felt the power of the sword take control of him. The short sword came down in an overhead slash, and Jayfor swung his sword in an arc above his head. Like butter, Jayfor's sword sliced through the bandit's blade.

The blade clanged to the ground, and the bandit was left holding a hilt with a pathetic stub of metal on top. He looked at Jayfor in fear, but the look didn't remain for long. Jayfor kicked the man in the stomach, then once he doubled over, he held the blade of his sword in both hands and thrust the pommel into the man's head. There was a deep thud, then the man's eyes rolled back, and he fell to the ground.

One down, eight to go, Jayfor thought.

The rest of the criminals weren't happy to see their comrade fall. Their confidence turned into anger, and changing tactics, they ran towards the two men with bloodthirsty battle cries, weapons raised high in anticipation. The bridge quivered with the weight of eight boots stampeding across it. Jayfor gritted his teeth. The odds were extremely against them, he knew. Four against one was a tough number.

He should have known better than to help the stranger. He should have been more on guard and not have let his pity get the best of him. But there was nothing to do about it now. The bandits drew closer, their cries louder. Then they were on top of them.

It was all they could do to deflect the blows that came swarming towards them from the bandit's weapons. The criminals were crafty. They spread out in a semicircle around each man, so that four of them could attack one simultaneously. They also attacked in patterns so that Trenson and Jayfor couldn't counterattack; whenever one bandit swung his blade and hit Trenson's, that bandit immediately disengaged and another one attacked at a weak spot. The odds were for the attackers, and all they had to do was tire their targets until they were too tired to resist.

At which point, they would kill them.

Trenson heard the staccato clangs behind him as Jayfor deflected blows. It was the only assurance that he had that Jayfor was still alive. His sword blocked a sideways arc, Trenson ducked under another blade rushing towards him, he pushed aside a thrust and aimed for a counterattack, but another blade came at him so fast he had to swing his sword the other way to save his life.

The bandits were winning, and they knew it. Trenson couldn't see it, but he knew they were smiling sadistically as Trenson's strokes became less and less defiant, with less and less speed and accuracy. He still felt the power of the sword, but the longer the fight went on, the less he trusted in the sword's ability. This led to the sword's power diminishing, which in turn made him doubt it more. It was a vicious circle, but he couldn't stop it. Doggedly, Trenson pressed on, sweat flooding his face, getting into his eyes and partially blinding him, but there was no time to wipe it away.

Trenson's intuition told him he might be gaining the upper hand, as he returned a slice with an explosive counterthrust, which rendered the bandit off balance. He was just about to capitalize when something hit his mind. He had been too focused on the fight to notice it, but now that he did, it filled him with sickening dread.

The sound of Jayfor fighting behind him stopped.

He knew that turning around would leave his back exposed from four blades, but he had to know. He spun around. There was no Jayfor. Instead, there were four bandits standing there, and a new fifth one, a bigger and stockier one, and they all had their eyes turned to one side of the bridge with twisted satisfaction. Trenson only managed to see Jayfor's feet fly into the air before Jayfor toppled off the end of the bridge and into the water.

"*NO!*"

***

Jayfor hadn't seen it coming either. His mind was laser-focused on his fight, countering blows and dodging thrusts, that he didn't notice when another man walked onto the bridge. If he would have, he would have been concerned, as this man was nothing to laugh about. He was average height, but his bulk made him menacing. He strode across the bridge. There were deep lines across his face, some from battle scars, others from his permanent scowl. He had a club strapped to his back, but he made no motion to grab it and he walked calmly into the fray.

He walked at an angle to where Jayfor was standing so that he was blocked from Jayfor's sight by one of the bandits – until the last second. After Jayfor had countered another attack, he suddenly had a sense of dread overcome him, that something bad was going to happen. He saw the massive figure for no more than two seconds as the large bandit pushed aside his comrades and brought a massive fist slamming into Jayfor's head.

The blow was so powerful that it made Jayfor stumble backwards — just close enough to the edge. Pain exploded in his face. He was only conscious for a few more moments, but in those moments he had the sensation that he was stumbling backwards, then falling backwards, then felt a cool presence as he splashed into the water. Then he blacked out.

***

Trenson felt the tip of a sword press against the back of his neck. "Drop your weapon."

Fury welled in Trenson. He gripped his sword tight. He wanted to keep fighting. He wanted to make these men pay for killing his friend. He wanted them to hurt just as much as he did. He gripped his sword tighter. If he died in the process, at least he would have vengeance.

But not so. The bandits knew what Trenson was thinking, and the one behind him kicked him in the knees. Trenson fell forward on his knees, and the sword was taken from his hand as he fell. All vestige of courage left him on losing his sword.

The bandits were all in good humor now. "That was too easy!" One of them said with a laugh. "I thought these two were supposed to be dangerous."

"They are," another replied. "Or at least, they were. Now look at 'em. One took a swim, the other's groveling at our feet!"

Another round of laughs passed through the crowd. Trenson held his head low. He felt completely drained, finished, done. He had failed. Again. Could he never do anything right? He hadn't been able to save Loronis from Xavson's insurrection, and he wasn't able to preserve what was left of the kingdom now.

The larger bandit that had knocked Jayfor off the bridge, who was evidently the leader, stepped forward. The laughter hushed as they waited to hear what he would say. The leader stared hard into Trenson's eyes, void of pity or sympathy.

"Now, boys, how should we go about this?" He crossed his arms and started walking slowly in circles around Trenson. "We could just do it quick and easy: slice his throat and into the river. But then again, that wouldn't be any fun, would it?"

Every bandit shook his head in agreement.

"Let's see... So long as he's out of the way, I don't care what we do with him. Our contractor told us to kill both of them." The leader looked down the river, the current carrying the distant figure of Jayfor down the river. "One's breathing, one's not. How do you think we should deal with this one, boys?"

He directed the question among his comrades. Eight voices spoke at once.

"Let's hang him!"

"Fill him full of arrows."

"No, let's tie his feet together and watch him try to run *as* we fill him full of arrows!"

The possibilities were endless. They bickered about how to get rid of the person who was on his knees right before them, listening to everything they said. Trenson tried not to think about the imminence of death or the fact that Jayfor was dead. Instead he kept his expression blank. He knew the killers would only thrive on any appeal to mercy.

The leader stood behind Trenson's back and smiled a grim smile. He knew exactly what Trenson was trying to do: remain stoic so as to deprave them of any enjoyment. He had seen it countless times. He had also seen them break when the moment came and cry out for pity countless times. Unfortunately for them, pity was an emotion the leader didn't feel.

The creative ways they came up with to kill Trenson was startling. The last one he heard was tying him to a tree upside down with his mouth just below the water line while shooting him full of arrows — apparently arrows were their favorite technique. Then the bandit leader snapped to attention.

"Quiet!" He ordered. Immediately all sounds ceased.

Except for one. Trenson heard it too: repeating itself over and over again. It was distant and almost imperceivable, but he still heard it. It was a faint creaking sound, and a rumbling noise accompanied it.

The leader's face turned to the others, a cunning smile playing on his lips. "Maybe we can get some coin out of this after all."

The bandits looked at each other knowingly, each one of them silently smiling at each other and Trenson. Trenson wasn't sure what they were getting at.

"Get him on his feet," the leader ordered.

One man ran forward to Trenson's side with mock tenderness. "Gladly." He grabbed Trenson by the arm and heaved him to his feet — only for a few seconds. Then he threw him down onto the bridge again. The bandit immediately began kicking him hard. "Get up! Get up!" he yelled with each kick. The bandits howled with laughter. Trenson did not, instead groaning every time the hard tip of the boot cracked into him. He slowly got to his feet amid the onslaught, and he was forced to walk forward down the bridge, the iron grip of the man preventing his escape.

As the group walked forward, one man ran up to the leader. Trenson could hear the conversation. "This wasn't part of the deal. We were told specifically to kill both of them. He's supposed to be dead."

The leader shrugged. "I see no harm in earning a bit of coin from our labor. Besides, how will our contractor ever know that he still lives? He'll be long gone in a few weeks."

The man was still skeptical. "I don't know. I have a bad feeling about this."

The leader grunted. "You'll have an even worse feeling if you don't keep that mouth of yours shut."

The man didn't press any more. Instead, he shook his head and mumbled something about never being listened to.

They crossed the bridge and walked down the road a little way. The creaking sound became louder, and in little time, Trenson found its source: a merchant caravan, just like the one Phantas drove. It was almost the same in many aspects: two horses, a wooden wagon, a man driving it — but there was something else that dumbfounded Trenson, something that would have made him stop in his tracks if he could he have.

Slaves. There were people, about a dozen of them, all chained single-file to the back of the cart. They all had scanty clothing and looked as though they had gone days without food. They were surrounded by guards with spears. What were slaves doing here? Slavery was unheard of in Faldon!

"Greetings, sir!" The leader of the bandits called out to the driver. The driver turned to the sound and, once he saw an entourage coming towards him, he stopped the convoy and looked sideways at the bandits, obviously guessing their occupation. The guards held their spears towards the group in a warning gesture. There were an even number of guards and bandits.

The leader held up both hands to show that they were empty. "Come now, we mean no harm! All we're looking for is a little business!" His voice became formal and appealing.

"Business, eh?" The wagon driver was a middle-aged man who had deep lines on his face, probably from deeply scowling all the time. "I know just what your 'business' is. You don't come no closer, sir."

"I assure you, our intentions are honest. I was hoping to do a little trade with you. See, I have a man here," He motioned for the man holding Trenson to step forward, which he did, and pushed Trenson forward for the man to see. "who's in excellent condition. He's resilient and works with little complaint. Surely such a man would sell for a good price at the market?"

From what little Trenson had heard of slave labor, he knew that merchants would gather slaves in their travels and bring them to auctions, where they were sold to many different people. But that was only in Kallary and Elara. Faldon had severe laws against slavery. Then he reminded himself there was no Faldon anymore. There was no king. And as a result, the unthinkable became reality.

The man scrutinized Trenson, looking him up and down. He had been in this business for a long time, and knew a good worker when he saw one. This man wasn't ideal, but he would probably sell for a decent wage at an auction. The only thing that worried him was the spark in his eyes that told of hidden resolve and courage. Slaves that had minds of their own were bad business. But overall, this wouldn't be a bad purchase.

"Very well," the driver said eventually, "how much are you asking?"

The guards around the caravan relaxed and set their spears to the ground, although still holding them tight in case something changed.

"Hmm... Well besides the fact that he's a fine specimen of a man, there's also the fact that he has gear on him. Valuable gear." He motioned to the man who had taken Trenson sword and, after taking it from him, held it up. The sword didn't look particularly appealing — it was simple and modest, although Trenson knew the power it held, and his heart leaped when he realized he would have to part with it.

"There's this sword, and—" he yanked the satchel off from Trenson's arm, and started rummaging through it. "A fine assortment of traveling gear in here as well. I'll be selling all this with him, as one deal."

The driver nodded once. "I see." He knew the sword wouldn't go for much in today's market, and that the *fine assortment* was probably just a jumble of cooking items, which he wasn't wrong about. When it came to selling things, the driver knew, there was always a little bit of truth stretching. He moved on to the point he wanted to know most. "How much are you asking for him?"

"Three-hundred crescents," the leader replied without missing a beat.

The wagon driver laughed scornfully. "I see how it is, now! You think you can just make a fortune off of some green young buck! Well you've another thing coming, as it turns out I like to eat too. I'll give no more than one-fifty."

The leader mocked the driver by laughing in the same scornfully tone. "You can keep your crescents if you think I'm going to give him away from practically nothing! Two-fifty."

The bidding went back and forth. It was a wry thought, but Trenson felt a little undignified with how low they were setting the price for him. He was worth more than that, he thought, at least four digits. That would be fair, especially for a fine young man like himself. But the range always shifted no lower than one hundred and no higher than three hundred.

All joking aside, Trenson used the bartering as an opportunity to look for avenues to escape. The bandit holding Trenson by the arm noticed what Trenson was doing and gripped his arm even tighter. Trenson's arm started to fall asleep from lack of circulation. However, the man had no reason to fear Trenson trying to escape, as Trenson knew that it would be worthless. There was an entourage of bandits behind him, an armed caravan in front of him, and nowhere to run to the left and right. Now was not the time.

Finally, a price was settled: Trenson was to be handed over for two hundred and thirty crescents — including all his gear. A measly amount, Trenson thought, but no one asked his opinion. One of the guards of the caravan walked forward and handed the leader his money. The leader took it eagerly, and the man holding Trenson threw him forward. Trenson stumbled forward and, for a second, was glad that his arm was free from the man's iron grip.

That didn't last long. The guard immediately grabbed Trenson's other arm and started leading him to the back of the line of slaves. The slaves glanced at him as he walked past them, and Trenson shuddered; the expression of defeat and hopelessness on their faces was chilling.

He was quickly brought to the back, where, conveniently, there was one extra pair of cuffs dragging on the ground behind the last slave. The guard snapped the cuffs over Trenson's hands dexterously, this not being the first time he had done so.

The bandit and the caravan leader looked to be exchanging final words. Trenson couldn't hear their talk, but the bandit leader was walking backwards with a casual smile. The caravan driver was as sour as ever and threw some curt words at the bandits. The leader shrugged, and he and his party started to walk back into the woods. The leader threw one last look at Trenson and waved bye to him with a huge smile. The other bandits laughed and waved too. Trenson ignored them and just stared at the ground.

The horses started pulling the cart forward, in turn pulling the slaves forward. Trenson fell into step behind the man in front of him. He walked away from Jayfor, away from his mission, away from everything he had suffered for. Instead, he walked towards a different future, one of servitude and slavery.

Some hero he was, he thought as he mechanically placed one foot in front of the other. Some hero he was.

XXXVI

WHEN JAYFOR WOKE UP, he was face down on the sandy bank of the river. As he gained consciousness, he quietly groaned. He felt like he had just fallen into a river. Then he realized he *had* just fallen into a river.

He slowly rolled over on his back. The sun dazzled his vision, but his eyes slowly adjusted until he could see the tops of the trees on either side of the river, swaying in the breeze. It was a peaceful scene. But for Jayfor, he didn't feel at peace at all.

He tried to get up, testing his muscles to see if they worked. Finding that they did, he sat up on his elbows. He instantly froze at what he saw.

A man, sitting on a fallen tree and drinking from a mug while staring at a fire, was seated close to Jayfor. The man was shrouded in a long cloak, one that covered his entire body. The cowl was thrown over his face, and it was just long enough that the light from the fire only illuminated the space under his eyes, while his eyes were hidden, giving him a mysterious look.

"You slept a long time." The voice was deep and carefully articulated. The man didn't move his head to look at Jayfor. He set the mug down beside him, then put his hands together and rested his forearms on his knees as he continued to stare at the fire.

Jayfor didn't move. He wasn't sure if he could trust this man or not.

"Since you're wondering if you can trust me, I think I should point out that I fished you out of the river and saved you from drowning. Throw yourself back in if you don't believe me."

Jayfor grunted, pushing aside the strangeness that this stranger had answered his thoughts exactly. "No thank you."

The man didn't move. Jayfor, deciding that perhaps he was in no danger after all, sat upright and looked around. He wondered where the bridge was.

"The bridge is about a mile upstream." Once again, the stranger answered his thoughts.

Jayfor stared at the man, carefully assessing him. There was something vaguely familiar about this man. "Who are you?"

"I am called many things. Different people have different opinions. But right now, I am the man who saved you from drowning. And also, the man who hasn't been thanked for his trouble."

Jayfor slowly rose from sitting to standing, his legs sore but still allowing him to move. "Thank you," he said simply. It sounded empty, but he didn't know what else to say. There was something about the man's presence that made it tougher to break the silence.

For the first time, the man smiled, his lips curving up around a closely trimmed beard. "It was my honor, Jayfor."

Jayfor stared hard at the man. "How do you know my name?"

The man shrugged. "That is your name, isn't it?"

"It…" Jayfor considered telling him it was Conrad, then realized he had just ruined it by responding to his name in such a way. "It is."

The man didn't respond. His smile disappeared as he kept looking into the fire.

Jayfor patted himself down to make sure he still had all his equipment. His satchel was still at his side, with all its gear, although it was a little wet. Nothing seemed to be missing except for one thing — his sword.

"Looking for this?" The man seemed to just conjure the familiar sword out of nowhere as he offered it hilt-first to Jayfor.

Jayfor stared at the man a few seconds before taking the sword and sliding it into its sheath. Obviously, this wasn't an ordinary man. "Are you a—"

"Senver?" A hint of a smile played on his lips. "No, I am not."

"But you know who I am. And you seem to know everything about me."

"Keen observations," the man replied smoothly.

"So who — or what — are you?" Jayfor stared hard at the man.

There was a brief period of silence. The hooded man kept looking into the fire, ignoring Jayfor's stare. Finally he replied, "Like I said, I have been called many things, I am currently called many things, and will someday be called many more things."

Jayfor huffed. He didn't like this verbal sparring. This man was confusing him on purpose. He was about to ask the man to be a little clearer, when the stranger spoke first.

"It would be best if you got back to the bridge. Trenson's now a slave and is being hauled to an auction. He'll be sold into further bondage unless you rescue him."

"Trenson — what?!" Jayfor suddenly remembered that Trenson had still been fighting the bandits. And he had lost? And now he was sold as a slave?

The man nodded. "The slaver is taking him west, into Kallary, to be auctioned in the city of Talikan. You can follow the caravan there and intercept it in the city."

Jayfor looked upstream. Far off, a little speck in the distance, he thought he could see the outline of the bridge. He would have to walk back up the riverside to get to it and get back on the path. "Then I know what to do next." He turned to look at the man. "How do you..."

But his words drifted away, as the man had disappeared.

EPILOGUE

"**H**E HAS NO IDEA who he was just talking to, does he?" Reginold commented to Erador as they watched Jayfor walk across the bridge again. They were concealed out of sight by underbrush on the side of the road, and watched Jayfor from behind as he briskly made his way down the road.

"No," Erador replied, "he doesn't."

Reginold shook his head. "That's a shame. It's not every day the Hero of prophecy appears on Ralladin."

Erador didn't reply. He was lost in thought, musing if Jayfor would have acted differently if he would have known who the man was. He knew he himself would have for sure. But then again, Senver thought differently than people, or so he was told.

"Their journey certainly took a turn." Reginold broke the silence again.

Erador stopped his musing. "Indeed. I never expected anything like this to happen."

"But they will survive and succeed, right?"

Erador shrugged. "Only Va'ar knows. I personally think they will, but maybe they won't, and this will pave the way for something else. Va'ar knows what He's doing."

Reginold nodded. "He sure does."

Erador let the silence hang for a few more seconds before he looked at his comrade. "Well, we best be heading back. The King is waiting for us."

Did you like this book?

THAT'S GREAT, THANK YOU! If you really want to help me, please leave a review for my book on Amazon or Goodreads. Those reviews really make a difference.

I also love to hear from readers and hear what they thought of my book! Reach out to me through my email, contact@gunnerl ong.com, and let me know what you thought!

If you want to stay updated on my books and learn more about my life as an author, follow me on Facebook or Instagram @Author Gunner Long.

OR: Subscribe to the email list for updates delivered straight to your inbox!

Also by Gunner Long

1. Insurrection

2. Endeavor

3. Destiny (*Coming Soon*)

About the author

G UNNER LONG ALWAYS READ the works of C.S. Lewis and J.R.R. Tolkien, and was moved by the stories and messages they conveyed. Dedicated to the Lord, he was always searching for age-appropriate books that offered the same thrilling tales and adventures, but without the immorality that seemed to plague modern action books. So he decided to change that. He created the world of Ralladin and started his first book, *Insurrection,* when he was just thirteen, driven to create something that not only kids, but people of all ages could enjoy. He hopes that people read his books and leave with not only a story, but a message. He lives with his family near Brunswick, Georgia.